## PRAISE FOR MAX BYRD

"Max Byrd is an expert at mingling real historical
figures with his invented characters."
—*THE NEW YORK TIMES*

"Lock Byrd's cage and throw away the key—until he slips
out a few more thrillers." —*THE PHILADELPHIA ENQUIRER*

"Max Byrd's plots, like his wit, are sinister and charming."
— DIANE JOHNSON,
bestselling author of *The Shadow Knows*

"Max Byrd is a fine and forceful writer."
—LAWRENCE BLOCK, bestselling author of
*Eight Million Ways to Die*

"Max Byrd is in the first division of American crime writing."
—*THE NEW YORK TIMES*

"Sharp writing . . . exciting . . . fulfills the promise of its
title."
—*PUBLISHERS WEEKLY,* for *California Thriller*

# FLY AWAY, JILL

# FLY AWAY, JILL

## A MIKE HALLER MYSTERY

# MAX BYRD

T U R N E R

Turner Publishing Company
200 4th Avenue North • Suite 950 Nashville, Tennessee 37219
445 Park Avenue • 9th Floor New York, NY 10022

www.turnerpublishing.com

Fly Away, Jill

Cover design: Glen Edelstein
Book design: Kym Whitley

Cover image: Masterfile

Library of Congress Cataloging-in-Publication Data

Byrd, Max.
   Fly away, Jill / Max Byrd.
      p. cm.
   "A Mike Haller mystery."
   ISBN 978-1-61858-028-3
   1. Private investigators—California—San Francisco—Fiction. I. Title.
   PS3552.Y675F59 2012
   813'.54—dc23

                           2012022563

Printed in the United States of America
12 13 14 15 16 17 18—0 9 8 7 6 5 4 3 2 1

*There were two blackbirds*
*Sitting on a hill;*
*The one named Jack,*
*The other named Jill.*
*Fly away, Jack! Fly away, Jill!*
*Come again, Jack! Come again, Jill!*

*—English Nursery Rhyme*

# CHAPTER 1

K ENSINGTON WOULD HAVE BEEN MORE FASHIONABLE, I suppose. Chelsea would certainly have been tonier, or Hampstead or Carnaby Street or wherever the hell the beautiful people had been blown this year. I braced my hands against the window sill and stared out at the rain coming down in the usual English way, squeezed out of the dirty gray sponge of the sky in an endless drizzle. Beneath the window, a trailer truck ground its gears together, grunted, and coughed black diesel smoke. Then it turned slowly at the corner, and dowdy old Bloomsbury Square reappeared below me in the rain, a dim green face staring up.

Bloomsbury. The Levittown of George the Third. You can't find many sights like it even in London anymore: three full sides of a city square bordered by uniform eighteenth-century red-brick townhouses, still trim, shapely, and calm, built to a human scale that left no room for air conditioners, TV antennas, or any of the other dental frontwork of modern architecture. I liked it better than, say, the new Hilton, which I couldn't afford anyway, despite Carlo Angeletti's expense account. Besides, the oldest structures I ever see in California are Chevrolets with running boards.

An old lady with a black umbrella stumped across the square. Just ahead of her, on the east side, facing my window, rose the block-long Great Northern Assurance Company, ten stories high, a pale twentieth-century mass of squinting windows and granite facade. A neon sign ran all the way around the top. In the square, the hackberry trees swayed with an invisible breeze, and on the sign, the dull red letters ASSURANCE came and went, just like the real thing.

I turned around and yawned at the untouched bed. I needed a nap. I needed a two-day nap. The flight from New York had taken seven hours, and the flight from San Francisco before that had taken five. But Carlo Angeletti was paying me to find his missing lady, not to stretch out and sleep. Cherchez la goddamn femme. I shoved my suitcase to one end of the bed and sat down to make a phone call from my list of numbers. When I hung up, I yawned again and read the little folded card on the nightstand that said the White Horse Hotel was not responsible for lost valuables, theft, fire, flood, or anything else unpleasant that might happen to you in the city. Cheers. I patted my empty jacket pocket where the gun would go and locked the door behind me.

Soho is never entirely deserted, day or night. But at ten A.M. on a rainy Monday morning, the signs of life along Rupert Street had dwindled to two cats skulking in a broken food crate and the tired flashing lights around the doorway of Raymond's Exotic Revue. As I faced Shaftesbury Avenue, a heavyset redhead swinging a light paisley suitcase in one hand came briskly in my direction from a side street. A stripper, probably, with her change of costume in the suitcase, heading for Raymond's. By some quirk of British unionism, only a dozen or so women make up the whole Soho strip force, and you can see them at all hours hurrying from club to club, making the same dreary rounds six or eight times a day, sometimes just ahead of the same dreary customers. An endless grind, my partner Fred would say.

She sailed past me with a professional look of contempt for loitering men in slightly faded raincoats, but her red hair had already reminded me of Dinah, and I stood in the drizzle a little longer being reminded.

Dinah had driven me to the San Francisco airport two days before, when I thought I was only going to New York and when my ancient blue Mercedes was in the shop for one of its periodic cures. While we had waited at the curb in front of American Airlines, a low-rider had driven slowly past, eyeing us and gunning his motor with a sound like a Howitzer clearing its throat.

"Do you see his bumper sticker?" Dinah asked in fascination. "It says 'Kill Them.' Just 'Kill Them.'"

"Probably left over from Christmas," I said. The driver had a steering wheel made out of links of stainless steel chain. What looked like a real bone was hanging from the mirror where the plastic bootie should have been. "He looks like raw material for you," I said as he slammed the car into second and drove away. We crossed into the terminal. Dinah is a psychiatrist at the Washington General Hospital. She is also short and plump and redheaded and the other half of what her older brother, the last square peg in the mellow round state of California, uncomfortably calls our "relationship."

"Or you, Haller," she said. I am a private detective, a specialist in missing persons. I am also an uneasy transplant from the East, from Cotton Mather's Boston, though I've been in

California long enough for my brain to have turned into a hot tub like everybody else's. In the plate glass window beside the long counter, while the clerk checked the credit line on my Visa, our Mutt and Jeff reflections shimmered and wobbled like two transparent shadows. Once upon a time, I was a newspaperman as well, and a security cop, and a college dropout. Dinah's medical colleagues, who put a premium on stability and high credit lines, tend to think I should be her patient instead of her relator. Dinah herself just smiles and introduces me as an incurable romantic.

My ticket stamped and bags checked, I led her upstairs to the sky lounge, where we could watch the planes take off and land and the luggage cart drivers dash around like finalists in a bump-car derby.

"You don't have to stay," I told her as we followed a 747 lifting off the runway. "I can't even board for another half hour."

"I want to check out the stewardae on your plane," she said, watching the plane climb. "You've been such a grouch for the last month that I want to size up the competition."

"Won't Mendelsohn be annoyed that you left the office early?" Shirley Mendelsohn is the senior resident in the department of psychiatry. A three-time divorcee and mother of five, she specializes in marital problems and once wrote a book called *The Nuclear Family Must Be Shut Down,* which had been published by a vanity press in Berkeley.

"Mendelsohn is with her women's action group against sexism today. I have the rest of the day off." Dinah sipped her Brandy Alexander through a plastic straw. It was 2:00 in the afternoon. "They're debating a revised version of the Lord's Prayer for the Berkeley schools," she said. "It begins, 'Our Resource Person who art in heaven.'"

"I may have to go on from New York," I told her. "I don't

know where. Maybe even Europe. I could be gone for two or three weeks." I don't know why I was trying to give her a hard time, but I was. I had in fact been a grouch, and there was a part of me that thought she might be the reason. She and I. Us. There was another part of me, of course, that looked at her round face and warm eyes and realized that, if I were tired of her, I ought to see a psychiatrist.

"Is Goldilocks going to take a long time to find?" she asked. She had seen the photograph of the missing girl that Carlo Angeletti had given me and promptly called me a cradle snatcher. I shrugged. "If I didn't know you were an aging and prudent youth," she said, "I would figure that you have gone temporarily gaga over that girl. Over the picture of that girl."

I shrugged again, annoyed, and pulled out a cigarette. "A routine case," I said. I don't know why I lied. This particular Goldilocks had skipped out of the house too fast, and one very large, very dangerous papa bear wanted her back. It looked about as routine as heisting the Golden Gate. I don't know why I kept quiet about the picture either, since Dinah was obviously right. My tongue picked up a shred of tobacco from the end of the cigarette, bitter and sharp. Aging youth, she had said. They age whiskey and ham to improve them, not unmarried men trotting out of breath toward 40. What compulsions were stirring beneath my surface, like massive, shadowy sea beasts crawling along an ocean floor, I couldn't say. I had had glimpses of them before, and would again. Goldilocks's face had floated out of a forgotten dream.

"A routine case," I repeated pompously.

"A witchhunt," Dinah said. "While you're gone I think I'll drive over to El Cerrito to see Daisy." Daisy is her brother's teenage daughter, "But I'd better read up on angel dust and the more exotic forms of marijuana first, Billy tells me.

He's worried about her." She finished the Brandy Alexander with a slurp.

"You don't do drug therapy," I said in surprise. "She ought to go to some teenage drug center."

"Mike, anybody who does psychiatry today does drug therapy, just the way any internist in San Francisco does alcoholism counseling. It's the '80s."

I grimaced and watched a single-engine plane take off in the wake of a big jet. It wobbled in the tailstream like a baby bird pushed out of the nest. Then it banked and vanished into the cold, gray fog that was billowing over the city, as gone as the girl in Angeletti's picture. I pushed back my chair to get up. There is always cold, gray fog in San Francisco in August, and I would be glad to get away from it.

In the cold, gray rain of London, the redhead turned off Rupert Street and started down Shaftesbury Avenue. I raised my raincoat collar and walked past the West End Adult Bookstore ("Rubber Goods a Specialty") to a grime-blackened building that had been new when Queen Victoria was a tot. On the ground floor lurked an Indian restaurant named, like every third restaurant in London these days, the Taj Mahal. In the window, a greasy, villainous-looking slab of lamb—or possibly cat—turned slowly on an electric spit, accompanied by a few flies enjoying the ride. Underneath a white silhouette of the Taj Mahal itself, somebody had hand-lettered the word "Kebab" over and over across the length of the glass. And underneath that, "E. Hamid, Prop."

I took a deep breath of street air, pushed the door hard against the wet frame, and went right on in.

It was darker and damper inside than out and completely deserted, but I took a chair along the wall, like a real paying customer, away from the roasting flies, and eventually a morose young waiter with a turban came over and worried a few things into place on my table.

"Lunch, sir?"

"A pint of bitter, and tell Hamid that somebody wants to chit-chat, will you?"

"Thank you, sir."

The pint came right away. Hamid took his time. I was aware of eyes peering through bead curtains at the back of the room and occasional singsong murmurs. I drank my beer and opened a pack of Players.

When Hamid appeared, he sat down without a word. I pushed the cigarettes toward him.

"Bloody back again, mate?" Hamid grinned.

I loved hearing him use his fake Cockney accent. It fit his narrow olive face and heavy-lidded eyes about as well as a Santa Claus suit, an insolent little tribute to his adopted country. Or just the nervous tic of a born mimic. He claimed to be Pakistani, though I had heard more than once in the old days that he was a Berber Arab who had slipped out of French North Africa in an illegal hurry and used a borrowed visa to scuttle into England. He certainly spoke French, and people who knew said he spoke Farsi and Kurdish as well. I had first met him 15 or 16 years ago, when I was trying to squeeze a living out of UPI by writing features about English lowlife and he was widely regarded as the best-informed petty criminal in London, a cheerful tutor for any reporter with cash in hand. Now 70 at least and smooth-skinned as a gypsy baby, he still knew most of what went on in the expanding Pakistani and Indian underworld; but ever since the Middle East had brought its violent politics to town and stirred up the Metropolitan Police, he had dealt mainly in girls and guns, staying cautiously away from the center of action. Both police and terrorists considered him more useful than dangerous, so far.

I thumbed my lighter for his cigarette. "Can't keep away from the food, Hamid. How's tricks?"

"Nice enough till I see your bloody mug again."

It was three years since I had been in London and we had done business. He probably remembered his profit to the penny. We exhaled blue smoke together over the table, and he smiled the way I imagine a hornet would.

"Still playing crime stopper then, Haller?" He deepened his voice and went into his Indian Basil Rathbone imitation. "Bloody Giant Rat of Sumatra, hey? Good God, Watson, it's the shadow of a bleedin' gigantic hound!" Gales of laughter, white teeth bursting against olive skin, finally wound down into a spasm of coughing. Meanwhile, the young man with the turban brought us plates of prawns, brown glop sauce, and fried bread. Hamid thumped his chest with one hand to stop his coughing and with the other hand waved away some curious flies.

"Still playing, Hamid," I told him. "But I need more toys. You can't get anything bigger than a paper clip through the buzzers at Heathrow these days." I took a prawn with my fingers and bit one end gingerly, like a man testing a coin. Hotter than sin.

His eyes narrowed theatrically and the fake Cockney accent returned, thicker, part of the act. I had never heard him speak in a normal voice. "Christ, Haller, why should I 'elp you? You picked the bloody flesh off my bones last time you came around here. Bloody flesh off my bones. Besides, the fucking Irish have got every bobby in London pissing down his leg. Dropped another bomb in a letter box in Bayswater yesterday. You can't just pick up hardware on call anymore. They'll twist your soddin' balls off."

A careless fly circled his plate and paused for an instant on an edge. Hamid clapped his hands together in a blur, then slowly wiped his palms on the dark tablecloth.

"They take off bloody backwards, you know that?" he said.

"A Smith and Wesson .38," I said through the prawn. "I can get wildlife lectures at the zoo. With a box of ammunition and a shoulder holster. Don't bother with a pillow." For some reason, silencers were a standard item with the English sporting set, usually thrown in without asking, even though the best ones in the world are no good after two or three shots. A nation of good manners. "And I'd like it this afternoon."

"I'll put in a requisition with Margaret bloody Thatcher," Hamid sneered.

"For £70."

"100."

We settled on 90, and he wrote an address in East London for me on a paper napkin.

"What is it?" I asked as I got up. "One of your kinky specialty brothels? Lounge chairs and leathercraft?"

"You'll feel right at 'ome, cocky," he grinned. "Take a cab back if you get winded."

I took a cab both ways, because of the rain and because I was impatient. People will argue that a London taxi is the most civilized form of public transportation in the world. But then people will argue that everything about London is civilized, that she's still the grand old lady of cities, lifting the hems of her skirts and tiptoeing reluctantly into the squalid twentieth century. The cab got bogged down in the thick midday traffic heading toward Temple Bar, and I tapped my fingers on the seat and wished that this time it weren't so civilized and sluggish.

Why the hell did I think I needed a gun anyway? Not

to chase down one erring bride, hardly old enough to have bought the license. A girl half my age. Goldilocks. But she had run too fast from California. And from New York. And people who worked for Carlo Angeletti probably got in the habit of wearing guns.

On my left, the Bank of England sailed impressively by in the rain. Threadneedle Street. The next signs were for Eastcheap and Cornhill. I sat back in the cab and relaxed a fraction. Anyone who speaks English starts out with a feeling for London, I suppose, when every street sign seems to pop out of a nursery rhyme or a novel. For me, it had the added attraction of nostalgia, since the two years of my UPI stint were long enough ago to seem perfect and unrenewable. I managed a smile to myself. It had also been raining on the day I first arrived in London, 19 years old, fresh off the boat train from Paris, and I had stood on the ramp outside Victoria Station with a map and a guidebook asking stranger after stranger how to get to a bed-and-breakfast house in Russell Square. I knew perfectly well how to get there, of course—the map in my pocket had it circled—but I couldn't believe that all those people really had English accents, and I kept asking just to hear them talk.

I shook my head. Nineteen years old, as innocent and emptyheaded as a guppy. And now I was being chauffered to a brothel to buy a pistol. Freud or Dinah would have a field day.

The meter ticked off ten pences like a clock in a hurry. The streets grew narrow and ugly, even in the obscurity of the black rain, as we left the financial district of the City and entered the part where the tourist buses never run, the immense warren of East London, explosively crowded with a few million dark-skinned immigrants of the empire and a few million more resentful whites. Misery doesn't like company. East London is a melting pot that regularly boils over into gang fights and race riots. It is also the birthplace of Punk. I leaned forward and wiped condensation off the window. Row after twisted row of blackened stoops and bricks. There were parts of London it seemed impossible anybody ever found twice.

The cabbie turned and circled purposefully for ten minutes more, then pulled over in front of a nondescript block of flats as impassively as if we had stopped at Claridge's for tea. Nobody was on the street, and a pair of open garbage pails let the rain drum in monotonously.

"Number 63," he pointed. "Want me to wait, guv? Nearest tube is five minutes' walk."

"Keep the meter running. I won't be long."

He nodded doubtfully and took a £5 note as security. I got out into the bleak rain.

It looked like a brothel, all right, but not for the jet set. From the sidewalk, I saw a door with three sets of locks, sooty brick walls that ran like cheap mascara in the rain, a double window discolored with unidentifiable smears, and a tattered *Playboy* foldout taped to one pane. Next to it, in a plastic candleholder, somebody had stuck an oversized red light bulb, Christmassy or tumescent, depending on your mood. I climbed the steps and stood jamming the bell-press with my finger until an overweight Indian woman in a dirty orange sari opened the door.

"Too early for girls," she said with a giggle. "Not till 2:00."

"Hamid called about me. Mike Haller."

She glanced over her shoulder into the dark hall, squinted and then bobbed her head five or six times.

"You have to wait a little time." She grinned. "He just called. We have a special room."

"I bet you do."

But the special room turned out to be in the back of the building and nothing more than an airless plasterboard cubicle where the customers could lounge. Its furnishings consisted of a stack of folding chairs, like a funeral parlor, and a line of unemptied plastic ashtrays on the window sill. Near the chairs, somebody had abandoned a cheap cup and saucer still half-filled with coffee. The whole place smelled of wet dogs.

The woman gestured vaguely with another giggle and went out. I pried a Players from the pack to deaden my nose and waited. In the hallway outside, a blond young Englishman was vacuuming intensely, bumping the wall molding rhythmically as he rolled the machine over and over the same small space. He wore a bra and panties.

Two cigarettes later, I had learned that flies do take off backwards, just as Hamid had said, and I had unfolded one of the rickety chairs for what was beginning to look like a long wait.

"You agreed with Hamid for a hundred guineas?"

An Indian man about my own age stood in the doorway, gripping a plastic Marks and Spencer shopping bag in front of his belt with both hands. Giggles peeked over his shoulder. I got up gratefully.

"I agreed with Hamid for 90. Pounds, not guineas."

He shrugged with the air of the perpetual small-time loser and handed me the shopping bag. I gave him a packet of £10 notes, which he counted slowly twice while I looked at the pistol and checked the date on the ammunition box. Then we nodded at each other distantly.

"Cheers," Giggles said with a smile.

CHAPTER 2

"Which part of Angeletti's story don't you believe?"

Magnus had just sent back a bottle of wine—
something I had never actually seen done before—and asked
the waiter for Chateau Lynch-Bages '64 instead.

"I don't suppose the club lets you take it home in a dog-
gy cask," I said, buttering a stony dinner roll and wondering
whether to send it back.

"My dear Michael," Magnus murmured with that forgiving
air so many Englishmen take on when they talk to Americans.
We were bent over New Zealand lamb and frozen vegetables
in the Reform Club, his club, just off Pall Mall, though the
heavy oak woodwork and thick dark drapes muffled the outside world so effectively that we might have been miles away
in the country. The Reform Club, Magnus had told me, was
founded in 1832—making it one of the newer ones—by supporters of the first Reform Bill for Parliamentary elections, rav-
ing democrats according to the standards of the day. Not the
slightest taint of democracy, however, had reached the room
where we sat, a long handsome dining hall mostly filled, like

a taxidermist's showroom, with elderly men in gray wool suits and neckties of rousing colors like black and olive green. Why the English male still flocked to these mausoleums I couldn't say, unless it was the wine. No women belonged—Reform has to stop somewhere—and apart from Magnus, the membership so far seemed limited to the better class of zombie. The waiter returned with surprising quickness, before I could figure out a truthful answer to Magnus's question, and started to pour the new wine reverently, frowning at the sediment that drifted up the neck of the bottle.

"'And Time that gave does now his gift confound,'" Magnus recited with an apologetic quaver in his voice to let me know it was poetry. The waiter twisted the bottle at the last moment, so that the sediment just reached the lip, then stopped.

"Auden?" I tried.

He shook his head.

"I dropped out of college around Beowulf"—I shrugged —"as you know."

"My dear Michael, drop out you did indeed. But you have probably read more books of this and that than half the dons at Oxford. Unsystematically, of course. You are not a systematic man." He sipped the wine and nodded dismissal at the waiter. "Shakespeare," he said, turning the full force of his smile on me. "One of the sonnets. We don't quote modern poets in the club, you know. Godawful lot of corpses, aren't we?"

Magnus Harpe. The least-likely zombie in London. He pushed my glass along the table with another smile, and I took a sip. When I first met Magnus, I had been on a summer vacation in Europe after my freshman year of college. The trip was a present from my father, a reward for making it through the first year of his Ivy League alma mater without disgracing him, and the Harpes were old family friends I was supposed to look up. For three days, I had resisted calling anybody in London remotely associated with Boston, but on the fourth night, homesick and lonely, I finally picked up the telephone. And Magnus, to my surprise, turned out to be a figure of great glamor then—15 years my senior, dashingly handsome in a blue-blooded way, an Oxford bachelor with the run of Mayfair debutantes ("a free hand," he called it) and a famous general for a father. Dazzling stuff to a 19-year-old an ocean away from home. "We are going to knock the rough edges off," he had announced, inspecting my clothes and my haircut. "Starting with the opera," he had said after inspecting my empty head, and the next night. I found myself bundled in the back of a long blue Bentley and deposited with Magnus at Covent Garden.

The rough edges were there to stay, but if the world held anything more beautiful than the duet at the end of the first act of *La Bohème*, I had never heard of it, and I spent the rest of my time haunting all the other operas in London and tagging along after Magnus for more revelations. On my last day in England, he had driven me to a celebrity charity shoot in Essex, where potted earls tried to blast flying crockery out of the sky; then to Keats's house in Hampstead, where he made me read "Ode to a Nightingale" in the garden where it had been written; and finally to a black-tie casino and whorehouse in Grosvenor Square, where he had given me £50 and a pat on the back. England in a nutshell, he had called it. The result, of course, was that when I should have boarded the boat to Boston and my second year of college, I had stayed back and taken up *La Bohème* in earnest, living with a second-string blond soprano in Paris and ignoring my father's unhappy letters. A year later, I came back to London to work for UPI."

"Big nose," Magnus said, twirling the wine in his glass. Some old friends you meet awkwardly and never seek out. But Magnus's was the first number I called when I came to London. My worldly tutor, who still sometimes made me feel like a clumsy younger brother around him. The perfect, unrenewable past.

But time sticks out his foot for all of us. Although Magnus had kept his considerable charm, at the age of 52, his good looks had started to crumble in wrinkles and patches, eroded by drink and inactivity. The tall, elegant body had started to look angular instead of lean, the wide shoulders had begun to droop like the wings of a heavy plane. A new moustache was in compensation for the hair, I suppose, a flight officer's clipped brush that made him look a little like Terry Thomas with his teeth fixed; and he was dressed more than ever like a Jermyn Street dandy, creating an effortless patrician effect with a club-bable gray suit cut to perfection, a powder blue tie that puffed out over the Turnbull and Asser silk shirt, shoes from the dark rippled leather of some extinct beast. In the Middle Ages, he would have been an up-and-coming cardinal, a pope's emis-sary, traveling his diplomatic rounds with the easy security of the quick and well-born. In the declining years of the twen-tieth century, he was something called a consulting architect. A troubleshooter, he had once explained indifferently to me, a fixit man who flew off at a moment's notice to Manches-ter or Reading or Surbiton-upon-Crawley or wherever a big project like a shopping center had suddenly run into trouble. His specialty was evidently electrical circuitry, the care, feeding, and rerouting of it, though I had always thought his success was probably due more to his ability to manage people than to technical wizardry.

"Now," he said, leaning confidentially toward me, wine and food all properly arranged. "Now. Which part of Angeletti's sto-ry didn't you believe?"

He really wanted to know. The family connection had been

fathers—my father had worked for his father in the war, running small-time intelligence operations from various anonymous flats near Hanover Square—and Magnus had always considered that I was carrying on the paternal line of work, while he had lapsed into the inelegant world of commerce, letting us all down. Besides, like everybody else, he thought a private detective mixed with a far more interesting class of people, slept late in the mornings, and shared his trenchcoat with Lauren Bacall. I need my illusions too, so I sat in his club, drinking his wine, and I told him about Carlo Angeletti. And Caroline.

"Angeletti. Kind of a snake," Fred had announced two weeks before, after spending an afternoon checking with whoever it is he checks. I'd sat back to listen as he'd paused to roll his cigar into the corner of his mouth. Willie Mays never swung a bat as big as one of Fred's cigars. When he had retired from the San Francisco PD three years ago, I had talked him into helping me out as part-time personal assistant, gadfly, and grandfather figure. He had argued for a while—tracking lost kids was too depressing, he just wanted to loaf—but he had finally come around. You can be an ex-cop, but you can't be an ex-Irishman. He missed the talk, he had explained, more than the money; the talk and the life on the streets. I watched him tip his pork pie hat up from his big Irish nose and hook one thumb under his belt.

"Angeletti's got some riceland in the Delta near Stockton," he said. "Angeletti Farms. But he's not a farmer. Most of his dollars—and there's five or six million—come from three oil tankers that he works freelance all over, but mainly in Europe." He looked at a brown envelope covered with notes. "Marseilles, London, Bremen. Like that. Makes him kind of an absentee owner, but apparently that's the way a lot of small tanker peo-

ple operate. Set up an office in Monrovia where the boat buys
its flag, then you go retire to the Alps and bank by mail. He's a
widower, late 60s. Came across in 1947 from the old country
on a French visa—Italians sometimes did that after the war if
they had political problems—never been back, which means
either he likes it here or he had problems. Got bad asthma and
a gimpy leg. Got one son, 24, went to Stanford, bums around
now. Got two Sevilles he buys every October, always dark blue,
same color as Nixon's suits. Got a houseboat, a powerboat, an
office in the Wells Fargo building on Montgomery Street, and
a permanent suite at the Mark Hopkins. But the houseboat is
where he lives, maybe on account of the asthma, maybe on account of the Federal Reserve bank inspectors."

"Is that the snake part?"

"Yeah. He's got controlling stock in a couple of Valley savings and loans, and the Feds have been wondering for years
why so many guys come from so far just to open accounts
there. And why they usually make their first deposit from a
grocery bag."

"He runs a laundry?"

Fred shrugged. "It's not against the law to accept cash in
your bank," he said. "You know that, Mike. You can take anything from anybody. You just got to make a report to the FDIC
on any cash deposit over $10,000. Angeletti's banks make ten,
12 reports like that a quarter. Mostly hippies, the Feds figure,
bringing in the hash money, or whatever." He rolled the cigar to the other corner. "Hell, there's a lot bigger operations
than that. There's a couple of banks in Miami don't deposit ten
personal checks a year. 'Course they're holding hands with the
Cubans, who grow more goddamn dope than sugar cane under
Castro. Now Angeletti, he's not Family, or hooked in with the
racket, but he's not a softball player either." He had taken out

the cigar and sucked his teeth noisily. "I can't imagine what you got that he ain't already bought."

Three hours later, I was stopped on a narrow asphalt road in the heart of the Delta and staring at a simple wooden sign-post that had "Angeletti" painted neatly across the top. Parallel to the road on the left ran a high bank of brown earth, 15 or 20 feet high. On the right, the roadbed slumped into brackish mud and tall, coarse pampas grass, then rose abruptly into an-other levee. Beyond that were the endless mazes of brown dikes and green waterways and locks that make up the 500 square miles of the Delta, the swampy mass of roads and canals just east of San Francisco, where the Sacramento River meets the bay. After the sample of its convolutions that afternoon, I felt like a laboratory rat that couldn't find the cheese.

In the gold-miner days, there used to be Mississippi-style gambling boats floating up and down the Delta from San Fran-cisco to Sacramento, and more than one floating brothel. Now there are a few bait shops and package stores, a few settlements of tubercular Chinese, descendants of the ones who came to build the railroads, and some scattered hippie communes that live on fish and herbs and bootleg drugs. Them and Carlo An-geletti. The cheese stands alone.

I sighed and started to nurse the Mercedes along the road, wondering if its 1958 paint job was going to blister and peel in the August sun. The last temperature I had seen was on a bank in a little town with the wishful name of Winters, ten miles back. 102, it had read. When I came to another signpost, I stopped again. Next to it sat a small white guardhouse, like a bus stop shelter, and a ten-foot cyclone gate in the levee.

I leaned out into the fierce heat. Overhead, in a sky the color of chromium, a few black shadows circled. Hawks.

"Haller? Michael Haller?"

A rangy man in sports shirt, slacks, and his early 30s bounded out of the guardhouse, much too energetically, and walked to the car, bending toward me with a bright, toothy, professional smile. Even the little alligator on his shirt was smiling.

"Haller," I agreed.

"Right on time." I was half an hour late. "Mr. Angeletti can see you in about five minutes." He peered into the car, not carelessly. "Mind if I ride up to the house with you? It's damn hot out here."

He waved to the guardhouse before I could answer, and a dark-skinned man in a security uniform emerged to swing open the gate. I watched the barbed wire glint along its top while the smiling man got in.

"My name's Hunter Merriman," he said pleasantly, pumping my hand and smiling again. "Mr. Angeletti's attorney. Just drive straight ahead and pull up by the left side of the house. We'll go right to his office."

On the other side of the levee was a deepwater channel, black and sparkling. Maybe a quarter of a mile across it stretched a long line of grass, beyond that other lines of grass crisscrossing, and finally the distant shadows of the coastal-range mountains, humping out of the black water like gigantic shadowy fish. The road, all mud and rut now, ran along the channel to another gate, left open, and then to a flat, beautifully tended lawn.

"Just park right there with those others," Merriman instructed, and I sailed us in next to a snarling Maserati convertible that looked as if it needed to be defanged. Merriman's, I figured. People who smile that much usually want to bite. Next to it stood somebody's Buick, then a little apart, looking straight ahead like solemn watchdogs, was a pair of dark blue

Sevilles. On the grass in front of them, some grackles browsed. Then a hedge of bottlebrush, a short dock, and at the end of the dock, smug and white as a Georgia plantation house, floated Carlo Angeletti's houseboat.

"A beauty, isn't it?" Merriman said, swinging his door open. "Mr. Angeletti can't take the damp in San Francisco anymore—arthritis—so he had this custom-made."

"Who was the architect? Robert E. Lee?"

Merriman squeezed out a chuckle. "It does look Southern, doesn't it? He had one of those old Sacramento riverboats converted. The paddle wheel was his own idea, and the steampipes. It never leaves the dock, though." The grackles took off with a squawk as we slammed our doors. "The office is on the second floor."

Angeletti made us wait five minutes, to keep things clear. Meanwhile, Merriman dealt me a cup of coffee from a sideboard and I looked around admiringly at the office, a big room comfortably stuffed with desk, leather club chairs, bookcases, filing cabinets, and expensive knickknacks. The floor was covered with a red and blue Mishkin rug like the one in Shirley Mendelsohn's office, the kind the Iranians won't sell to us anymore. The walls had a few paintings of landscapes and castles, beautifully framed in carved wood, and a big travel poster of the Coliseum in Rome, probably hiding a wall safe full of Confederate money. Half a cup later, somebody coughed outside, the door whispered open, and Carlo Angeletti himself limped in, followed by a tall young man in a suit.

If I had been expecting the godfather, I was disappointed. Angeletti turned out to be a bony, horsefaced old man, tanned the color of cardboard, a harmless Italian papa in Hawaiian shirt and khaki trousers. He bobbed his head and shook hands with a smile, showing a gap on the right side of his mouth where the teeth used to be, and hobbled on the bad leg to his desk. The young man went to the other side and sat down. What hair Angeletti had was neatly trimmed in a gray wreath around his ears. His face was furred with a two-day stubble of beard. The mouth kept smiling as he sat down, pink and moist like a baby bird's beak.

"Merriman is here to see that everything is arranged right," he said in a thick accent that sounded as much French as Italian to me. Merriman slid an espresso cup in front of him. "Money, travel, whatever. I want you to find my boy's wife."

He jerked his hand toward the young man who had come in behind him. Piero Alberti, but known as Peter A. at Stanford, according to Fred. Less of a snake, apparently. An economics major of no particular academic distinction, graduated two years ago with a varsity letter in gymnastics, swinging on the rings. All set to take over the tanker-banker business one of these days, maybe sooner rather than later. He was already dressed for the part, beige tropical suit, brown loafers, checked sports shirt, and one of those very trim haircuts. If he wore a tie, it would probably light up and say "preppie." Right now he just wore the sullen look of the very young and wealthy. Merriman let him get his own coffee.

I glanced at Peter A. and sat still. People talk more, Fred is always saying, if you don't.

"She disappeared on July 28." Merriman took over. "Last week. She drove into town to do some shopping, at the J. Magnin's on Arden Way. In Sacramento. She took Piero's car, the Maserati"—I sloshed coffee in my cup—"which we found the next day at the Sacto airport in the short-term parking lot. But no Caroline, not a trace."

"Did you call the police?"

Angeletti spread his hands wide in a Mediterranean gesture of fraternity, and I looked back at him. "Mr. Haller." He smiled, very serious, very friendly.

"Mr. Haller, I'm the old school, you know? You see how I live out here." The hands took in Mt. Vernon, the glistening water outside, the long flat horizon of canals and scrub vegetation. "We like our privacy, Mr. Haller. You know?"

I nodded back fraternally. He probably had millions of good reasons in the bank not to call the police.

"And so naturally you prefer a private operative."

"*Prego,* Mr. Haller." The hands fell back. "I prefer you."

"Did you try to track her?"

"Merriman did."

"She took an Air West flight at 11:30 to San Francisco," Merriman said. "After that—zero. She could have flown off again, she could have gone into town. We didn't check any airlines or limousines. That's not my kind of work."

*Prego.* He made it sound menial and distasteful, which isn't far wrong sometimes.

"Did she take anything with her?" I asked. Merriman cocked an eyebrow and I explained: "Cash? Jewelry? Traveler's checks?"

"Oh. She had a little over $800 with her. Pocket money."

"Sure." I enjoy lawyers. "Credit cards?"

He looked at Angeletti.

"I give 'em both American Express," Angeletti said with a flip of his hand toward Piero.

"We won't know if she used it until the bills come in." Merriman again. "This is her picture." He handed me a manilla folder. "Vital statistics, background."

I held it unopened in my lap and shifted slightly toward Piero. "Was there a quarrel between you two? Bad feeling? Any kind of immediate cause for her to leave?"

"Nothing like that." Merriman answered for him too. I was

getting a little tired of Merriman. "Caroline was a girl Piero met in South Tahoe working as a cocktail waitress in one of the clubs." He smiled as cheerfully as if she had been a debutante from Hillsborough.

Piero said, "Yeah," and stroked his chin in embarrassment. Not so great in the Stanford alumni news.

"The marriage was fine," Merriman said. "They had the usual spats, but Mr. Angeletti was content."

"How long have you been married?"

"Six months," Piero mumbled.

"January 19th," Merriman said.

"So why me?"

"I'm sorry?"

"Why not Bums or Pinkerton or somebody with a big organization that can work ten airports at a time?"

"We've heard of you, Mike," Merriman said. Angeletti showed his gums in approval of this friendly informality. You get first names only in most of California now, anyway. Some say it defuses hostility. Dinah says it's because of short attention spans.

"Michael," I said, just to be a snot.

"Michael." You could bounce rocks off Merriman's smile. "You've built up quite a reputation for finding missing persons. It seems to be your specialty, right?" He didn't expect an answer. "And you have the qualifications for this. Caroline is English, you see, and Mr. Angeletti and Piero have the idea that she might have returned to England. Homesick, maybe, some problem back there she didn't want to talk about. They wanted somebody who has experience in Europe." He gestured toward a pile of papers on Angeletti's desk. My folder, I assumed. "You spent one year working in France, then two more working in London for the wire services. You spent a year with Interpol, some time in the Army, then three more years in LA before you came up to San Francisco and opened your own office. You left LA because of a fistfight with another reporter, Carlton Hand, over a woman. You spent your year with Interpol on the French-Italian border."

"Uh-huh."

He tapped the papers with his finger. "You scored 590 out of 600 on the State Department French exam in 1972, but never followed it up."

"There were two gold fillings in 1958 you missed."

"Mr. Angeletti likes things thorough"—smugly. He folded his arms across his chest, indicating that he was going to talk about money. "Mr. Angeletti is prepared to pay you a $3,000 advance, $200 a day, and expenses. Within reason."

Mr. Angeletti was just then toying with a foot-long polished mahogany model of an oil tanker that must have cost twice the advance. It would make a wonderful cigarette lighter, I figured, or you could just use it to spill oil in the bathtub. The brass plate on the hull said "Luchon."

"Two-fifty," I said. "And I have two questions."

Merriman didn't even glance at the desk. "All right. Your questions?"

"First, why do you want her found? You could have any marriage less than a year old annulled under California law, no community property, no financial liability. Second, what do you want me to do if I can find her?"

Piero flushed. Papa turned the model tanker around and pointed it toward the far wall, as if he could give it a push and watch it float through the air. Merriman tilted his head significantly toward the manilla folder I held. I turned the cover and looked at the first picture of Caroline Angeletti.

She looked back from beside a swimming pool at somebody's house, one hand on the diving board, one hip cocked

and aimed at the camera in a gesture she meant to be pro-
vocative. But she was much too young to carry it off—no more
than 20—and the effect was oddly beguiling, innocent, like a
little girl in lipstick and playing dress-up. Medium height, long
blond hair. Small high breasts. No smile, just the too wide,
heartbreaking curve of mouth you often see in the English,
sensual and sad. A colt.

"She's a lovely girl," Merriman said.

"She's a beauty," Angeletti growled. He was holding the
tanker extended between his palms now, the way you might
measure a fish. "Piero wants her back." Piero squirmed. "I'm
the old school," his father continued. "These are just a couple
of kids, that's all. But I don't like to see them break up a marriage. You marry, you stay married." The accent sounded more
Italian every minute. I nodded to show I would remember.
"And I don't like my boy to be unhappy," he said, tipping his
head toward Piero.

"All right. What do you want me to do if I find her?"

"You should report to me," Merriman said, "every two
days. My office and home numbers are in there; an answering
service will always reach me. We—Mr. Angeletti—wants no
action taken. Simply report where she is."

Angeletti put down the boat and stood up. We all stood
up too. "She's not a bad girl, Mike," he said. I looked around
at the indentations on the backs of the chairs, hoping I could
give Piero my empty coffee cup to put away. Merriman took it
instead. "You find her," Angeletti said, "we talk to her, get her
back home. That's all. Very reasonable." Merriman swung the
door open for me. "But, hey!" Angeletti's voice went hoarse,
holding me a moment longer. "You be damn sure you don't
find her with somebody else."

He showed me his empty gums and laughed to take the

bite off, but on the way out, I still wondered if that was an instruction or a warning. I also wondered what a nice young Stanford graduate was doing wearing a pistol holster in the small of his back.

"She's pregnant," Magnus said. "The old man wants a grandson. The Italians always do." He finished his wine and made a face. "The general used to be the same way. Too late now."

I ignored the reference to Magnus's less than happy marriage and spooned some of the dessert onto a plate. A syllabub, Magnus's recommendation. Wretched sweet stuff that made my two gold fillings rattle.

"Damn pretty girl," he said, handing the photograph back.

I smiled at his English reserve. When I had shown the picture to Fred three days earlier, he had wiggled his eyebrows up and down and given a long, loud whistle. "That one makes my socks roll up and down," he had said. "I feel 50 again." And he had studied me thoughtfully for half a minute. "You and women," he had said, putting the torch to another of his cigars and folding his hands over his middle like a pot-bellied stove. "You and women. You're not a womanizer, Mike, but, for a rough and ready bachelor, you've got a dreamy streak." He puffed smoke. "And a domestic streak. You'll wake up one morning a family man yet." He puffed again. "With Dinah."

"I'll wake up one morning face down in a Delta bayou," I had said, not bothering to deny either charge.

"It's listening to all those operas," he said. "You start to think you're a white knight."

"I start to think I'm a detective."

Magnus coughed loudly and brought me back to London. "How is your girl Dinah, by the way?" he asked as I refolded the photograph and tucked it in my jacket.

"She's annoyed with me," I said. "She says that going to the opera is my only proof of a sense of humor."

Magnus chuckled.

I pushed my syllabub toward the center of the table. "You should have a Reform dentist in attendance with this stuff," I said.

"The old man was lying, wasn't he?" Magnus persisted.

"Somebody usually is. He knows, or his son knows, why the girl left home, and it's important to them. It's just not important to tell me."

"And does that bother you?"

"No," I said half-truthfully. "I'll find out why when I find her."

"As you no doubt expect to do very shortly."

"I've traced her this far," I said. "Sacramento to San Francisco. San Francisco to New York. One day stopover—I don't know why—then Alitalia to London. But London—there's no way even to start on London, 15,000,000 people, 10,000 hotels. So tomorrow I drive up to Ely to interview her parents. When people bolt, they usually head for familiar territory at first, though you'd think the opposite. For the same reason, they usually change their names but keep their initials." I finished my wine, placed the glass beside my empty dessert plate, and started tracing the Reform Club monogram idly with my fork.

"And you know that her home is in Ely because . . . ?"

"She was born in London, in 1960 in fact, according to her marriage license. But her parents have moved away. At least they're not in the phone book. Her passport application two years ago gives an address in Ely but no telephone."

"Um," Magnus said, straightening and grimacing. "I thought that sort of thing was confidential. I mean, you can't just walk into the Home Office and ask for a file."

"England ought to pay her civil servants more."

"Dear, dear," he said, somehow without making himself

sound spinsterish. "You bribed the passport clerk." He loved it. "I can see why Angeletti hired you."

"Angeletti's lawyer recommended me," I said, "and Angeletti has probably gotten in the habit of doing what his lawyer recommends."

"And if I looked closely inside your jacket, would I see an illegal gun which his lawyer recommended?"

"Not with my tailor you wouldn't," I said, feeling the weight of the pistol along my ribs. "Sir Robert Hall. But I'm wearing a gun because I always do. And because I'm not certain that Angeletti isn't having me followed."

Magnus looked incredulously around the dining room. The zombies continued to graze.

"I've seen nothing and nobody," I told him apologetically. A waiter materialized and took away one plate in each hand. "But it's what some people would do in his place, with his money."

"A stalking horse," Magnus nodded. He liked American slang of a certain vintage. It sounded like cloaks and daggers and derring-do, the Great War come round again. "A stalking horse for the girl. Let you do the work and find her, then dismiss you, step in himself, and—smack!" He clapped his hands softly, looked down at them, and shook his head in admiration. "The Italians never change, do they? Most jealous, possessive people on earth." Another waiter appeared with a chit, which he signed, and we stood up. "There's one way to be sure you aren't followed to Ely tomorrow, young horse," he said.

"What's that?"

His face lit up in a conspiratorial smile. "Let me fly you in the company plane."

CHAPTER **3**

SAVAGE PEOPLE, THE ENGLISH.

Just because they stand in line for buses, everybody in America talks about British civility and fair play and *Masterpiece Theatre* on the BBC. Take them out of the bus queues, on the other hand, and plunk them in their cars and the whole country drives like sun-crazed Druids late for a sacrifice.

Magnus certainly did, like the high priest himself—ferocious, unsentimental, very fast, and bloody-minded. Rain had grounded the little single-engine plane he flew himself from job to job, so he switched us at the last minute to his big white XJ touring Jaguar, raising my status considerably at the White Horse Hotel but making us about as inconspicuous as the Batmobile as we snarled across Bloomsbury Square.

Nobody followed us anyway, nobody that I could spot in the heavy morning traffic and the unending gray rain. We fought the Battle of Britain again up Tottenham Court Road, peeled through the maze of streets around King's Cross station, and, shouldering aside an Austin Mini and a lorry full of chickens, finally jumped at 80 miles an hour onto the A-1 motorway toward Ely. There the Jaguar's 12 cylinders took over, and we drove in companionable silence through the lush green countryside, in and out of pockets of rain. From time to time, I scanned the cars behind us, but caught no sign of anything unusual; Magnus studied his mirror soberly, far more alert.

Mostly I thought of California, to tell the truth, California and England. I had driven to Carlo Angeletti's houseboat through the kind of landscape that simply doesn't exist in Europe, apart from a few desolate square miles in central Spain and the northern Hebrides, a landscape almost untouched by people. Once upon a time, somebody had come into the Delta, built the levees and roads, and gone away again, leaving Nature ready to take a swipe with her paw and level it whenever she felt in the mood. But everywhere I looked from Magnus's car, I saw houses, hills, orchards that had been populated for centuries, a landscape as humanly shaped and softened as an old coat. Maybe Caroline Angeletti had simply looked around once too often at the flat angles of the Great Central Valley and bolted for home. California could do that.

Magnus swung the car around a kamikaze dump truck and passed a real Tudor cottage by the side of the road, its white plaster strapped together with thatch and oak. There was one like it in Redwood City, except it was three times the size, a Best Western motel, and had a miniature-golf course in front. I could sit in my Green Street apartment in San Francisco and watch the Pacific sink its teeth into the raw Marin hills and understand Caroline's disappearance, all right. But before I started whistling "Rule, Britannia," I thought about her father-in-law's big gesturing hands and her new husband's idea of sportswear. Goldilocks could have other reasons for leaving.

"Still like England as much as ever, Michael?" Magnus asked suddenly, gesturing at the marshy horizon of East Anglia.

"More than ever." The Tudor motel in Redwood City, I remembered, had a plaster copy of Venus de Milo on top of a fountain of colored water.

"It's a wonder we haven't gnawed this bloody island bare," Magnus said. "You can wear out a country the same as a car, you know." He pointed one big finger at a sign that hurtled past on the left. "Have a look at Ely cathedral, if you like. Half an hour detour this time of day, through city center. The spiritual flagship of East Anglia."

"Another time, Magnus."

"Quite right," he said. "Falling apart anyway, like everything else in England. Like yours truly."

"Picturesque, I'm sure," I said, never sure how to answer the inverted English pride in national disaster. "Both of you."

"Be a bloody ruin in a few more years. Both of us. The nave is full of decapitated statues of saints, you know, all their heads chopped off by Oliver Cromwell. Your chap Angeletti would love it."

"More the thing for a consulting architect, Magnus."

"Missing heads are rather different from missing persons. No remedy for them." He turned to look at me, amused, affectionate. The daylight cut deeper lines in his face than the Reform Club gloom had done last night and brought out the tiny brown liver spots across the backs of his hands. Time that gave. "You never stop thinking about business, do you, Michael? Not money, I mean. But work."

"*Lieben und Arbeiten,*" I said, the only German I know. Dinah had taught it to me.

"Freud," he looked back at the road. "To love and to work. The only test of maturity, Freud said." His face turned heavy and blank, and I knew he was thinking of Susannah, his wife. "Age, of course, is not the same thing as maturity." Pompous in someone else. Sad in my old friend. Whatever had gone wrong there had taken its toll of him, boring through that urbane facade. What do you do when your marriage is a long, slow failure? Drive too fast and hang around with men you think are happier? Magnus just had a negative self-image, they would say in California. The trick, they would say, is to get in touch with your feelings. The trick, I thought, is to get your feelings to shut up.

"Collin lives in a place called Caldwell Gardens," I said after a moment, faintly embarrassed. "On the north side of town."

"I shall have you there," he said, pressing the accelerator and smiling with his old charm, "in ten minutes or less, buster. The only way you could be followed would be by rocket."

No rocket, no tail. Ten minutes later to the dot, we pulled through the meager stone gate of Caldwell Gardens and set about looking for number 47. Gardens meant subdivision, of course—real estate jargon is the same everywhere, like thieves' Latin—and we found the father outside, puttering around a tiny slip of lawn in front of his semi-detached rural villa, as the developer no doubt described it. A few neighbors down the row of shabby houses looked up curiously as Magnus parked the Jaguar and we got out.

"Mr. Collin? Anthony Collin?"

He was a tall man, thin and birdlike. Older than I had expected, 70 at least, with runny blue eyes and a slight stoop. He straightened and watched us come through the little gate. "My name is Haller," I said, handing him a card. "This is Mr. Harpe, my associate. We're engaged in legal work for a client in the United States and wondered if we could ask a few questions about your daughter, Caroline."

He wiped his hands deliberately on his corduroy work pants

and took my card, reading it longer than seemed necessary. Then he glanced at Magnus, taking in the expensive black and white houndstooth jacket, the gray trousers, the gleaming handmade shoes. The English would try to establish the social class of an angel. Finally he handed the card back to me and spoke in a high-pitched, rheumy voice.

"She's not in trouble?"

"No, sir. I don't think she's in trouble. Could we step inside, perhaps, and talk for a moment?" I let my head tilt toward the watching neighbors. After another pause, he nodded and led us the five or six steps into the house.

Inside the small, darkened parlor, over-furnished with cheap tea-tables and stuffed upholstery, he looked even more birdlike, less substantial. No lamp in the daytime, he explained, retreating to a chair across the room, electricity is expensive. We sat down formally on the couch, and Magnus, touching his moustache with one finger, looked in obvious dismay at the shelves of cheap porcelain figurines along one whole wall, almost all variations in different colors of the early-Christian fish symbol. One short stretch at the top was given over to Western paperbacks of the Max Brand variety. Below, on the coffee table between us and the old man, sat a huge Jerusalem Bible, half a dozen fringed bookmarks protruding like quills; beside it lay month-old copies of *House and Garden* and *The Missionary,* arranged at careful right angles to the table. Upstairs a television muttered angrily. A woman's voice called something incoherent.

"My wife is an invalid and doesn't leave her bed," Mr. Collin said, ignoring the voice. "You can tell me what you have to say."

I explained that his daughter's father-in-law was concerned about the fact that she had left their home and her husband two weeks ago. He thought she might have returned to England and had hired me to find her.

He pursed his lips into a beak. "We were not invited to Caroline's wedding," he said, going straight to an old wound. "One might call us estranged from our daughter." His eyes turned constantly to Magnus as he talked, as if to defy him to find something wrong with his accent, his choice of words. Magnus frowned down at the table. "We lost touch with her when she went away to university. She won an exhibition to Cambridge, you know, but she never finished her degree . . ." His voice trailed off. A shadow lay in his lap like a baby. Magnus coughed. "Caroline is an only child, a December child. Difficult to manage at our age. Perhaps if you told me why she has run away?"

"To be honest, I don't know, Mr. Collin. Neither her husband nor her father-in-law could say. There was no quarrel. She simply disappeared voluntarily about two weeks ago, taking a plane to New York and then, I think, to London. We're not sure."

Collin blinked his runny eyes at me for a moment before he spoke again, bobbing his Adam's apple in a swallow.

"She's in England, I reckon."

Magnus looked up and stirred beside me. I motioned him still with a hand.

"Are you certain?"

"Yes. We received a . . . letter from her two days ago."

"From London?"

"It wasn't actually a letter," he said, turning his gaze toward the shelves of figurines. Sadness crept into his voice, settled into his face. "She sent us a postal money order, for £50, without any message. We haven't actually heard from her since the notice of her wedding. But it was her signature."

"Do you still have the money order, Mr. Collin?"

"No," he said, looking hard at the shelves. "I took the bus into town yesterday and deposited it in my bank. I'm a pensioner, you see. I retired from the Ely Missionary Trust three years ago. The money was welcome." He licked his lips with a gray tongue that popped out like a mouse. "The money order was drawn on the Trinity Street branch of the Cambridge Post Office, if that information helps you."

"It does indeed. Thank you." Magnus and I stood up. "If she writes again, you would do me a favor by ringing me, collect, at my London hotel." I wrote on a card and placed it on the table, on top of *The Missionary*. Anthony Collin regarded it suspiciously, as if he wanted to ask a question. Instead, he sat silently, bony fingers curved around the ends of the chair arms. I glanced around the room, where the fish now seemed to be swimming in a box of shadows, and we let ourselves out.

"Brrrrr." Magnus shook himself as he slammed the Jaguar's door on Caldwell Gardens. He stiffened his legs and turned his long, handsome face to me. "'It does indeed,'" he mocked, "'engaged in legal work for a client'—my God, I didn't know you could sound so much like a bloody lawyer. Positively gruesome. I thought a private eye was supposed to growl out of the comer of his mouth and slap his suspects silly, instead of trading pompous phrases like the Lord High Chancellor in his wig. You've ruined all my illusions." The rain had begun again, slanting against the windshield. "He was fiddling, wasn't he?"

I shrugged and lit a Players, only the third of the day. "There was either a message or more money than he told us."

"I bet on the money."

"So do I. Correspondence is a dying art."

Magnus thought about that and listened to the rain march up and down the Jaguar's roof. Then he turned the key in the ignition and whipped us around in a U, spraying water onto the narrow sidewalk. "Hold tight for just an hour," he announced, "and I shall deposit us both in the finest bar in Cambridge, in front of two beakers of the true, the blushful Hippocrene."

"Keats," I guessed.

"Gin," he said.

"If you had traveled in the Middle Ages," Magnus asked, "how would you have known you were approaching a city?"

We were approaching Cambridge on a branch of the A-4 more than an hour later, thanks to tie-ups in Ely. The rain had vanished once again, leaving a pleasant haze in the air and a smudge of industrial smoke. I looked blank at his question.

"Great black clouds like this," he said. He waved a hand at the smoke, scattering the crumbs of an Oxford education.

"Smog?"

"Not far off. Flies actually. The first urban pollution. Could see them for miles apparently."

I made a note to tell Hamid.

"But really, Michael," he said, as if returning to a previous question, "why do you do it? Why specialize in tracking down missing people? Persons, as Americans insist on saying. Banging into pensioners' flats, living in third-class hotels. There must be more lucrative branches to the detective trade."

Magnus had not enjoyed our visit to Ely, I thought. Angeletti, Hamid, Collin—I had had enough of old men, too.

"I suppose I just drifted into it," I finally answered.

He shot the Jaguar around a sluggish Rover, his hands cupped loosely at the bottom of the steering wheel as Englishmen are mysteriously taught to drive. "No one just drifts, Michael," he said with a sideways glance at me. "There is a tide in the affairs of men. Bloody undertow, too," he added after a second. "But still, you're not really the sort for business espionage or divorce cases, are you? Too impatient."

"A psychiatrist would probably say I identify with the people I track." Magnus looked over, interested. "Most of them suddenly throw off the accumulated weight of a whole life," I went on, "even a whole personality. It's everybody's occasional fantasy, but these people actually do it. They just jump off the ends of their lives and go off to be something completely different. The police call them rabbits, bolting for a hole."

"And you catch them, old hound, and spoil it."

"It's not really possible," I said, thinking of San Francisco and Dinah, and how ties turn into knots. "Only a powerful fantasy. Besides, I don't always catch them." There had been James Barkan of the Oakland flatlands, for example, 53 years old when he ran away for no demonstrable reason in the world, a butcher whose wife wanted him back. There was no girlfriend, no debt, no terminal disease. Just a bad case of what the church used to diagnose as despair. Now it's a mid-life crisis that goes off in the middle of a passage, according to a timetable in *People* magazine. The 42:05. But passages just go to other rooms. The police had pulled Barkan's head out of a gas oven in Seattle. A rabbit.

"You quit school, old man, and chased across half of Europe. Then you quit reporting and took up missing persons," Magnus said. Traffic beeped and swayed.

"I didn't vanish anywhere," I pointed out reasonably.

"California," he said firmly, "is off the map." I smiled, but he went on seriously, tapping some nerve of his own. "You've felt that pressure, too. It's not merely imagination. What are you now—38, 39? Just starting to feel it really. I'm 15 years older. It starts about then, where you are now, and it doesn't stop. At 40, you begin asking yourself about all that time that's simply gone, run right through your fingers, about as memorable as yesterday's empty bottle. You think about all the things you've done and you've left undone, as the Prayer Book says. At 50, you start asking where's your bloody *hair* gone, but you're really talking about what a proper mess you've made of your life and how little time you have left to take control of it. What a *waste* it's all been." His eyes moved mechanically across the traffic as we sped up again. "Father's generation had things easier, you know. The war took care of that. Changed everybody's life at once. Let them start all over again, like your rabbits. Gave it some point." We rolled past light gray Gothic buildings, the first of the Cambridge colleges. "They say a man's life is shaped like an hourglass, wide at the top and bottom, pinched in the middle. You're feeling the pinch, all right." He switched lanes abruptly. "I know I bloody well am."

I looked out the car window. We were still in the midst of what English weathermen, in a wonderful phrase that sounds faintly magical, call a sunny spell, and the light splashed off the old buildings in a lively dance. Through a courtyard, I caught glimpses of a distant river and what looked like church towers.

"Caroline Angeletti is younger than most of the people I track," I said after a moment.

"Indeed she is. And prettier too, if that photograph's any good. No mid-life crisis for her, by God. Good old-fashioned villainy, cops and robbers, and Mafiosi in-laws. Splendid."

I sat admiring Magnus's emotional agility, the capacity to spring from mood to mood like a performing flea. After a moment, he tilted his head in my direction and added in his best avuncular tones, "Just be sure, old lad, that you're not confusing your high-minded mission with a case of the middle-age letches. She has that vulnerable look you romantic Puritans always fall for. Innocent as a sacrificial lamb."

He turned left, following a sign that said City Centre and passing close to a great arched gateway. "I wish I had gone to Cambridge," he said in another leap of association. "Much more beautiful buildings than Oxford. That's Christ College there on the right, the gate. John Milton's college. You'd like him. Another steely-eyed romantic Puritan like you. A damn meddling rebel." We stopped at a light and Magnus twisted in the seat to face me, all the old banter back in his voice. "Now give us the truth, Michael," he said. "When you find this girl, do you really plan to tell Angeletti?"

The gin was served up at the Blue Boar Inn on Trinity Street, not far from the Post Office branch and next door to Heffer's, which billed itself in the window as the biggest bookstore in the world. Along with the gin came roast beef sandwiches and a nostalgic monologue about Magnus's college days, leading by stages to more complaints about the present state of Susannah's bitchiness, then the dreariness of a new design he was rehabilitating for a shopping center near Brighton. His interest in Caroline Angeletti seemed to have blown away with the weather.

"Brighton's near your country place anyway, isn't it, Magnus?" I said, polite and restless. The Blue Boar grandfather clock read twenty to three, and the day outside had turned warm and muggy.

"Oh yes, only 20 miles away. Best-known tourist spot in England once, Brighton; all the American troop trains in the war used to stand there for hours, waiting to be rerouted."

"Forget the troop trains," I told him, putting down my coffee cup. "Let's go stalk missing persons."

But Magnus begged off, to my surprise. There was bugger-all business in London, he said, there was the extra time he had already taken, there was the great bitch Susannah. I rescued my overnight bag from the Jaguar, relieved as much as irritated, and promised to call when I got back. With a rueful face, he slid the Jaguar effortlessly into the summer traffic.

Work. Magnus was a fascinating man, one of my oldest friends, and when he was up, nobody's conversation could be more richly stocked or interesting; but I was tired of old men and tired of middle-aged men on introspective binges; I wanted to stretch out and work, work alone. The sleuthhound doesn't run in a pack. I checked the bag at the desk of the Blue Boar and started to walk the half mile to King's College, where Caroline Collin had been a student for two years. Won an exhibition, as her father said, and vanished.

Even in August, of course, the students were there. All of a sudden, the world is permanently swarming with students, the way the Middle Ages were swarming with flies. But in Cambridge, they seemed amiable enough, whirling down the narrow medieval streets on their bicycles or spilling off the foot-wide sidewalks in talkative, idle groups. Some of them even carried books, which made a change from California. Nobody noticed an aging youth. I crossed a street, circled a church, and entered the wider thoroughfare of King's Parade. To my left stretched Victorian storefronts, miscellaneous offices, a precious-looking coffee shop named "The Whim"; to my right, the dignified cream-colored stone of the college buildings, punctuated by an occasional Gothic archway and a glimpse of bright green grass.

Soho is my idea of a center of learning, I guess. There had been a sign on the quadrangle gate of my famous old New England college that said solemnly, "Enter to Grow in Wisdom." But I had told my father it was on the wrong side of the gate. College towns don't make me nostalgic like Magnus, just impatient.

I tried to picture Caroline in Cambridge as I walked. A ripe adolescent, barely 17 when she arrived, according to the folder, newly sprung from a missionary cell of invalidism and

Bibles, as ready to skitter into the 1980 version of freedom as a ball of Silly Putty. California, here I come. I understood the temptation to drop out, all right, and go off to the land of hot tubs and sunshine. And I understood landing in trouble sooner or later. But the troubles were different for her generation. Teenagers in San Francisco now sport magnum pistols loaded with dum-dum bullets; grammar schools have drug counselors. In 1960, when I had turned my back on respectable oppression, not one kid in 1,000, I suppose, had tasted marijuana, let alone the new fast food of higher education, the angel dust, LSD, coke, and quaaludes that I regularly pull out of the pockets of runaways and that Dinah counsels her niece against. In 1960, I would have gone into a head shop to buy a hat. Caroline had dropped out into a rougher world, with no Magnus to offer happy landings. Instead, by the luck of the draw, she had dropped in on Carlo Angeletti.

Just before I reached the imposing gate of King's College —no inscription about wisdom that I could see—a young man in Levi's and shoulder-length hair detached himself from a wall and trotted over to hand me a flier. It announced a rock concert to end apartheid. Over his head, over the green college quadrangle, rose the famous chapel, 600 years old, built for a willful king. Henry VI, I thought, the one who was later beaten goofy by Joan of Arc. I could ask Magnus. I took the flier and walked inside the gate, where some Japanese tourists were gaping as a solitary white-haired don ambled across the lawn, the folds of his black academic gown flapping like a bat's wings in the breeze. At the edge of the lawn, a neatly painted sign announced that only Fellows of the College were allowed to walk on the grass. England is a tight little island, I thought, but its distances are great.

Ian Lange, Esq., lived in a fortress called Bodley's Court, near the river. He answered the door on the second knock and looked down a red nose and several cascading chins in displeasure.

"You're not Alan," he said and started to close the door again.

I gave him a card, the one with the tommy gun rampant, and three fast sentences about what I wanted.

"I haven't time to see you," he pouted through a faint Scotch burr. "I have someone due in five minutes."

"She *was* your student, Professor Lange?"

"Doctor," he corrected automatically, "not professor. Vulgar Americanism. All right, five minutes, until he comes."

He spun on a heel and a toe and led me through a dark hallway to the sitting room. Opera drifted softly from a record player on a table, laughter from students on the river bank below. He walked the length of a wall of books, stopped beside a fair reproduction of one of Cezanne's rounds with Mt. St. Victoire, and turned to face me, posing with one elbow on a shelf. Impatience on a monument. Across the room, covering a round oak table, stood the tea things, a kettle, china, crustless sandwiches, assorted goodies probably catered by The Whim. The English say high tea the way Catholics say high mass.

"I remember the person, Mr. Haller. Caroline Collin. Without an S. She was reading English literature; she left after two years without taking her degree. I was her tutor. She wanted to travel, I was told."

"She appears to have traveled back to Cambridge."

"So you say." He glanced ostentatiously at his watch, a pudgy little man constructed along the lines of a dumpling, dressed in a tan jacket with a dark shirt and a plaid tie. His pants were straw-colored and bell-bottomed. His hair fell down across his crown in long, pale red stripes, showing a lot of freckled skull between the lines. Even from where I stood, he smelled like the tonic shelf in a barber shop.

"I hoped you might tell me something about her, Doctor Lange. Had she been in trouble before, for instance? Were there any particularly close friends that you remember?"

He sniffed, a little less bored. Trouble would interest him.

"Nothing serious, of course," he said after a moment. "But she went around with a bad lot and was said to be rather wild. A parson's daughter, I think. They often go giddy when they break loose from home for the first time." He shifted one of his chins. "Bit of a tart, I should have said, actually. Other tutors thought she was an innocent, a babe in the woods, one of those lost children." He pursed his lips to show what he thought of other tutors. "And there was a minor incident with drugs, her second year, when she evidently sold marijuana to someone in the town." He finally brought his arm down from the book shelf and shook it out, pudgy hand fluttering in the air for a moment. "Not that I get terribly excited by that, you know. A pill to swallow, a cigarette to smoke—we all have our little ways."

The record stopped at the end of an aria, so he crossed the room to turn it over.

"Ponchielli, isn't it?" I said, needling him while he aimed the phonograph arm. "Third act of *Gioconda*?" He looked over his shoulder in irritation. The English hate for an American to know things like that.

"Your time is almost gone, Mr. Haller. Is there anything else?"

"What kind of student was she?"

"Oh." One hand rippled. "She had a good mind—not absolutely *first-rate*, of course—but then she wasn't too keen on getting ahead academically. Rather too much enjoying her freedom. I suppose she's pregnant or something nasty?"

I opened my mouth to speak, but a knock at the door interrupted me. Lange flounced past and down the hall.

In a minute or two, after a whispered conference at the

door, he returned leading a tall, hipless young man who had curly blond hair as thick as lamb's wool and a gold medallion on a gold chain hanging down his cashmere décolletage. Don we now our gay apparel. He blinked his lashes at me by way of greeting and went to coil around the tea table, while Lange stood with folded arms at the hallway entrance, foot tapping the carpet. Bit of a tart, I should have said.

"You didn't say if she would have friends who might still be in Cambridge," I reminded him halfway down the hall.

"Most unlikely. Her crowd were all one or two years ahead of her and they would have gone down by now. I haven't any idea, Mr. Haller. She was only my student, not my daughter or my lover." And the door hurried shut behind me.

I chewed a cigarette all the way back to King's Parade, did not throw the match on the Fellow's grass when I lit it, and decided about a quarter inch from the filter to go to the cops.

The central station, the kid with the apartheid fliers told me, was on Leighton Street in City Centre. I threaded my way through an open-air vegetable and flower market behind an old church and entered an ancient cobblestone street that curled in a long, irregular half-moon. Halfway down it, I paused to admire a sign that hung in the window of a fish market: Notary Public. I had cast my first ballot in a French fish market like this one years ago, an absentee vote for a president, never mind which one. The fishmonger had summoned his whole staff out as witnesses; wiping their hands on their aprons and grinning at the patriotic young Yank, they'd looked on as he had spread out the ballot on a stack of shad and roe and watched genially over my shoulder while I voted. I don't think they noticed the smell in Boston.

The police station was at the end of the street, a huge Victorian redbrick facing a line of shops and a fenced-in motor pool.

In the lobby, I learned from the directory board that Sergeant Paul Russin was in charge of burglary, juveniles, and narcotics; and upstairs a thin woman at a typewriter said he could see me if he wanted to, no point asking her. She banged open a knee-high wooden gate by her desk and let me through. "In the corner."

I followed the jab of her pencil to a cramped pre-fab office, two panels of pale green wallboard, top halves frosted translucent glass, a fiberboard and veneer door that had been intended for some other doorway. Somebody had skinned the Giant Rat of Sumatra and thrown down the pelt for a carpet over part of the battered hardwood floor. Sergeant Russin, looking like the guy that could have done it, shook hands unenthusiastically without getting up from behind his desk. He waved me to a straight-backed chair and resumed eating a Danish and sipping tea that he poured from a stainless steel thermos. This would be low tea in Doctor Lange's book.

"Caroline Collin, hey?"

"About 24, 20 or 21 then. Got into trouble on marijuana when she was still at the university."

"And skipped out on a rich American husband now." Russin's accent was incorrigibly working-class. "Still acting balmy, isn't she? All right then, hands across the bloody sea. Let's see what we have."

He took his time finishing the roll and stood up beside a row of three dirty-green filing cabinets, wiping his fingers in a crumpled paper napkin as an afterthought. A big man, in his early 30s, a couple of inches taller than I am, wearing a rumpled blue uniform and the genial look of an athlete who's never run into anything so big or so hard that he couldn't handle it. But his weight was already sliding downhill toward his belly. He whistled tunelessly as he flipped manilla folders about the cabinet drawers.

"Here she is. In with the university lot, of course. Ought to file them by bloody colleges. Arrested 10 December 1978, possession of less than one ounce of marijuana, part of a group of 12 arrested at the same party." He turned over a sheet of paper and continued reading. "King's College authorities notified. Doctor somebody, head tutor. Can't read the name. Atrocious handwriting. Placed on probation for one term, no further charges, action dropped." He smacked the folder on his desk as he sat down again. "Strictly routine."

"Know anything else about her?"

"That's the file."

"Friends, rumors, suspicions—a missing persons job runs on marginal information, as I'm sure you know, Sergeant—contacts, habits. You'd not be likely to forget her if you saw her." I handed him the photograph.

"I saw her." His round face was still genial, but he handed back the picture slowly.

"And?"

"You carry a license or a piece of paper?" His eyes had gone chilly and metallic, the way they teach you on day one at every police school in the world. I took the photostat of my license out of the wallet and passed it over. He read it three or four times, probably looking for the invisible ink.

"We call them private enquiry agents over here," he said at last. "They can't have a gun or make arrests."

"Yeah, it's a wonderful country, and back home even the meter maid carries a Mauser. I know."

"Your girl ran around with a spotty crowd," Russin said, stroking one of his long straw sideburns and still trying to guess my weight with his eyes. I slipped the photostat back in the wallet between the machine pistol ammunition and the Crimestopper's Code. "Kind of a mixture of students, hangers-on, and working lads. Oil and water. Some of the lads were passing more than marijuana, and the girl was probably selling it in a small way to her college chums. Not worth trying to prove. What the hell, she was only 19—we didn't reckon she was the bloody French connection. She got off with a spot of probation, but three of the lot she was picked up with already had records for dealing. One of them was sent off to Dartmoor."

"Do you know his name?"

"I do. But it's not important to you. He's still there, last time anybody checked. Possession and sale of heroin, assault, assault with a deadly weapon, armed robbery, resisting arrest."

"All in one day?"

"The deadly weapon was a Ford Cortina," Russin said tonelessly. "Sent one of our people to hospital with a crushed pelvis. Lovely companion for a pretty young Cambridge undergraduate reading English poetry."

I started to ask a question, but the telephone interrupted. Russin listened, grunted, then swiveled his chair around until his back was to me. I looked at a hook of police mimeos on the wall, the most recent one dated last October.

"Right then. Number 318." He swiveled back and replaced the phone. "The hard boys were getting their stuff from London," he told me. "London leaks heroin like an old sewer. Your girl was just sitting there smoking her kicks, according to her, and kind of just not paying attention to what was happening on the other side of the room." He spun the cap back on the thermos and stood up. "The university chaps forget how little most of the working lads have to fall back on. A Cambridge degree will see you through some rough weather. A few years on the needle leaves an apprentice lorry mechanic nearer to hopeless." He was drawing a dark blue raincoat over his shoulders after a glance out the window at the end of the most recent sunny spell. Sergeant Russin had a heavy dignity that would take a long time to grow cynical. "You can come along if you like. Little job to do across town, but you can finish your questions on the way."

We tramped downstairs, through a corridor, and into the motor pool lot. Russin motioned me into a white patrol car, and we set out eastward, away from the university buildings and toward the grim rows of attached brick houses that march off into the reclaimed marshes of East Anglia. Beyond the train station, in a squall of rain, we circled a new shopping center that ought to have been reclaimed as well, a huge grid of concrete, orange fluorescence and blinking lights that signaled "Wimpy," "Woolworth," "Rexall," "Safeway" to a passing world.

"We call that Little America," Russin said as we shot past. "My wife reckons all of California looks like that."

"California's bigger," I grunted.

He smiled at some secret joke. We drove on through ancient, faceless streets intended to lead to a Victorian factory, in and out of a modern high-rise housing development intended to lead nowhere, and finally pulled up behind an orange-and-white ambulance cantilevered half on, half off the sidewalk, its roof light revolving slowly. Next to it was another police car, and on the sidewalk a large crowd of curious spectators. Russin parked farther up the street, and we walked back, reaching number 318 just as the door of the house bounced open and two medics staggered out with a stretcher. The crowd pushed back and then forward again.

"Who's here, then?" Russin asked as the stretcher reached the sidewalk. He leaned over in the drizzle, a curious blond giant, and examined dispassionately the face of a very young man, in his early 20s at best, complexion cracked with acne like old canvas, shoulder-length hair in black greasy bunches spread against the crisp hospital linen. Blood pumped out of the folds of skin around one dilated eye. A deep cut began under his ear and snaked out of sight beneath his collar. From his left temple, a bruise the color and texture of raisins spread out in a pool. Under the strapped blanket, his body jerked and trembled, and his lips moved soundlessly, frothing.

"Drying out, I reckon," said one of the ambulance attendants. "And had a proper punchup too." They put the stretcher down on the wet sidewalk and opened the ambulance doors. The boy turned his head carefully toward Russin and vomited, splattering his shoes and raincoat. The crowd murmured in admiration. Russin, his face expressionless, wiped his shoes and coat with a cloth from the ambulance, then led me through the crowd, up the stairs, and into the second-floor hallway.

"I was the first one here, Sergeant. All over now." A cop not much older than the kid in the ambulance hurried over to meet us at the apartment door—an excitable, fast-talking man in a crisp new uniform, eager to impress the sergeant. Winkler, P. C.—Police Constable—was printed on a plastic bar over his breast pocket. His eyes took in the stains on Russin's coat as he kept up his rapid-fire report, glancing at me curiously from time to time. "The tall boy over there held out on his heroin— probably going to resell it later—we found half a kilo—and the other lad went stark bonkers, screaming and pounding the walls, punching the girl all over the face. That's when the downstairs neighbors called. The lad they just took out got properly carved before I got here, though, nasty cut right down the ear and over the heart, quarter of an inch. Took a thumbnail in the squinter too. Felony assault along with the drugs, if you want; here's the knife, nasty little item, very trim, French."

Russin looked over Winkler's head to the other side of the room, where an older cop was standing beside a window. Sitting cross-legged on the floor nearby were a man in his 20s and a plump girl with a swollen pink face who looked about 16, both of them dressed in olive-drab U.S. Army fatigues. Little America. The apartment itself was early junkie: two filthy mattresses covered with nylon sleeping bags, a small efficiency refrigerator, a brown plastic leaf bag overflowing with empty cans, milk cartons, wasted food. No chairs, no sofas, no beds. No pink stuffed animals, no paperbacks of Vonnegut or Tolkien, no posters of Robert Redford or Kiss. The girl began sobbing softly, a sound like a kitten's mew, and Winkler twisted his neck in embarrassment. From another room, we heard a toilet flush, and then an older man in a business suit came in past the refrigerator, carrying a black medical bag. He nodded at Russin, showing a roadmap of broken red veins on a dour Irish face, and knelt beside the girl. She held out her arm mechanically, still sobbing, and kept her elbow straight while the doctor rubbed an alcohol patch on it and took a hypodermic from the bag. We all have our little ways, Lange had said.

"She's seen one of these before," the doctor grunted to no one in particular.

Russin sighed and walked over to the boy. I stayed with Winkler, the kid-faced cop.

"Girl's named Michelle," he said to me after a moment. "Like in the Beatles' song. The lad's got a record, I expect." I offered him a cigarette and he shook his head. "Not on duty. I get credit for the arrest, you see. Second one this month. He claims to be out of work. Used to drive a mini-cab in Bedford, he says, before he came to bleeding Cambridge, he says. You writing this up for the papers by any chance?" he asked, cocking his chin at me. "We heard at the station that *News of the World* were going to do a feature on Cambridge and drugs. Town and gown, they were going to call it."

"Or needle and pen," I said, my American accent telling its own story. "I just came along to keep the sergeant company."

"Oh." He looked back at the girl and the doctor. "Private enquiries, eh? You chaps don't often see this side of it, do you? The backstairs part of it, I mean."

I dragged on my cigarette and didn't answer. About half the cases I take on these days are runaway kids, and about half of them end up in scenes like this. Or worse. The Tenderloin in San Francisco makes backstairs Cambridge look like Boys' Town. On Eddy Street, you can buy a nickel bag at the Safeway checkout counter.

Russin came back, rubbing one big hand across half an acre of chin and bringing the faint, sweet smell of vomit.

"They'll give you a ride in the other car," he said. "I'm afraid I've got to stay with this lot. Going to have to write up a charge on the lad."

"Is this the sort of thing Caroline Collin was picked up in?"

"Not quite like this. A bit tonier, I think." He found a matchstick in his raincoat pocket and stuck it between his teeth. "She had King's to go home to, and mum and dad. I don't suppose she had much idea what goes on in the real world. Just worried about what lovely job to do when she left university."

"You've given her some thought."

"There's only so many types in the world."

"If she were back in Cambridge, would you know?"

"Probably not." He looked over his shoulder at the doctor. "Not for a while." He tipped his head toward the sad-faced cop. "Get Jerry here to let you off at your hotel. Come around again tomorrow morning if you want. Maybe I'll think of some names for you by then."

Jerry let me off at the station instead, and I spent the five-minute walk back to the Blue Boar wondering which step to take next. There's a rule book for every job, of course, whether it's breaking eggs or finding disappearing people. In a smallish city, you begin with hotels or rooming houses or taxicabs, depending on your guesswork, the state of your shoe leather, the size of your advance. In England, there are not only hotels, there are also things called service flats and people called estate agents who rent them by the day or week. If Caroline Angeletti seriously wanted to stay out of sight, she could have easily bolted into a service flat, cooked her own meals, and never been seen from one day to the next. The clerk at the Blue Boar looked puzzled, but he gave me a room key and a list of estate agents specializing in flats. I took a map from his basket of folders and set out for the first office at ten past five. I know, because I checked my watch against the hotel clock and thought briefly about wasting an hour on a drink in the finest bar, and because that was the first time I actually saw her.

I had turned down a narrow street just off a slightly less narrow one called Petty Cury and entered a block-square maze of bright new shops and offices, the kind of boutique explosion you find in California inside an old tuna plant. Marie Lipton, Rentals, had an office on the second floor, between Kites 'N' Things and The Wicked Candle, and I had just pushed the elevator button when I glanced idly back toward the street and the window of a Thomas Cook's Travel and saw her standing at the counter, fishing through her purse.

Sometimes it happens like that, if you pass up the extra drink or your birth sign is on the cusp that month, and then you throw away the rule book. I stepped back to look again. The shop lamps reflected the late-afternoon drizzle off the window, but it was Caroline Angeletti, no mistake, taller than I had imagined, wrapped in a clear plastic raincoat over a light summer dress, still as tanned as if she had never left California. She stuffed whatever she had bought into the purse and turned for the door. I went down a parallel corridor of open booths, straight to the sidewalk, thinking that I could cable her husband and go home now. Or else follow her through the wet Cambridge streets. Magnus had wondered what I would do when I found her. I suddenly realized that I didn't know yet. I would ask the lady.

A delivery van climbed onto the sidewalk as I reached it, blocking my view of the front of Thomas Cook's, and a bicycle and a car thumped each other a moment later in the street, bringing shouts of anger, a long blast of a horn. The crowd of excited shoppers darted like minnows in the wet light. I squeezed between the van and Cook's front window, slipped gracefully on the slick stone pavement, and rolled halfway into a puddle of dirty water that was overflowing the curb. A curse and another squeeze and I was past the van and near the door of Cook's. But the crowd surged busily up and down Petty Cury, and Caroline Angeletti had disappeared somewhere into the drizzle.

# CHAPTER 4

I CAUGHT UP WITH HER IN LONDON.

The clerk in Cook's had taken some persuading —with my oil-soaked raincoat and foot-long rip in the trousers leg, I didn't look much like the long-lost American friend that I claimed to be. But money changed hands, as it always does in a very civilized country with 20 percent inflation, and eventually I learned that she had booked a first-class train ticket for London that night and a suite at the Savoy.

Not the Savoy you stomp at. That's in New York, and long vanished anyway. The Savoy in London is one of the last enclaves of Victorian gentility, the Margaret Dumont of modern hotels. Magnus country. It lies just down from the Strand, on the Victoria Embankment of the Thames, about ten blocks and a thousand years from Rupert Street in Soho. Up front, on the Strand itself, as I left my taxi, was the Savoy Theatre, which was where Gilbert and Sullivan had started. It now plays interchangeable music hall farces to busloads of corn-fed American tourists—the marquee I passed said *There's a Girl in My Soup*—while the hotel proper waits at the end of a deep courtyard lined with Rolls-Royces and the flags of all nations. During the Empire, when they could afford it, the British used to stay at the Savoy themselves. Now it pretty much belongs to the dukes of oil, to the Japanese, the Germans, who like to come to England and shop and who love the combination of atmosphere and rudeness, and to the few Americans still rich enough to drop $250 a day for a fair-sized bed, hunting prints on the walls, and bath towels the size of carports. I wondered, not for the first time that night, how Caroline Angeletti had come so far on her stolen $800 and a credit card she ought to be afraid to use.

The man at the desk thought the rip in my pants clashed with the decor.

"We don't give out the room numbers of guests," he said, nostrils flaring in distaste.

"Mrs. Angeletti is expecting me. If you would just ring her room—"

"We have no Angeletti staying here," he said without looking.

"She sometimes travels under the name of Collin, for privacy."

"Nor Collin." He squinted in the direction of what I took to be the house detective's bench. A bull in a decent brown suit, no rip, looked up from his tabloid.

"I'll wait in the bar for her."

"The bar," he said in a tone of regret, "is open to the public."

Open it was, and as empty and silent as a Brooks Brothers store on the Berkeley campus. Arabs don't drink in public, and the Germans and the Japanese like authentic olde English pubs instead of softly lit chromium cocktail lounges. I took one of the two stools nearest the open door and perched, giving myself a good view of the four elevator doors and the mail desk. While I perched, the kid barman came back with a double malt Scotch and a pack of Players.

"What's all the fuss at the desk then?" he asked, leaning on his elbows over the bar and making an effort to be friendly.

"There's a rumor they found an Englishman in the lobby."

He snorted, helped himself to one of my Players, then looked over my shoulder. "Oh, oh." He vanished into the gloom. The bull in brown drifted slowly by, inspecting the stains on my raincoat and the £10 note I had left on the bar. I sipped the Scotch, genteel as a lord, and kept my suitcoat buttoned until he finally gave up and went back to his newspaper. They won't throw you out for dressing badly, even in the Savoy, but they can get touchy about customers who tuck pistols under their arms. I waved for another Scotch and sat watching the parade of nations across the lobby. Sheik, rattle, and roll. If Angeletti had a tail on me, I decided, he was wearing a tuxedo or a caftan; or he had missed the train down from Cambridge and had gone home to sulk. I could have done that too, at least gone back to the White Horse and changed; but once so close I hated the idea of letting her slip away again. Another two drinks and I could call it overtime.

I never made it to the fourth drink.

She came out of the elevator at 10:15, alone as far as I could see, and walked quickly through the lobby toward the taxi rank. I left the money and the Scotch on the bar and managed to get to the door ahead of her.

"Mrs. Angeletti," I said, pushing it wide for both of us.

Her eyes were much more beautiful than the pictures had shown, green and feral, and somebody in London or New York had been smart enough to cut and shape her blond hair instead of draping it down her back in universal college-girl style. Goldilocks. I had already seen the summer dress and the slender figure. What I hadn't expected was the coarseness of her voice.

"Who the hell are you?"

She stopped in the middle of the door and glared up at me. Various duchesses and Arabs squeezed around us. A doorman in a major-general's uniform looked over curiously.

"Carlo Angeletti sent me," I said. Then the fear brushed over her eyes, and I caught a glimpse of her father's face.

"Oh God," she said. "Oh shit. Leave me alone. Get away." She spun toward the lobby. I caught her left wrist.

"Why don't we go somewhere else," I said rapidly, "before the management comes over to help?" She followed my glance to the desk, where the clerk was regarding us coldly. The bull was already on his feet, hitching his belt with both hands. She shook her wrist free, looked desperately past me toward the cabs and cars. If there was anybody waiting, I couldn't tell.

"I followed you down from Cambridge this evening," I said. "I saw your father this afternoon." The bull was halfway to us.

"Carlo sent you," she said, turning her face to me, trembling. I pushed the door open again and the major-general held it.

"But he's not here, only me. Let's go somewhere and talk."

She licked her lips, glanced again at the cars outside, and nodded once. I dropped a coin in somebody's hand and followed her out, steering us into the third cab from the front.

"St. Martin's Lane," I said as we pulled out, past two drivers who glowered from their seats. "Anywhere at all, one of the restaurants."

Caroline sank back in the far corner of the seat and stared at the flickering traffic. "Shit," she said in her elegant British accent. "Shit, shit, shit."

After a minute or so on the Strand, the cab darted north through a network of narrow Soho streets, all relatively dark, and I watched through the rear window for whatever might be tagging along. When we crossed the bright neon patch of Leicester Square, I gave up and turned around, and two blocks later, at the top of St. Martin's Lane, I paid the driver and we got out.

"You pick the restaurant," I said.

There are half a dozen along that street, theatre restaurants mostly, equipped with bars and after-hours licenses and usually deserted at that time of night. She chose an Italian one halfway down, directly across from a revival of *Oliver*, and sat at a table with her back to the window; I sat with my back to the wall.

"Have you eaten?" I asked. She sat tight-lipped, scowling. "Two plates of fettucini," I told the waiter, "and a bottle of chianti." He moped away. "I only had a cheese sandwich on the train down from Cambridge," I said conversationally to Caroline. "The cheese tasted like shirtboard."

"Where is he?" she said in a small, almost inaudible voice. Outside the restaurant window, people strolled, chattering gaily in the evening air. A moony spell.

"Your father-in-law?"

She nodded once, hard.

"In California, as far as I know."

"He just snapped his fingers and said fetch?"

"I'm a private detective from San Francisco," I said, buttering a wedge of bread. "Angeletti's lawyer seemed to think I could help."

"Merriman."

"And your husband, of course."

She pinched and unpinched her fingers around the stem of her wine glass. The waiter rematerialized with the wine and plates of languid noodles that must have been ready since noon. He poured into my glass and I sipped carefully. They arrested a famous vintner in Milan a few years back for making chianti with absolutely no grape product at all: old ropes, Kool-Aid, inner tubes. He'd been doing it for ten years. When I nodded approval, the waiter poured again and vanished. I looked expectantly at Caroline.

"And my husband," she said finally, half a question in her voice.

"Not so forceful a personality as your father-in-law, I agree. More like the Howdy Doody of the Delta." I spooled some of the lukewarm fettucini on my fork. "But he wants you back too."

"Yes." She looked up and down the restaurant, at the window, her mind moving as quickly and nervously as a sparrow. "I suppose he does. I can almost believe you, you know. Otherwise, we wouldn't be talking, would we? Drinking wine and talking." She pushed her chair back six inches. "I don't see why I don't just get up and walk away. You won't dare stop me."

"Why don't you sit down and tell me instead what you took from him, Caroline?"

The green eyes went wider.

"What you took that he wants back so much?" The fettucini tasted worse than I expected, and I slid it to one side and took out my cigarettes.

"I don't know what . . . " she started and snapped her mouth shut.

"You don't know what I'm talking about." I lit a cigarette with one of the foot-long gimmick matches the restaurant provided on the tables, probably to reheat the food. "I haven't called Angeletti yet, Caroline, because I'm assuming he lied to me. Now that's not so unusual in my line of work. Most people lie to me. You're sitting on the edge of your chair getting all set to lie to me. Your father lied to me. I just had a cop in Cambridge lie to me. I even lie once in a while myself, so I won't start to feel self-righteous. I'm a voter and a veteran. I'm used to it. But Angeletti put a tail on me after the lies, a creepy-looking guy who resembles your present husband not a little in point of oiliness. He stuck with me all the way across the country, at least to New York."

"You were in New York?"

"Why not? So were you."

She sat forward on the chair, letting one hand cup the wine glass, the other hand brush back a strand of invisible hair. A pose from a perfume ad. I remembered the odd, similarly appealing pose she had struck for the photograph, a teenager masquerading as a vamp, vamping the worldly wise old man. Fathers must see their daughters like that sometimes and melt. "That man's gone," I said. "I lost him in New York, but twice so far in my busy London day, a green Austin Mini has popped in and out of my peripheral vision, different drivers, same plates. That's once too often in a city of 15,000,000 people."

She didn't look at the window, she didn't look at the bar or up and down the restaurant. "Did he follow you here?" she asked.

"Sterling Moss couldn't follow a cab through the West End. The interesting question is, how come your father-in-law, who could field half a tanker full of hard boys, first goes and hires a moderately obscure and two-thirds honest private eye and then pins a tail on him."

"I didn't take anything from him."

"The other interesting question, of course, is why you're not staring goggle-eyed out the window counting Austins on St. Martin's Lane."

"You're insolent." There was the faintest quiver of a smile at the corners of her long lips. Brave girl. "And your tough-guy act stinks."

I shrugged. "I do Jimmy Stewart better. How much money did you send your father from Cambridge?"

The smile trembled away. "I sent him £200. Why?"

"He told me £50."

Silence.

"And why did you trot off to Cambridge two hours after you landed in London? London's a lot easier to stay hidden in. Did you just want to see old college chums, revisit your tutor?" I blew smoke onto the table. "Score some dope?"

She looked up quickly. Tiger eyes, angry flush, a marvelous sexy child's face that flickered from expression to expression like sunshine and rain. She would have had a squirt like Peter Angeletti dangling from her hemline. An aging Lothario like me she could tie in a Windsor knot.

"Congratulations," she said with schoolgirlish sarcasm. "You've proved you're a detective. Wonderful. Sure I went to Cambridge to revisit college chums, only there aren't so many left there anymore, and my old queen of a tutor was never much worth seeing in the first place. I didn't need to go to Cambridge to buy a joint. You can walk two minutes in any direction in London and buy all you want. I'd just done one of the crazier things in my life, and I needed to be in some familiar place, somewhere stable and comfortable, to calm down. I couldn't go home. You've seen that apparently. All right then."

She took one of my Players and lit it while the flush in her cheek died down, then rubbed it out after one puff. "OK," she said. "I did. I took some money. It was half mine anyway, by community property, and I just thought of it as instant alimony. I wasn't going to get any more, that's for sure. Look"—a toss of the blond hair—"I met Peter in a bar in Lake Tahoe, a casino for God's sake. I was a silly English girl roaming the States for a lark. I'd had it up to here with college, so I tripped off to New York for a few weeks, then a spot of camping up north in Ontario, and finally drifted to California. It happens all the time. Peter was absolutely charming. Wealthy, cultivated, Stanford. He took me skiing one weekend, lots of nice restaurants, gambling. It was lovely, and I didn't see much else in my future but coming back to England and reading lit crit with Doctor Lange or learning to type or going on the dole, and Sunday night we both got jolly pissed and rolled out of bed and went straight down from the ski lodge to Reno, in that big sports car of his, and got married. At 7:00 in the morning, in an office building next to a Holiday Inn. I'm no dizzy romantic. I didn't know what I was getting into except that I liked him and it had to be a lot better than coming back here." She pulled another cigarette from the pack on the table, one hand brushing mine as she reached. "You probably think that's very calculating," she said. She lit this one and kept it going. "It just didn't work out, that's all."

"How much did you take?"

She turned her lips down in a Raggedy Ann frown. "$10,000, more or less. Peter and I had a joint account in Sacramento, at one of Carlo's banks."

"Savings and loans in California aren't allowed to hand out more than $500 in cash to a customer, and nobody mentioned a cashier's check to me."

"I know. I arranged for the cash a week in advance. They'll do it if you give five days' business notice." She was right. "Look, I tried, really. But Peter was like a different man around his father, a goon, a tough macho goon. And we had to live near Carlo, that was part of the arrangement. We had to be near him and entertain him on weekends in that unbelievable houseboat of his. Peter wouldn't hear of moving to San Francisco, the way I wanted to. He didn't even want to go back to Tahoe. He was afraid of his father, afraid of losing his goddamn money." She leaned forward. "I hated it there, you understand? The flatness, the canals, the heat, so bloody provincial. I stood it for six months, then I hopped on the first plane I could and ran like hell from that stinking, miserable valley."

I sipped my wine. She rubbed out her second cigarette carefully, touching my wrist with the tips of her fingers, then looked up at me again.

"Would you believe Carlo even made a pass at me? That old man?" She straightened her shoulders and stretched her torso subtly to show why. In body language, I decided, Caroline had written the book. I looked at her breasts jutting against the soft fabric of her dress, nipples like split infinitives.

"I believe he'd make a pass at a lamp base, Caroline. I even believe that you didn't care much for Tara West and that Peter A., who looked to me like he couldn't sign his name to go to the bathroom, somehow got all impulsive on a ski weekend and woke up married to you. What I don't believe is that a gangster like our pal Carlo is going to waste good money hiring me to get back a lousy ten grand. Not even if you slapped him silly for pinching. Not even if Peter got down on his knees and sang 'O My Papa.'"

"He's Italian," she said stubbornly, sounding for an instant like Magnus.

I made a gesture of disgust.

"I can't tell you any more," she said. "That's the truth."

I didn't say anything. I felt old and tired and fagged out. A fender-sized bruise on my hip had stiffened, and my dirty wet clothes smelled like the inside of an owl's mouth.

"Are you going to call Carlo?" Tight, frightened voice.

I put money on the table, Carlo's money. In the shadows of the restaurant, Caroline Collin suddenly looked old and far away. I saw her for an instant 40 years from now, nose hooked toward her chin, blond hair frayed to a thin white, shoulders pinched, bust like a skateboard. Sixty and counting. Forty years from now, I would be almost 80. And counting.

"You'll give me a chance, won't you?" she pleaded, trying to find the right combination of bravado and sexiness to hold me. "You put on that self-conscious tough-guy front like so many Americans, but that's not really you, is it?"

"I also do Liberace."

"Please. I like you."

I took a long pull on my cigarette and watched the smoke climb up the air in a thin, serpentine coil, answering an invisible charmer's flute. Caroline leaned toward me. I like to be liked. I had also made up my mind half an hour ago that there was one more question I should have asked Carlo Angeletti.

"I'll call you in the morning," I said. "I won't do anything before that."

# CHAPTER 5

CAROLINE'S CAB TURNED LEFT INTO THE GLITTER OF SHAFTESBURY Avenue and began the roundabout route back to the Savoy. I watched until it vanished, then my feet turned right, and I walked slowly in the other direction toward Covent Garden. Traffic hissed impatiently past, sending white sprays of rain over the curbs, but nobody on or off the sidewalk seemed remotely interested in me. At the top of one listless Soho street, I stopped and shook out my watch. Twenty past midnight. Nobody in London would be much interested in anything besides catching the last underground train or finding a social club that snuck after-hours drinks.

Just beyond the empty opera house at Covent Garden, I stopped again to pull up my raincoat collar and look at street signs. Wild Street, it said. Down these wild streets, a man must go. Three Greek sailors, arm in arm, staggered out of a chop house just closed, singing "Good Night, Irene" in the accents, I suppose, of Sophocles. They stumbled by and I shoved my hands in my pockets and walked on, going south, I thought, toward Fleet Street. Or maybe west toward Buckingham Palace. The street curved off to the left, and I hesitated before following it, momentarily confused. Lights drifted on the slick pavement. Philip Marlowe never walked a step in Los Angeles, I thought. A city of great drive, which was why I had left it. All designer freeways and indefinitely expanding borders. Ninety miles wide and two inches deep. London, on the other hand, had rearranged her central ten square miles a couple of times a century for the last 1,000 years, leaving a map that looked more like a scrambled plan of the brain than a field of cloverleafs. The great gray Babylon, Magnus called it, no doubt quoting somebody. Fifteen years ago, after two seasons with UPI, I could probably have strolled anywhere in the West End without a pause, from Hyde Park to the Bank. But the city seemed to have gotten older.

At the next corner, to my surprise, Wild Street suddenly jogged into St. Mary's-le-Strand, the lady in the lake, and I knew where I was again. A few blocks past the church, Fleet Street began, normally one of the busiest parts of the city; but traffic had thinned now to an occasional late bus or cab, a solitary car, so that I had the dark wet streets to myself for minutes at a time. London was yawning, stretching her stout arms, and preparing to sleep. I marched on, jumping at every car that passed, toward the last small job of the day. And maybe the answer to my question.

Behind the black letters "United Press International" on the door, the night shift was slumped into its usual tableau. At the desk nearest me, a bald man dressed in a dark suit but no tie hunched over his telephone, one hand doodling slowly on a pad. Beyond him stretched ten or twelve identical metal desks, interrupted by two rows of flat plaster pillars that propped up the ceiling where builders had enlarged the room. Here and there, a few other pale men—and one carrot-haired woman—typed or read under the grumbling fluorescent lights, or slouched and stared blankly at the dull green walls, waiting for a story to call itself in. A working-class version of the Reform Club, with all the vitality of an empty train station. So much for the reporter's glamorous life.

Dinah says I am a sentimental man. Person. And she must be right. I looked around the dingy newsroom with a rush of genuine affection. Other people's early 20s may smell like footballs and near beer and Brylcreem. Mine smell like linotype, ink, and newsprint. I inhaled the fine pungency of a million gobbled cigarettes and cups of coffee. The unrenewable past. For two years, I had worked in this very room and afterwards in another just like it in LA, during the time when I should have been tunneling through college and then, according to my father's plan, rolling up my sleeve for medical school. The man at the desk glanced over at me without interest and shifted the phone to his other ear. I had quit the *LA Times* after two more years because, as I had announced without blushing to my editor, I wanted to be a writer. And I rightly figured that newspaper work had almost nothing to do with writing—three-sentence paragraphs, get your numbers straight, check out the lead the other guy was using. Nothing there for a 26-year-old would-be poet who wanted to make his dactyls dance like dervishes and bring tears to the eyes of pliable women. "Don't Get It Right, Get It Written" was what my editor had framed over his desk. He thought Keats was an ex-senator from New York. But to tell the truth, most reporters aren't interested in language or style. They like to watch people in action. They like to be in crowds, observing, pretending to be objective, feeling a little smug and self-righteous at the messes other people get into. And as it turned out, I wasn't a writer myself after all but really a lapsed reporter at heart. Which probably explains how I had drifted on to detecting.

The red-haired woman abruptly started pounding on a sheet of yellow legal paper, a dervish, her manual typewriter sounding like a military drill team in the big room. I wove cautiously between the desks, still looking over my shoulder for Austins, and walked toward the far corner and the door to the teletype room. A black janitor came out towing a canvas trash bag suspended on casters and a metal frame. I went around him, around the last rank of desks, and into what used to be the night supervisor's room.

It still was. And Archie Owen looked up cheerfully from a bag of Wimpy's hamburgers and a sky-blue mug of coffee.

"Michael Haller! Little Mikie! As sure as a pig! Dear boy, dear boy, come in." He stood up, grinning with pleasure, and stretched a wad of doughy fingers across the desk. Archie Owen was one of the shortest and fattest people I have ever known, a little stuffed sofa cushion of a man. Before walking into UPI to ask for a job 30 years ago, he claimed to have worked as a carnival magician on the road in his native Wales, always ending his act, he once told me, by climbing into a steamer trunk and disappearing. When he had reappeared one day in London, tired of scraping by in the carnival and drawn to the great city like every other poor boy in the '30s, the bosses had started him off at the rewrite desk, counting inches on finished copy. But when they saw how he could cut and edit a story—brevity is the soul of profit in the wire services—they had bounced him straight to supervisor. Fattest man, trimmest prose. He rarely left the building so far as I knew, except to go home to his cramped bed-sitter in Islington. If he had ever actually covered a live news story, there was nobody around anymore to remember. But here he still was, waddling past the corner of his desk, tubbier than any two trunks, laughing and talking at top speed and showing me the three or four rotting gray stumps of teeth still left in his mouth by the National Health.

We had always gotten on well when I worked for UPI. Maybe because at 21, I was too shy—though Dinah says that's impossible—to joke about his size. Maybe because I thought from the first that he knew more about sorting out fact from blubber than any half dozen teachers at my famous college.

Like many desk-bound people, however, Archie was an inveterate gossip. Still chattering a welcome, he dug out another blue coffee mug, looked critically at its edges, shrugged, and sat me down to hear ten minutes of slanderous news from the small, furiously social world of British journalism as if I had never left it. Then, Fleet Street scuttled, he leaned back with the cold disc of a Wimpy and between noisy mouthfuls asked what I wanted.

"Not to say you're not welcome, dear boy. Old friends the best friends—when were you last here, after all? Almost three years ago, wasn't it? Not to say you have to be off on one of your morbid cases either. But when a detective chap drops into my office past midnight wearing a bunged-up raincoat and torn trousers and a glint in his eye like a Welsh hangman, I do reckon it's more than social. Eh, dear boy? What do you need from old Arch beside another cuppa?"

I curled my palms around the warm cup and asked him the favor I had been thinking about for more than an hour.

"I'd like to use a telephone to call the States, Archie—I'll put it on my credit card—and then I'd like to use the wire-photo line for something from San Francisco. The transmission shouldn't take more than a minute, but I won't start it for a couple of hours."

"Is that all?" He waved the hamburger with a flourish.

"Dear boy, use the one in here. I've got to go around and feed the teletype some fodder anyway. There's a train smash in the Midlands the world wants to hear about, and some silly bugger calling it in who ought to be back in third form. I'll tell the lad in the telex room to let you have what comes over for you. Make yourself at home, and I'll be back in half an hour. Have the other burger while you wait."

He padded out still talking and I closed the flimsy door behind him. The noise of the typewriter outside rattled through as easily as before. I lit one more tired, stale cigarette and pulled the telephone toward me.

Fred answered from the office number on the second ring.

"Mike Haller's office. This is Fred."

"This is Mike."

"Goddamn, Mike, where are you? Still in New York? Dinah's been calling twice a day."

"I'm in London, Fred, come to look at the queen."

"You could have stayed in San Francisco for that."

"I finally caught up with the Angeletti, just the way papa Carlo thought."

"Yeah. Does she look like her picture?"

"She's too skinny. She won't eat. Who else called?"

"There's a guy from Phoenix, stockbroker, who wants you to find his son. Kid left home in his brand new BMW last week, and they're sure he's in Berkeley popping pills and reading Che Guevera. 1 told him I'd look."

"Anybody else?"

"Another guy wants her doctor tailed." I sighed. About the third most common call a p.i. gets is from a husband who wants his wife's gynecologist followed. "I told him to call Blue Cross."

"OK."

"You didn't call from London to check the books, Mike."

"No. Am I right it's only 4:30 there?"

"Close enough."

"Good. I need you to drive down to Palo Alto for me and do one little errand. This is what I need."

He listened without comment, but I could hear the scratch of his pencil as he took notes and the squeak of the old swivel chair at the desk. Outside, the fog would have cleared and it would be windy and bright, the way it almost always is at the end of an August afternoon in San Francisco. My office is down by the water almost under the shadow of the Bay Bridge, in a neighborhood of old warehouses and shabby office buildings still unscarred by urban renewal. Sooner or later, of course, the condominia will sprout like mushrooms and the boutique explosion will lob us down to Daly City. But, for the moment, Fred could still look up from the clunky old desk and see over a warehouse roof to the wide expanse of the bay and beyond it to the green-brown horizon of the Berkeley Hills, pretty much the same outline that old Juan Bautista de Anza first saw when he plunked down his tiny mission for the Indians on Yerba Buena. Or that Mark Twain saw 100 years later from the roaring docks. I looked up from Archie's phone at the pale green wall board where he had taped a magazine photograph of Glamorgan Castle in Wales. I felt far from home and lonely, a big kid.

"That's all you need, Mike? Just the one?"

"That's it. Remember. David Bender, UPI on Market Street. And if you miss in Palo Alto, you'll have to go to Motor Vehicles—you still got your friend in there?"

"Don't worry, guy. Give my love to the queen."

We hung up, and I sat staring at Glamorgan for a long minute. Then I took a bite of Archie's Wimpy. It tasted like somebody's sock. I put it down and crossed the little room to the shapeless brown moleskin chair Archie had bought at the flea market on Portobello Road the Sunday his wife had left him. I sank in it with a grunt, stretched out my legs, and went instantly to sleep.

The ringing of the telephone woke me with a jump. I blinked my eyes clear and took my hand off the pistol butt as Archie extended the telephone over the desk.

"You want me to leave, dear boy?"

"No, stay, Archie. Hello. Yeah, Fred, what's up?"

The connection was poor this time, and fluffs of static kept blowing across Fred's voice. He almost shouted to make himself clear.

"I'm up at UPI in the city, Mike. Your friend Bender is going to start transmitting in about five minutes, just as soon as they get through with the governor and some visiting Chinese. He's been telling them about spaceship earth and they've been buying up Fresno."

"I'll be waiting. Any problems?"

"Piece of cake. Whole thing took about ten minutes. I got to take the book back on Monday, but they didn't seem too worried."

"Thanks, Fred. I appreciate it."

"I'm going over to Berkeley tomorrow. You ought to call Dinah."

I hung up again and told Archie that my transmission was coming over. He was hunched over a square aluminum foil dish of what looked like Sara Lee brownies, digging out chunks with a fork. Once, years ago, I had seen him make a sandwich out of two slices of bread and a Hershey bar. Without looking up, he nodded and asked if he could help.

"You could get me another cup of that motor oil you're drinking."

"All you like. Mind if I tag along and see what you're using the company line for?"

A polite question with only one answer. He polished off the last of the brownie cake and led me out through the newsroom and down a hallway on the other side crowded with fuse boxes, cables, and wooden cartons. In a cramped room halfway down, we found what looked like a pregnant Xerox machine and a wall of metal supply cabinets.

Archie looked at the watch on one fat wrist. "The lad's on his break," he told me. "Just as well."

Together we bent over the controls on top of the machine: a green plastic screen that looked like a television set, a line of numbered knobs for adjusting ink flow, six or eight switches for things I could never remember, and an abbreviated version of a typewriter keyboard. On the plastic screen, messages in telex code marched steadily by, like the news headlines in Times Square, telling datelines, story titles, photographers, and sizes. Someone reading it in London could decide whether to take a sample photograph out and show it to customers or whether to let the thing travel away forever in an electronic void. Or someone could send directly from one set to another, as the boys occasionally used to do with dirty pictures. After a minute of reading, we saw LON SPC LN 14-997 ONLIN PIX TO FOLLOW. London Special, I mentally translated; picture to follow on line.

Archie leaned over the keyboard and pecked with one finger: LON READY 14-997 TRANSMIT.

"They've got a new IBM model in some of the bureaus," he said, standing back. "You can put the picture right on the telly screen and hold it. Then you can enlarge or trim or pick one comer. Does everything but go out for coffee. We'll be getting one next year. Much better definition than this old heap."

It was true that the picture now sliding out between two rubber rollers on one side and into a wire basket was not remarkably clear. The grainy texture of the paper and the big black dots made it look pretty much as it does in your morning newspaper, flimsy, primitive, underexposed. But it was clear enough to use. I spread it on top of the machine. Archie looked over my shoulder with interest, breathing brownie down my collar.

"And that's all you wanted, dear boy?"

"Yep. What I expected, if not what I wanted," I said without looking up. I felt very tired. In front of me lay an eight-by eleven-inch blowup of a photo from the Stanford University yearbook of 1979. *The Cardinal.* The type below the face read "Peter Anthony Angeletti, Sacramento, California. Economics. Varsity gymnastics '78, '79. Sigma—" the transmission border had cut off the rest, so I couldn't read about Peter Angeletti's fraternity, clubs, ambitions, or whether he had been voted most likely to cop a plea.

But then, I didn't really want to, since the face looking pleasantly up at me from the telex machine bore no resemblance at all to the man I had met on his father's houseboat.

CHAPTER 6

"ALL SET?"

"All set." I folded the wirephoto sheet and placed it in my inside jacket pocket, next to the pistol. "When you come to California, Archie, I'll return the favor."

"I never leave London, dear boy. When a man is tired of London, you know."

I didn't know. I was busy thinking about the possible good reasons Angeletti could have had for introducing another man to me as his son. There were no good reasons. Somebody is always lying a little bit, I had oh-so-smugly told Magnus.

Archie smiled his kindly smile, cocking his round head and showing the four stumps of teeth, and we shook hands. Then with one last glance at the cavernous newsroom, I started for the stairs.

The UPI offices were—and are—on the third floor of a late-Victorian building off Fleet Street, dingy and incompletely modernized, one of those nondescript London redbricks that have been carved up over the years for more different purposes than a boarding-house turkey. I had lived in a moldy building just like it off Gower Street. Not a softball player, Fred had said. Angeletti could be hiding his son from something. Or he could be looking for him as well as Caroline. Or instead of her. Either way, it was no longer a romp down memory lane. I could get down to business or I could find myself one morning looking up into the front end of the false son's pistol.

A tiny self-service elevator, little more than a bird cage, runs up a wire-mesh shaft in the central stairwell of the UPI building; a heavy-duty elevator for equipment covers a back wall. Not liking elevators, open or closed, and figuring the exercise would keep me awake, I walked down the fire stairs to a side door, skipping the lobby and going out into Chancery Lane. Wondering if the kid with the gun was one of Angeletti's hoodlums or if he had rented him for the day from the Harvard Club.

The rain had stopped again, and only a few gray clouds were brushed back like a forelock from the bleak English sky. No California city street is ever that dark and empty.

At 4:30 A.M. Chancery Lane had no Orange Julius to light up the morning, no Latino low-riders, no all-night liquor stores or pancake houses. Just a dark stretch of brick and shadows about 30 generations old. People had been bustling up this particular branch of real estate while Boston was a collection of wigwams, while San Francisco was just a place the fish talked about. My heels tapped and splashed in pudlets as I walked north, trying to remember what you were tired of when you were tired of London. I had just begun to think that you could come back after all, that I could exchange San Francisco for London if I wanted and to hell with Angeletti, when two men stepped silently beside me at either elbow and one of them rammed a hard, sharp point into my back.

"I'll stick this through your bloody gut, I will."

I froze. They quick-stepped me into the shadows and spun

me spread-eagle against the walls, like cops rousting a wino. Quick efficient hands reached under my jacket and removed both the gun and holster. Other hands patted me down from crotch to heel. Nobody touched the photo or my wallet. The man on my right stepped back and blinked a penlight once toward Fleet Street.

"He don't say much, do he?" the one with flashlight said.

The other one grunted.

I stood with my cheek mashed against cold stone and thought about jumping one of them. Then moved my head and thought about jumping the other one. They crouched back too far on either side, knife sharp against my kidney, pistol barrel against my shoulder. Professionals. A matched set. I wasn't good enough, not good enough to even think about it. And while I thought about that, a car motor purred to a stop behind me, a door creaked open, and I was half-shoved, half-booted backwards, turned and tossed into the back seat of a cramped English car, belly first over the transmission hump. One man climbed in the front. The other sat in the back with his feet planted firmly on the inside of my knees and the knife point now against the side of my neck, hard enough to draw a trickle of blood, warm like a baby's lips.

"Keep him there until we stop."

The driver had a French accent—at another time I might have started guessing south of Paris and west of Nice—and his voice sounded loud and hollow in the empty street. He let out the clutch and we rolled wordlessly up Chancery Lane, turned swiftly two or three times and finally, minutes later, halted again in darkness between street lamps. The man in front got out quickly and flung open the back door. Somebody else told me to crawl out backwards, slowly, and stay on my hands and knees. We seemed to be in a side street somewhere off Holborn, but I had no time for more than a glance before stiff hands jerked me to my feet, jammed each wrist into a half Nelson, and shoved me stumbling around and through a high folding metal gate set across one end of an alley. Behind us, the driver closed the gate with a bustling metallic clang.

We entered a door in the alley and started down a set of dimly lit stairs, but there was still light enough for me to glimpse a flash of white tile walls and the familiar red-circle-and-blue-bar logo of the London Underground. Somehow I guessed we weren't going to stop for a ticket.

Through a winding, narrow corridor and down more steps —about every tenth bulb lit—the man in front used his pen-light, swinging the little beam from wall to wall. Five minutes at least of steady descent. Then he pushed open a metal fire door and we suddenly walked into the tube itself, past stacks of buckets, fire extinguishers, fuse boxes, to emerge at the end of a passenger platform. We had evidently come down a service stairwell to the front of the station. Ahead of us, an empty train five or six cars long sat on the track, all doors open, small interior lights scattered at regular intervals in the thick darkness. Farther down the track, where the tunnel and the train curved slightly to the right and vanished completely into blackness, I could see more dim lights above a staircase and the first steps of a steep escalator. Nearer, in the yellow-ish glow of the train lights, the word "Holborn" could just be seen on a sloping wall. Nothing moved. No light blinked. The train simply sat, somewhere near the third circle of the inferno, and listened to the umbilical hum of its power rail snaking through the darkness.

"Down to the front of the first car."

We pushed along the platform, hearing our heels click loudly and the fabric of our coats and trousers rustle, until we reached the first door of the first car, just behind the driver's compartment, and went in.

On one of the dingy upholstered benches opposite us, another man sat, muffled in a topcoat and snap brim hat to keep off the chill. His cigarette tip glowed, sending off the crisp aroma of Gauloise and brightening the bottoms of gold-rimmed tinted glasses. His left hand was in his pocket.

"Sit down." Another French accent. "Everything good?" The other two nodded and took up standing positions a pace away from me on each side. I was pushed back on the bench facing the Frenchman across the narrow aisle. In the dim light, he had a complexion like dirty ice. "All right, Monsieur Haller," he said tonelessly, "tell me what you know."

"I know this is a no smoking section," I said, pointing at a placard over the seat. The man on the left backhanded my face with sudden power, as if swatting a fly, and my head snapped back against the window with a thud. I tasted a drop of blood along my upper lip.

"Mister Rampal's got no time for your jokes, 'aller," the one on my right said.

"Sure," I said. "Is he related to Rampal the flutist?" And he hit me again, harder. Life, I thought. When you're tired of London, you're tired of life.

"Let's be quick, Monsieur Haller. You met a young woman tonight in the Savoy Hotel and took her to a restaurant. I want to know why you did it and what she said to you."

I made some genealogical suggestions in idiomatic French, and this time the dapper Frenchman himself stepped over and slapped me carefully several times, letting his rings tear the skin around my nose and mouth and smearing my cheeks with blood.

"A 'ard case," the talking Englishman remarked with satisfaction. Everybody watched me straighten up on the train bench again. Under us, the third rail whined faintly to itself, whistling in the dark. Around us, the dim lights flickered for a moment as a distant generator shifted gears.

"Aren't you boys worried about a night watchman down here?"

"The night watchman is well taken care of," the Frenchman said, leaving two possibilities hanging in the air, neither much comfort. He sat down again. "Suppose you tell me what I ask you before I have put out your eyes with this." And he flipped open one of those plastic tube cigarette lighters with his left hand, thumbed it lit, and leaned forward. It burned bright under my right nostril and flamed in reflection on his tinted glasses like a smoking ghost. I closed my eyes reflexively as the flame scorched my nose and cheek. A strong grip stopped my hand as it came up.

"Don't," I said, twisting my head away from the heat as far as I could. "Don't do that."

He chuckled and pulled the lighter back a few inches. "Amateurs," he said. "They never know what to do when they meet a professional . . ."

I never heard what kind of professional he meant because I kicked him as hard as I could in the groin with the toe of my shoe. He screamed and I flung myself up and into a crouch, driving an elbow toward the belly on my left. The second Englishman whirled me around in a bear hug. I shoved my hands up his chest, scratching for his throat. The other one hit my neck with a fist like a waffle iron and knocked us both sideways and into a balance pole in the middle of the aisle. We staggered apart a few steps. The Frenchman kept screaming. The bear-hugging Englishman marched toward me while the other stooped and doctored.

I circled around the balance pole, heading for the open door, the platform, the wonderful darkness. "Drink Bovril," a smiling girl said by an overhead light, "for ten kinds of vita-mins." The Englishman grabbed the pole with one hand and I shuffled sideways. "Down with Guinness." He stood flatfooted in front of the door with fists about shoulder high. Good. He didn't know what the hell he was doing without a knife. "Vote Labour." I faked a right and swung under his hand with a left that caught him in the diaphragm and bounced him sideways into the first row of seats. Sting like a butterfly.

Two giant steps and a "May I?" brought me to the door, raincoat flapping like a drunken bat, before the other man sucker-punched me through it and dribbled me off the black, hard concrete platform.

When I shook my head clear and looked up, the barrel of his pistol was no bigger than a coal chute. My own Smith and Wesson. Guns don't kill. People do.

"Bring the son'bitch back here."

The Frenchman was calling from the train car, where he sat now on the bench again, holding his belly or thereabouts and doubled over sideways. The Englishman he had called Asher motioned me up with the pistol.

"Stand by the door, Rog," Henry said, and the other Eng-lishman, honking like a punctured accordian, squeezed behind him and stood blocking the exit. Henry folded me roughly back into my seat, then stood with the pistol while the Frenchman slowly straightened and set his mouth in a clamp. He must have wanted to retch, but not in front of the help.

"We're not going to get anything out of him," he said in a rattling voice. Shaking fingers adjusted his gold rims. "Marteau need not be bothered." He looked at Asher. Overhead in the shadows, a placard announced an exhibit of delicate porcelain at the British Museum. The power line snorted beneath us. "It's past 5:00. Take care of him," the Frenchman said. He handed over a pint bottle J & B Scotch from his topcoat pocket. "You know what to do."

Henry nodded, and the Frenchman got carefully to his feet and left the car. We could hear his footsteps echoing down the platform until he went through the door to the service stairs and there was nothing but the power hum and the chill darkness outside again, a long black cavern lined with tiny smudges of straw-colored light, like stars going out. I had never seen so little light and so much space.

"Get him over there."

I was jerked backward against the seat and half turned so that the man behind me could grip my arms in a nelson and still find space to grind a knee in the small of my back. While he breathed a rancid cloud of saliva and tobacco into my ear, his partner, my gun still in one paw, twisted the metal cap of the bottle with a thumb and two fingers.

"Keep him still, Rog."

The grip tightened.

Henry stuffed the gun in his belt with a practiced move, pinched two grimy fingers across my nose, and as my head tilted and my jaw sagged, he jammed the bottle in.

I held out for a few seconds, maybe a full minute. Then I gulped for air and the first swallow kicked its way down my throat. My eyes burned and watered at the same time. The bottle emptied in bubbling sobs as Henry held my nostrils and smiled slightly into my face. The last mouthful made me gag convulsively, and I spit most of it out, dribbling the warm Scotch down my chin and shirt. Henry didn't seem to mind my manners. He slipped the empty bottle into my raincoat pocket and Roger let me sit up again, though my head pitched instantly toward my knees as I tried to clear my throat and chest. Firewater, right enough. My ears rang and popped, my stomach quivered like a trampoline, and I knew it would only get worse.

"Don't like your grog, Yank?" Henry said.

"I was hoping for Bovril," I whispered.

"This one is going to die laughing, he is," Roger said behind me. "Bloody Benny Hill." He wheezed tobacco breath. "It's 5:20, Hen. You want to hurry it along now. The bloody tube opens at 6."

"Got to wait till he's properly pissed, Rog." Henry leaned forward, pressing his gray, pitted skin close to my face. "You know what, Yank? Rog and me is going to crabwalk you to the end of the car and crack your bleedin' skull against the track." He sneered, the chipped teeth of an Englishman, breath like a dead mouse. "Kick a poor Frenchman in the balls. When they find you, Yank, you're going to smell like a bleedin' power rail."

"You don't want to do that, Henry," I muttered, still balancing my head on my hands like a melon and feeling my belly heave.

"Five thousand volts when the mains comes on," he said. "I could run my bloody shaver off you."

I closed my eyes. Henry kept talking. My mind swam away. There had been a kid in my army barracks who died one Saturday night before our eyes. A teetotaler. A born-again Baptist from Nebraska. Sergeant Ray Alan Booth had bet him ten dollars and the kid had drunk a quart of vodka in five minutes, collected his ten dollars, and then passed out. Forever. Alcohol anesthetizes the brain, the battalion doctor had told the barracks later. Too much alcohol can close down the respiratory system, like slamming a door, so that you simply suffocate yourself. Dinah had once shown me a paper she had written in medical school on how cowboy surgeons used to give whiskey as anesthetic when they operated. Give him a bottle, was their motto, hold down his leg, saw as fast as you can. But half the patients died from alcohol suffocation, she had said, instead of gangrene or blood loss or fright.

Somebody asked a question. My mind reeled and staggered back to the present.

"Ready, Hen?"

Both men were standing over me, shadows in the dim light, watching my progress.

"Another minute, Rog."

Rog and Hen. A professional twosome, solicitous and chummy as your local TV news team. An anthology of pros. Who the hell was Marteau? And where was Caroline Angeletti? Had she sent him? I pushed my mind away. You metabolize alcohol at the rate of an ounce an hour, more or less. One ounce every hour and you don't get drunk. Sixteen ounces to a pint. In about ten minutes, unless I came up with a stomach pump, I was going to be too drunk to stand, too drunk to run. Dead drunk. Another stray tourist down the tube.

"Now."

One of them hauled me to my feet, and I slipped and fell back toward the seat. My ears beat like tom-toms.

"All the fight's gone out of 'im, Hen. Some of these big ones don't hold it better 'n a bird."

"Bring 'im then."

Roger hoisted me up with both arms and wrenched my right hand back against my shoulder blade. With his free hand, he pulled out a knife and let me admire it, an eight-inch ivory-handled switchblade. They're illegal in England. I could call a cop.

"Move along, sod." He prodded my raincoat with the knifepoint and I stumbled toward the open door. Outside on the platform, pale as Hamlet's father, Henry twitched his pen-light beam.

"Come on, move your bloody ass," Roger growled.

We went forward, listening to the amplified sound of our shoes and clothes in the empty darkness. After we had passed the front of the train, the platform extended only another ten or 15 feet through the stacks of buckets and fuse boxes we had already passed. I looked up. Henry stood in front of the stairwell door that the Frenchman had taken, a single dim bulb just above his sandy hair. Beside him narrow wooden steps dropped to the floor of the tunnel. Beyond the little circle of illumination—black space, an open throat. His penlight swept us toward the steps.

"Down you go, Yank."

I stared at the stairwell door, swaying. The only way out for me. There was no chance I could take on Roger or Henry alone, not to mention together. But there was no chance I could get to the stairwell either. Roger jogged my arm impatiently. I stepped into the path of the beam amid the workmen's litter, five feet from the steps, and did the only thing I could do. I kicked the bucket.

"Bugger!"

Roger and Henry both jerked their heads for an instant to see the paint bucket bounce across the tracks, spitting a tongue, of sparks, and carom off the far wall. Not a long instant, but long enough. I grabbed Roger's knife hand with my arms tangled chaotically. Roger grunted in pain. I jumped toward the stairwell door, missed my footing, and Henry grazed my temple with the side of his pistol, throwing me off balance, over the wooden steps, down with a thump to the tunnel floor five feet below.

"I'm fuckin' bleedin'!" Roger bawled.

Henry shot once at my head, but the bullet smashed off the wall beside me and ricocheted over and over down the tunnel, screaming like a banshee.

"For God's sake, Henry!"

Sucking in a cloud of nauseous cordite from the pistol shot, retching Scotch down my shirtfront, I rolled and half-crawled, half-loped toward my right, away from the feeble lights in the train and the single bulb over the stairwell door. Henry's penlight was nowhere to be seen. Roger groaned again in the blackness above and behind me, and the stairwell door opened briefly, filled with shadows.

"Bleedin' like a pig, I am."

The door swung shut. I stopped. Roger had fallen, tripped, somehow ripped himself with the switchblade. Roger had gone. Had Henry? I listened in the darkness, hearing only the hiss of waves sloshing across my skull, tides of Scotch rising. The tunnel was utterly silent except for the subliminal hum of the power rail, still on its minimum volts. If Henry had stayed behind, I could neither see nor hear him.

The silence stretched on, thinner and thinner. The blackness sank around me like a mask. I was perhaps 20 yards from the head of the train, from the last dying ripples of light. Could Henry see me? I squinted, tried to concentrate. Raincoat tan, suit dark. I squatted slowly in the center of the track, balancing my knuckles against the wooden crosstie. About a foot and a half to my left would be the power rail, elevated a little above the other two on a running brace. I shivered and edged my knuckles sideways. Somewhere farther back in the gaping darkness might be cross-tunnels, stairs, platforms. I slipped one arm from the raincoat and began shrugging the other arm loose. In the stillness, the whisper of fabric boomed like the Michigan marching band. Close to the train, to the glimmer from the stairwell bulb, I heard a single ping. Drop of water? Tap of heel? Someone's in the kitchen with Dinah. I was drunker than any ten Irishmen. One hand slipped on the rough crosstie and I slumped suddenly left, jerked myself upright, let the coat fall free away from the power rail, a crumpled shadow. Scotch boiled in my throat. I wanted to lie down, close my eyes, stop the spinning. I wanted to break Henry's neck like a stalk of celery. I wanted to reason together.

You never know until you have to. Cats and dogs tumbled in my belly, my balance blew back and forth in gusts, but I closed my eyes, forced my feet to life and turned. I was facing nothing, nothing at all but blackness: black, black, unimaginable blackness. Behind me the ping came again, louder.

"Yank."

He couldn't see me. Nobody could see anything in the maw of the tunnel. He could only shoot at sounds. Shoot at what he ran into. I lifted my right foot, balanced, pushed. The track was littered with filth, odd shapes and points that snapped at my ankles like teeth in a nightmare. He might see the pale tan of the raincoat if he came close enough. Even in the darkness. He might not shoot if he saw it. He might just beat it unconscious against the track. I swayed, stumbled.

"Yank."

Much closer. Henry would not have to pick his steps slowly, inch by inch in the blackness. Henry wasn't exploding with Scotch. Henry had a gun. His feet scuffled nearer. A stalking horse. Dinah blow your horn. I squeezed my eyes tight to stop the spinning. A mighty fine line. My left foot slid off the crosstie, my trouser caught on something mid-calf level. I stopped, trembling from heel to neck in the cold emptiness. *The power rail brace.* In my drunkenness, I had got it wrong, got it completely wrong. With all my tiptoeing caution. *The power rail was on this side.*

"Yank!"

Ten feet behind me. I twisted my neck to see black on

black, a sliver of light on metal, the pale tan of the raincoat. Henry jumped toward the coat. Lights blazed overhead and flickered once as Henry screamed, as the whiskey churned and erupted in my chest, as I pitched forward and started to fall.

# CHAPTER 7

**M**ORE ICE?"

I shook my head about a quarter of an inch each way. My ears fell off.

The homicide man put the Styrofoam ice bucket back on the table and folded his hands comfortably across his lap. I lowered my lips a few feet and wrapped them around the edge of the glass. A quart of water an hour, the doctor had said, plus the odd aspirin when I felt like it. I had swallowed six of them since the cops had arrived.

"We found a gun on the track, you know, near the body," the homicide man said after a lengthy pause. He was the friendly one. His red-faced partner had come in late and sprawled into one of the plastic hospital chairs with a glower. Now he rattled his copy of my statement and snorted. I drank another quart of water. The friendly one was little. About five-eight and a hundred and thirty or forty. Neat in a tweedy jacket and a salmon cardigan underneath it that somebody had knit for him. The domestic effect. A man with two or three daughters, a bustling wife, a sensible garden. His partner was as big as people usually get, in all directions. A head the size of a watermelon, shoulders and belly rolling like the slopes of the Sierra out of the flimsy chair, feet planted widely apart in old brown shoes that looked like tree stumps.

I sat motionless in my chair, hoping that when the big one's turn came, he would whisper.

"A gun," the homicide man repeated.

"I'm not surprised," I said. "He spent a lot of time pointing it at me."

"An American gun," he said. "A Smith and Wesson .38 police special. It looks to have come from one of the Pakistani or Indian suppliers in East London. Or there's one or two in Soho. They get the guns from the Irish, who get them from bloody-minded American supporters and sell off the extras for profit."

"International intrigue," I agreed. The homicide man rummaged through the cardigan and came up with a briar pipe, already filled. His partner had a matchstick jammed between his gums, but he didn't offer a light. Cardigan patted himself down while the big guy continued to glower; then he found a box of wooden matches and set out on the elaborate routine that pipe smokers have to follow. Light, suck, puff. Some airplanes get tested faster. I didn't mind the wait as long as he did it quietly. I didn't mind because my mouth tasted like the inside of an army boot and because my brain had turned to taco sauce. I had the Mount St. Helens of hangovers. My stomach felt like a sack of snakes. A fat gash on my left calf, inflicted by an unknown part of the Central Line, throbbed rhythmically. Otherwise, things were dandy. I was glad to sit around in hospital pajamas and bathrobe all afternoon and listen to official chit-chat while what was left of Henry's Scotch metabolized quietly. Sooner or later, of course, the chit-chat would turn ugly.

"You're from Boston," the homicide man resumed when he had his fire going.

"I'm from San Francisco," I said, sipping more water, "and I'm as Irish as the Pope."

"Did you try Alka-Seltzer with that?" he asked, pointing the stem of the pipe toward my water cup.

"I couldn't take the noise."

He nodded gently and turned his head to the other one. "Read over Mr. Haller's statement yet, Brian?" He got a grunt for an answer and turned back to me. "Inspector Stock is from narcotics."

"Sure." I looked again. Inspector Stock had the sour, suspicious face of a man who cultivates a state of permanent irritation, a doctor who hates to be around sick people, a cop who hates people in trouble. Bugger your bleeding heart, his face said; bugger yourself. He frowned at me and shifted the matchstick from one corner of his mouth to the other. His nose and cheeks were mottled with burst capillaries that might have got that way from drink or weather, or more probably from temper. His mountainous shoulders slumped inside a cheap rumpled suit coat off the rack from John Lewis or one of the other British chains. Nobody had knit him anything. Around 50, short of patience, short of hair, short of class. He would have risen about as far as he was going in a police hierarchy that looked for polish and the public relations touch. Unlike his neat, pipe-fiddling buddy, Inspector Stock looked as if he had put in a lot of bad hours on the mean streets. But then narcotics cops usually do.

"What's narcotics got to do with me?" I asked.

"Nothing, don't we hope," he said unpleasantly. His voice was loud and his accent was defiantly working-class. We watched as he cranked his bulk out of the armless plastic chair and walked across the small room to the window, blocking most of the sunlight. Six-four at least, 250 pounds. Contrary to popular opinion, men that big are often irascible, not gentle, as if bewildered by carrying so much extra body around like a ball and chain. He turned around and sat on the sill, arms crossed. I had to crane to see his face.

"What do you know about Charles Marteau?" he said.

"I don't know anything about him."

"Your statement," he enunciated slowly and formally, like a teacher to a doltish student, "says that one of the assailants mentioned the name Marteau."

"Yeah, one of the perpetrators." I wondered what else I had put in that statement before the good doctors of St. Raphael's had trotted out their tray of emetics and started to sober me up. "Somebody said the name, but I don't remember more than that. I never heard of him." The homicide man crossed and recrossed his legs briskly, and the one in the window cleared his throat as if he wanted to spit. They didn't much believe me. I didn't much blame them.

"Henry Dean," Stock said with the same controlled impatience, "the man you killed, worked for a French narcotics distributing organization directed by a man named Charles Marteau."

"I didn't kill anybody. I was five yards away when he jumped on the power rail. I was minding my own business."

"You killed him, luv."

"Name of a cognac, isn't it, Brian?" the man in the chair asked. His pipe had gone out and he was poking it with the end of a match. "Marteau?" They had played this hardball, softball routine before.

"You're thinking of Martel. Marteau means hammer in French," Stock said. He spat the matchstick into a Styrofoam cup and pulled a fresh one from his jacket. "And it won't be his real name. Some kind of code, like a bloody paramilitary. We think he works from Bordeaux, exporting heroin to England. Not a major supplier, but a steady, clever one. The French police have been tiptoeing around for years and never touch him. They keep losing interest."

"Drug addiction isn't illegal in England, you know, Mister Haller," the homicide man told me.

"No," Stock said, disgusted. His neck had been injured somehow long ago, I decided, and he held his big head stiffly, unable to turn to the left. "But unlicensed sale of dangerous drugs is. There'll be a hamper full of marijuana somewhere right in this hospital, for treatment of glaucoma patients. The National Health also manufactures about 200 pounds of heroin a year for terminal cancer patients and for registered addicts. Make it out at a plant in Chigwell. The patients get injections by their doctors at ordinary clinics. But the Pakistanis and Indians and the blacks won't come to a drugs program office. They're suspicious," he sneered. "They smell a white man's plot." Even in the half-shadow, his face flushed with indignation. "Bloody stupid wogs. They buy it on the street and use it and pass it on farther north, to Manchester or Leeds."

"What happens there?"

"They use it. They stick it in their arms and feel good and forget about living in a filthy one-room walk-up with three other families on the dole. And after a while, they drop dead. That's what happens there. Some of them pass it on to the docks, too, and it gets sent right across the sea to your lot, and they swill it up in Harlem just as fast as it comes, and they drop dead too."

He jammed another matchstick in his mouth and looked out the window.

"Brian is more or less asking for your cooperation," the homicide man said mildly.

"I'm just looking for a missing wife, Inspector. I don't do drugs."

"You were picked up by professional criminals who tried to kill you."

I shrugged and drank more water. *"C'est la vie sportive."*

"Who's the wife, tough guy?" Stock rasped in his nasal accent. "Give us names."

"This is the first break in the case Brian has had for over a year," the homicide man said, leaning forward, hands on knees.

"I can't tell you that," I said carefully. Even half befuddled with painkiller and sleeplessness, I didn't see any percentage in inviting the police into Carlo Angeletti's business. I would find Caroline again, without the police, and I would find Rampal and Roger too. Especially Roger. Mario Thomas and the psychobabblists would call my attitude macho. I like independent. Forthright. Self-destructive. "Under British law," I said, "I don't think I have to tell you that."

"By God!" Stock exploded. The other man held up a palm.

"It's a confidential matter," I said wearily. "I'm licensed and hired to use my own judgment. I don't think the missing wife has anything to do with this. She's just a kid."

"Bugger under British law!" Stock shouted.

"Just another big-city mugging," I muttered. My brain had shrunk to the size of a Brazil nut. I wanted to lie down and wake up in my own little bed in Green Street.

Stock bounced his 250 pounds off the floor and paced to the door, making the small room shake. The man in the chair puffed at his pipe and watched me, expressionless. Two or three daughters and two or three cats, I decided. Nothing in life would ever surprise him.

"Haller." Stock came back and stood in front of me, all eight feet and two tons of him. His face was like a clenched fist.

The rumpled suit gave off the acrid aroma of laundry solvents, roiling my belly; he put his big paws on each side of my chair, shoulder high, and lowered his eyes to mine.

"Haller," he said venomously. I saw nothing but saliva, teeth, bursting veins. "You dumb cock-sucking bloody-minded bugger." Homicide murmured a protest. "You don't have to file a bloody complaint," Stock said. "You don't even have to stand by a statement the half-witted constable took when you were under medication. But Inspector Nelson here can plant your bloody arse in the bloody chokey until our inquiries on Henry Dean are completed. Under British law. For weeks. If you don't have a barrister, my American friend, you'd bloody well better get one."

Someone knocked and Stock slowly raised the huge burning moon of his face from mine. And into the room stepped Magnus.

"My God, Michael! They told me you were assaulted in the Underground. Are you all right, dear fellow?"

Stock wheeled away and snorted to the window while Magnus hurried in, crisp and elegant as if he'd stepped out of a Burberry ad, as slick as three earls. The policemen took in his linen jacket, his imperial purple cravat, his Jermyn Street tailoring, and Bond Street barbering and seemed to stiffen. Magnus belongs to what the British government officially calls Class I-A, and at the best of times his bearing and accent are usually enough to infuriate 90 percent of his countrymen. He glanced at me, at the two men with Official stamped over their workaday faces, and turned it on.

"A nurse called me at home just an hour ago, dear fellow," he said, inspecting my face and back for bruises, knife blades. The vowels trotted out, clipped and manicured as thoroughbreds at Ascot. "I stopped by your hotel for clothes." One hand raised an overnight valise to show me. Stock filled his cheeks and puffed.

"I'm all right," I said. "Just a case of mistaken identity. They thought I was Muhammed Ali."

"I'll drive you home." Authoritatively. "The doctor downstairs said you were ready to leave now. Susannah's made up a room."

Stock turned back in his stiff-necked way from the window and glowered. The homicide man stirred in his chair. Magnus glanced at them, as he might glance at a stray dog, and, wrinkling his nose, waved pipe smoke away from his face.

Englishmen wouldn't introduce themselves to each other in a lifeboat. I flipped one hand to indicate Stock and Nelson. "Magnus Harpe," I said. "The police."

"Inspector Nelson, CID," the man in the chair said, rising and tipping his pipe.

"Have you caught them yet?" Magnus asked.

"Actually . . . ," Nelson began.

"Surely you don't think they're at large in the hospital," Magnus said sarcastically.

"I'm afraid I'm still assisting the police with their inquiries," I told him, using British newspaper jargon for being under suspicion.

Magnus looked at me, at Nelson, at Stock. The room we were in served as a lounge or waiting room for interns. In addition to three or four armless plastic chairs, shaped like giant orange shoehorns, there was a white wooden table with cheap enamel tea things, a tiny two-foot-square refrigerator plastered with notes about the prices of cream and sugar, and an accordioned wall of thick beige fabric that could open to an adjoining lounge. The whole place would have fit in a corner of the Reform Club loo. Against its institutional shabbiness Magnus seemed all the more patrician.

"Is there a complaint against Mr. Haller?" he asked through his sinuses.

"We're considering holding Mr. Haller as a bloody material witness," Stock said loudly, letting a syrupy, mocking rhythm creep into his thick accent. Pretty soon I could ask for subtitles.

Magnus blustered, swelling his face and hitching his lanky shoulders. His solicitor, Sir Somebody, he began, and Stock answered shrilly, heated—two big men cramped into a small depersonalizing room and starting to snap their claws at each other like lobsters in a pot. My eyes felt feeble and tired from too much smoke, too little sleep, too much English. I watched the face of the only one in the room with any power.

"We're not holding Mr. Haller," Nelson said in his mild voice, cutting through the fracas. Some inspectors are more equal than others. Stock swore and jammed the matchstick back in his teeth. Nelson wouldn't be impressed by Magnus's Oxbridge act. Neither would Stock if he could control his emotions. I had been a cop just long enough to know what he would say next. And what he would do later.

"You're free to go, Mr. Haller," he said slowly. The pipe needed attention. He puffed once or twice with great concentration. "There will be a magistrate's hearing in about a week at which you must be present. We're keeping your passport as a precaution until the hearing is over. You're not to leave London for any reason without CID permission, and I have to warn you that we may withhold permission. You are entitled to police protection if you want it, in view of the circumstances." He looked up from the pipe. I shook my head. "I didn't think so. I ought to add that neither Inspector Stock nor I am fully satisfied with your cooperation."

He nodded curtly, probably fully satisfied with his grammar, and turned to go. Stock pushed past my chair and opened the hall door. The surveillance team would be waiting at the hospital entrance when I left, as good as he could make them, and that would be pretty good. Most cops in divisions like burglary or homicide, whether English or American, never learn to shadow a bar stool. Their crimes are reported by victims, and whatever information they need, they ask for. But all across the world, cops in narcotics and gambling and vice, the victimless crimes, don't get many hits reported. They have to generate their own information, either from slimeballs, which is what they call paid informants, or from surveillance. Narcotics cops are usually experts at shadowing. Between the Criminal Investigations Department and the Friends of Carlo Angeletti, I was going to be leading a parade right there in River City, straight to Caroline and Roger. Little Bo-Peeper, wagging his tails behind me.

Magnus stepped closer to me, his handsome face troubled with questions, and started to speak.

"Haller." Stock interrupted, leaning back in at the door. "If you're holding out on me, I'll tear your bloody fat American head off. I will."

Magnus tried to persuade me to go back with him to Chelsea, but I insisted on the White Horse instead.

"You could use the upstairs guest room." He was still grumbling as he held the door of the Jaguar open to the sidewalk. In the late afternoon sunlight, Bloomsbury Square looked fresh, green. In the reflection of Magnus's bright car window, I looked green too. "Susannah is going out tonight to some damn reception," he said. "I could give you soup and sandwiches. I could help you."

But I thanked him, backing away and waving, cautioned him not to repeat the little I had said, walked stiffly through the hotel lobby and three flights up. Macho as the man in the moon. My neck was a piece of knotty pine, my head was an egg balanced on it. I was hard-boiled all right. An Underground hero. Was it Roger's fist or Henry's that had caved in the back of my neck? I couldn't remember. It didn't matter. A bellboy twice my age frisked up the stairs and opened my room for me. Inside, after tossing Magnus's valise on the bed, I found my shaving kit and got out the dented silver flask I had bought from Haverhill's during my first year with the *LA Times*. A good old boy named Carlton Hand and I had drunk Yellowstone bourbon from it in Dixie cups while we manned the paper's graveyard shift. I winced at the mirror by the bed. Bad phrase. First I would take pen and paper like Lord Peter Wimsey and make a chart of all suspects and clues and a map of the house. First I would have a drink. I stacked aspirin on my tongue in a hecatomb to the gods of sobriety and raised the flask. Then I stretched out full-length on the bed and fumbled for my wallet, where Hunter Merriman's phone number was nestling beside Angeletti's cash. When I picked up the telephone, the operator said, "Yes?" Nobody in England has ever said, "Are you there?"

"Overseas call," I said. "Credit card." I read her the number carefully, feeling my bruises tighten and the aspirin and booze start to mix it up. My mouth seemed to twist around each word. A yawn flew out like a bird.

"The number is busy," she chanted in a little while. "Please try again later." I held the dead phone in my hand and stared at the light switch on the wall by the door, one of those round mammary forms the English like to use, with a suggestive toggle in the center. A secretly sensual race. Their light switches reminded me of Dinah. I would try Merriman again, as soon as I had another swallow from the flask. But before my thick fingers could reach the dial, sleep rolled me under like a warm tropical wave.

CHAPTER 8

I T WAS ALMOST EIGHT WHEN I AWOKE. AS A TREAT, THE WEATHER gnomes had cast another sunny spell, and Blooms-bury Square was fairly preening its old limbs in the unaccustomed summer warmth. Outside my window, strange English birds sang that the rain had gone away forever. In one of the paths across the square, another Churchillian old lady stalked east, carrying a yellow plastic shopping bag that said "St. Tropez" in big block letters. A dog barked over the traffic. I could always go back to writing travel articles for the wires, I thought. Guides to London museums. The best time to see the zoo. How to get around on the Underground. That way, I'd probably live long enough to collect a pension and buy a dog and sit in empty hotel rooms.

I washed the outer man with a hand-held shower that was as close as the White Horse came to twentieth-century plumbing, and then I worked my way through the breakfast that room service had sent up: tea, of course, poached eggs, tiny cooked tomatoes camouflaged with parsley, two strips of cold English bacon. They had put the toast in a wire rack guaranteed to chill it—you can get more flavor from a Frisbee—but I ate it all anyway, the first solid meal since Roger and Henry had bought me a drink in Holborn.

More tea bags were on the bedside table by an electric kettle. So was the telephone. I put through the overseas call I had started last night and ten or 12 rings later got an irritable Hunter Merriman on the phone.

"Haller? From London. For God's sake." He paused. "All right. Let me get to the phone in the den." I heard a woman's voice, a door slam, and the extension click dead.

"What the hell, Haller?" Merriman said, coming on the line again. "Do you know it's after midnight here?"

"I thought you might want my report right away, Merriman."

"Have you found her?"

"I found her and I lost her."

"What does that mean, Haller? Don't talk in riddles, man." Something bumped the receiver on his end, the scrape of a cigarette lighter. I told him what had happened, leaving out details like Roger, Henry, and Monsieur Rampal, dwelling instead on Caroline's dislike of the Valley and her fear of the old man.

"Christ," he said when I had finished. "What a mess. Look, you probably need more money over there. I'll deposit two more weeks to your account."

"That'll be nice. In the meantime, I'll keep looking for your girl, but she's almost certainly skipped out of her hotel, and she might even have left London."

"All right, got it. That's why we hired you. Keep looking, and let me know where you are. I'll tell Mr. Angeletti."

"Fine." I gave him the number of the White Horse. "And Hunter?"

"Yes?"

"Where exactly did you guys stash the real Peter Angeletti?"

There was a long pause, an exhalation of smoke. It was as quiet over the telephone line as if we were sitting in the same room, in the summer darkness, thoughtfully smoking, regarding each other like animals in separate cages.

"I'll get back to you," he said finally.

"Do that," I said and hung up.

The tea had grown cold, so I boiled another cup and dropped the bag in, lighting a cigarette while I waited and staring through the window at the bright, lively morning. There would be fog now in San Francisco, or drizzle. I hauled up the giant yellow section of the London telephone book that ran S-Z.

"Savoy Hotel."

"This is Mrs. Angeletti's doctor. Please connect me to her, in room 601."

A pause, then: "I'm sorry, doctor, our only Angeletti is in room 312. I can connect you to the front—"

"My mistake," I interrupted. "I can't read my own hand-writing. Would you ring 312, please?"

No answer. I cradled the phone slowly, and it rang once hysterically while my hand was still on it. The desk clerk told me in a bored voice that Mr. Harpe would like me to come around for cocktails at five. I thanked him and hung up again, still looking through the window at the morning rising up from Bloomsbury Square. Five would be fine, if the case hadn't gone down the tube before then. But it seemed like a long time to wait for a drink.

The limousines and taxis were busy ferrying passengers from the Savoy up the long driveway and into the real world. I stopped in front of the Savoy Theatre at the corner of the driveway and the Strand and studied posters. *There's a Girl in My Soup* was soon to be followed by a revival of *Hair*, they announced. As long as it wasn't *Subways Are for Sleeping*. I shivered in spite of the sunshine and threw a shifty-eyed glance down the crowded sidewalk, looking for cops. They could be three deep around me disguised as Japanese schoolchildren or they could still be hanging around outside the men's room in Charing Cross station, where I had taken a cab from the White Horse and made a fast, fraudulent exit through a john door and a left-luggage room. Either way, I probably still had company, Inspector Nelson's people or Rampal's.

I lit a cigarette and felt the smoke kick in the slats of my lungs. From Charing Cross, I had hurried up the Embankment to the back door of the Savoy, which turned out to be small and private and which opened onto the desk of a stern concierge reading the pink sheets of *The Financial Times*. When I had returned to the Embankment, across it, swinging gently at anchor in the old brown river, Robert Scott's *Discovery* was admitting a busload of Arab tourists down its gangplank. They would want to see a ship that had been to the South Pole, of course, for the same reasons that they flocked to London instead of Rome or Monte Carlo: cold, green, damp. Everything that Abadan isn't. I inhaled billows of tar and nicotine, glanced up and down the busy Strand sidewalk like Victor McLaughlin in *The Informer*, and thought about British fire laws for theatres. Then I stepped into the theatre lobby.

The straightforward approach, march right through the damn hotel and up to her room, had its attractions, especially with a ten-pound bruise on the back of my neck and a stomach about as robust as a soap ball. But straightforward would drag right along behind me whatever tails Nelson still had on. Plus the Frenchman. On the other hand, in 1922, fire had broken out in the Garrick Theatre and 14 people had been killed in the trample for the doors. Since then, London theatres had been built like sieves.

I examined more posters in the lobby until a line of buyers had formed at the ticket window. Two steps and I was over the fat velvet cord that blocked the staircase down. Another minute, three flights of stairs, past a closed intermission bar, and I found the men's room in the basement. Empty. No exit. To its left, farther down a corridor stood a janitor's broom closet and a set of metal fire doors with a bar handle and a bright red flag that told me not to open except in case of fire. Fine, fine. I don't relate well to signs either. I pushed the door open and stepped into a dimly lit service tunnel that looked far too much like the Underground station at Holborn. No alarm rang, nobody chased me. I started forward in what I guessed was the general direction of the Savoy.

The tunnel was about 30 yards long and must have run parallel to the driveway outside, connecting hotel and theatre basements. At the other end, I found a second fire door. Beyond that, a maze of short corridors and closets finally opened onto a service stairwell. I threw away the cigarette and, puffing, started up the stairs. Two minutes later, I stepped out at one end of the wide, completely deserted third-floor corridor.

No ticker tapes running. No poobahs in turbans and tunics. Just the usual sounds of a hotel at mid-morning drifting out from various rooms—buckets slapping, maids' voices, the occasional ring of the telephone. It wasn't the Holiday Inn, but, except for an Oriental runner down the center of the hall and gold fleur-de-lys wallpaper, it also wasn't the Hearst Castle. I straightened my shoulders and snapped my tie in front of a streaky antique mirror on the wall. You look like a million rials, kid. Then I walked quickly down the corridor reading numbers. At sudden voices, I froze, one hand halfway to where the gun used to be, and 304 suddenly threw a shaft of sunlight onto the wide red runner. A middle-aged couple came out discussing a map in German. They ignored me.

I took a deep, deep breath, knocked at 312, got no answer. A guy in North Beach, San Francisco, just down from the topless shows on Broadway—or silicone valley, as Fred calls it—once did me a favor by coating a duplicate Visa card with clear, heavy-duty plastic, industrial strength. I slipped the card from my wallet and into the brass Yale lock—it would be a cinch to break out of Yale—wiggled it 30 seconds and walked in.

The room was empty all the way through. I pulled the chain lock tight and finally remembered to exhale. In front of me was a window looking west toward Trafalgar Square and, wobbly in the bright haze, the towers of Houses of Parliament. To the left, a king-size bed with a green satiny cover that had already been made up; to the right, a desk, a color television, a closet, and the bathroom, door open to reveal another window. I stepped into the closet and started to go through things as systematically as you can if you haven't the slightest idea what you expect to find.

Two of the dresses hanging from the rack were from Bodger's Tailors in Cambridge, the rest from Magnins and Saks in Sacramento. The suitcase was new, Vuitton, and stashed neatly beside three pairs of sensible shoes. Sensible girl, Caroline. The plastic raincoat was gone.

On a polished Louis Quinze desk beside the television, the maid had arranged some books and papers in meaningless symmetry. I went through the books carefully, shaking the pages for loose baggies of heroin, I suppose. She was reading Kurt Vonnegut this trip, which didn't surprise me, and Dorothy Parker, which did. She had also been collecting airline schedules: at the bottom of a stack of currency-exchange receipts lay four blue and white Air France schedules. London to Paris, Paris to Nice, Paris to Bordeaux, Paris to Marseilles. A telephone number had been scratched hurriedly on hotel stationery and folded over. Serendipity. I would dial it, Rampal would answer and confess—what? I dialed it and got Boots Chemist in Piccadilly Circus, the only all-night drugstore in London.

You either like snooping or you don't. You either like opening bureau drawers in a quiet hotel and rummaging through strange women's underclothes, or you would rather be a dentist. I shut the bureau and went into the bathroom. Zero. As personalized and antiseptic as a letter from your congressman. Dinah tells me that a detective and a psychiatrist are much alike. They both poke around in more or less figurative private drawers and arrange what they find into a plot. Except a psychiatrist is more suspicious.

I looked at Caroline's toothpaste tube, squeezed in the middle the way their mothers teach them, and then in the mirror cabinet, where I found two extra toothbrushes still in their plastic boxes, a bottle of aspirin, a small floral-printed zipper case with two bottles of allergy tablets, and a plastic holder half-full of Ortho-Nova birth control pills. Everything had the label of a Rexall in Sacramento. Had Caroline sent the Frenchman and his helpers? Or had somebody else butted into the game?

I took two of her aspirin and went back into the bedroom. Maybe she had just strolled down to Boots to refill her prescription. Maybe she was at Air France buying a ticket for Marseilles. The phone rang before I could flip a coin, and I stood stupidly considering for a moment. If I answered, it was not likely anybody would want to chat very long or tell me where Caroline had gone, not even Caroline herself. On the other hand, if there were no answer, the caller, say a visiting Frenchman, might decide to come up and wait. And me with no party favors to offer.

No Smith and Wesson .38 to entertain with. The phone kept ringing. I looked out Caroline's window and saw far to the south a squat train crawling like a black caterpillar across Hungerford Bridge, where Moll Flanders used to cut silk purses from the gowns of bustling gentlewomen. The phone stopped ringing. It would do me no good to be caught in Caroline's room unarmed. I undid the chain and stepped outside.

I couldn't think of a reason to avoid the lobby on the way out, so I took an elevator down, still run in the Savoy by admirals in gold braided uniforms and tight white gloves, and five minutes later found myself back on the Strand, heading quickly west. One man cannot shadow an alert target for long without being noticed, even in crowded streets. Too many things can burn him, as the FBI always calls it—sudden street crossings, retracing steps in a hurry, shop-window reflections. But two men, if they're dressed in ordinary nondescript clothing, can do it with reasonable ease by taking both sides of a street and leap-frogging. Except that under Hoover, I remembered, the FBI couldn't have followed the Rose Bowl parade, because he made all the agents wear white-wall haircuts and dress in stiff white shirts and blue suits no matter where they went. The SDS used to count agents the way other kids counted Edsels. Three men can't be burned at all if they're halfway good.

At Trafalgar Square, I slowed down, walked casually past the National Gallery, and plunged like any other tourist into the pigeons around Nelson's column. Then I crossed abruptly against traffic and wound up at the bottom of Haymarket, next to the American Express office and its fixture of forlorn students loitering about and waiting for mail, all of them nicely equipped for city life in backpacks and desert boots and second-hand fatigues. A man in a mackintosh across the street looked familiar. And not especially interested in the menu he was reading in a window. At the end of the street, I ducked into an Underground entrance, not without a shudder, and hurried along a white tile corridor until I reached the giant, demented beehive that is Piccadilly Circus station, the largest, busiest, and nastiest in London. The same man started down the corridor. He could be on his way home to Brixton, of course, or he could be expecting rain. I shoved a handful of coins in a machine and took a 30-pence ticket good for any direction and any distance up to Camden Town or down to Earl's Court. Then I stepped on the long escalator that led down to the Northern Line, too jumpy even to give full attention to the bra and panty ads that the English use to dress up their subways. At the first platform, I left the slow moving stairs and struggled against the crowd to an entrance to the Bakerloo Line, walked the wrong way up a short escalator, and emerged on Regent Street beside a newsstand. Across the sidewalk, the red lights of the Windmill Adult Cinema Club winked and blinked. Where better to shake a tail? I dodged a double-decker bus and bought a £5 Overseas Visitor's Membership from a man with one eye. "Man Eaters" was almost over, he told me. But if I waited ten minutes, I could see the beginning of "Texas Cheerleaders." I couldn't wait.

At the top of a sticky aisle in a black, silent basement, I looked around for an exit sign. There was only one, down at the bottom of the theatre, just to the left of the screen. As I reached it and put one hand on the push bar, I looked over. Two naked women were pulling down a man's trousers and making a fuss. The camera moved in for a close-up. I left to see a man about a gun.

# CHAPTER 9

MAGNUS AND SUSANNAH HAD BEEN QUARRELING.

I walked into the living room and felt the air gone tense with anger. He stood in front of an antique sideboard that held a collection of liquor bottles and glasses, his fists bunched into apple shapes in the pockets of his jacket, his cheeks as flushed as if they'd been slapped.

Susannah couldn't have slapped him. She stood stiffly in a corner beside a bookcase and reading lamps, about as far from him as she could be in that room. The ice in her glass looked warmer than her face.

"Michael, darling! How wonderful!"

Their tableau, frozen for a heartbeat, shattered as the maid eased me into the room, curtsied nervously, and vanished. Susannah came forward with both arms outstretched while Magnus turned abruptly to the sideboard and rattled glass.

"Michael, it's been *years,* simply years." She gathered me in, flattened her cheek against mine for an instant, stepped back. I smiled foolishly and let myself be led into the room.

Susannah is three years older than I am, 12 years younger

than Magnus. In contrast to his rather pale, aristocratic handsomeness, she brought olive skin, exuberant black hair, the fleshiness of a Renaissance madonna. As she led me by one hand to the sideboard, I tried to remember the name of the publisher she worked for as an editor.

They had married ten years ago, everyone had assumed, because they were both Class I-A, because they had been to the same kinds of schools, country houses, and parties all their lives, because he was bright and languid and Oxonian and she was bright and languid and Girtonian. To thine own accent be true. But they had turned out to be as incompatible as ice cream and pepper, in Dinah's phrase. Susannah was the pepper, I thought, watching her swivel in the blue silk cocktail dress. An intense, moody woman, she often dominated by sheer force of feeling, rolling her moods over other people with the jolt of bare-knuckled ego.

"I don't see how you can touch another vile drop," she said, handing me the double gin I had ordered and Magnus had poured. Her fingers patted my wrist once and arched to straighten a strand of black hair by her ear. Under the polite mask she wore for her husband's friend, under the thickish makeup, her skin sagged a little with too many drinks, too much rich food, too many cigarettes. Her breasts and hips spread with the comfortable weight of maturity. She looked as If she had lived every day of every one of her 40-plus years, and I thought she was one of the sexiest women I had ever known.

"Some men are born to hangovers," I told her. "Others have hangovers thrust upon them."

She laughed and said, "Shakespeare" and turned on her heel, starting for the bookshelves again.

"Are you sure you're all right now, Michael?" Magnus asked behind me.

"All bones back in place, Magnus," I said, buttoning my coat tighter over the new pistol and turning to admire his camel hair jacket and fawn trousers off the rack somewhere on Saville Row. The living room opened through French doors onto a garden, which in turn was enclosed by a brown brick wall and, over its edges, by a luminous early evening sky peculiar to London in the summer. The light threw Magnus's outline into sharp relief, squaring his drooping shoulders and smoothing the skin of his pale, kind face.

"Magnus is annoyed," Susannah drawled from the corner, "because the police did not recognize him as an Important Personage." She flipped over books with one hand and waved her glass in our direction without actually looking. "He thought they should have tugged their caps and said 'yers, yers, milud' and begged his opinion of where to look for clues. He is bitten by the green-eyed monster. He wishes he were a private detective and got constantly coshed on the Central Line."

"Don't talk ruddy nonsense, Susannah," Magnus said. He drained whatever he had been drinking.

"You, I understand, Michael, were your usual magnificently insolent self, completely unflustered. But of course it's all in a day's work for you, isn't it? Tracing gorgeous heiresses—though I don't suppose she stands to inherit much now—flagging down hoodlums on the Underground with your trenchcoat." She snapped a last book back into the shelf and came toward me, smiling at her own patter. Her hand stretched out an empty glass stiff-armed at Magnus, but she continued to look at me. "What was the first thing she said to you, Michael?" she asked in a stage American accent. " 'Are you a man or a Mauser?'"

She shook her black hair with laughter and rode right over whatever feeble reply I might have started, taking her full glass back from Magnus with an automatic gesture and turning her head toward the books that lined one entire wall.

"I wanted to show you the book we just published this week," she went on. "But I can't find it. An American author, of course—the decadent English don't bother to write anymore—we're just reprinting it. A novel, if you can stand it, about the first lesbian astronaut. I have to rush off to a reception for the author in about 30 minutes—an *enormous* fat woman from Los Angeles who says she believes in biorhythms, reincarnation, and recreational drugs. Won't Kingsley Amis be delighted?"

"Now that you've managed to run down the men in the room and turn the conversation to yourself," Magnus began contemptuously.

"Don't be tedious, Magnus dear." The brittleness had come back in the room like a shower of glass. "Tell me, Michael," she said with a charming smile. She crooked one arm through mine and started us toward the French doors. "Have you married that pretty girl Dinah yet? The one with the gorgeous red hair? Or are you still living without benefit of clergy?"

"For God's sake, Susannah," Magnus said.

"Is that young Haller?" a voice interrupted from the door and we all wheeled to look.

"Father," Magnus said. "You're supposed to be napping. Jeremy won't be here to drive you for hours."

"Too damn noisy in London," the old man said and advanced into the living room, ramrod straight, thin silver hair carefully brushed back in the fashion of the '40s, shoulders almost as wide as Magnus's, eyes much bluer and colder. "I don't know how you stand it. How's your father, young man? I haven't seen him in 30 years."

"Cheyne Walk," said Susannah with the same mocking tone she had used on Magnus, "is not noisy, James. It is the most fashionable street in Chelsea. Carlyle lived on it, and Scott of the Antarctic." She walked away from the men, and Magnus followed her with a sad look of absorption in his eyes. Love or obsession. I don't know that much about marriage.

"Oh be quiet, Susannah," the general said. "Give me a Scotch, Magnus. Soda, no ice."

"He's fine, General," I said. "He talks about you often."

The old man nodded his head in a curt military acknowledgment, too stony-faced for me to tell if he was pleased or simply verifying what ought to be so. Brigadier General James C.E. Harpe, Ret., Magnus's very distinguished, very difficult father. He had entered the Royal Grenadiers straight out of Sandhurst, labored in the Middle East for the Empire throughout the '30s, and returned in late 1939 to take up a post in the military intelligence command, later to be the MI-6 of legend in the Supreme Allied Command. There, to his disgust, he had been handed a mixed dozen of wet-eared American draftees, all chosen apparently for their knowledge of German, and told to integrate them into the British outfits being set up to support Resistance groups in France and Belgium. My father was the only volunteer in the bunch, a first-year medical student on military leave whose rigid New England conscience wouldn't let him take a deferment from duty, and he had become personal deputy to the general. He had also become engaged a year later to my mother, an American volunteer in the same department. At the wedding, the general had given them a silver plate with the coat of arms of the City of London on it, which still sat in a glass case in my father's study. "The best years of my life" my father had said about once a month for as long as I could remember. "And the smartest old man in Europe."

"He writes me every Christmas," the general said. He straightened his lean frame. Magnus handed him a tall drink and he sipped once. He wore a sharkskin suit with a gold decorative button in the lapel. "Sometimes more often if there's an election on. Once in a while he writes in July—" he stopped abruptly and lifted his silver eyebrows. Beside me, Magnus coughed.

"He writes me then too," I said. My mother had gotten in the car one rainy July evening in Boston, when I was eight, taking my baby brother with her to a friend's house. Ten minutes later, her car had collided with a truck coming the wrong way on Storrow Drive and she and my brother were gone. The original missing persons, Dinah said.

"Never gotten over it," the general muttered.

"Father came up from Kent this morning," Magnus said to change the subject, "and his man drives him back tonight after dinner. He won't stay over in London."

"Fully of bloody wogs," the old man said, swallowing Scotch. The dewlap trembled over his starched collar. "The Pakistanis and Arabs have taken over and the whole city's in blackface."

"Come and hear Michael's story, James," Susannah said from the wing-back chair where she had settled. "He's uprooting London's criminal class singlehandedly."

The general simply snorted. Susannah was not a favorite with him. Most women weren't, in fact, but especially not childless women who should have borne him grandsons long ago.

"Have you found La Angeletti again?" Magnus asked as he steered us all to chairs beside Susannah. In front of us was a butler's tray table loaded with cheese and hors d'oeuvres, beyond it a small glassed-in fireplace and another wall of books. "Michael is still private detecting," he explained to his father. The general grunted. "He's trying to find a missing woman from California."

"California is so bland," Susannah said, swinging a long shapely leg impatiently back and forth and beginning another of her routines.

"Velveeta Valhalla," I said. Nobody is quicker to put down California than us transplants.

"I knew an Angeletti once, in the war," the general said in an old man's peremptory way. "Fillipo, Piero, something like that."

I put down my glass carefully on a silver coaster and leaned forward.

"My client's name is Carlo Angeletti, General," I said. "A man about your age, maybe a few years younger."

"Probably not the same man at all. Carlo. I knew this one down in the hills north of Nice, doing Resistance work he was, in '43 and '44."

"Father did the Allied coordination for Resistance groups in all of southeast France," Magnus said, taking on the shade of pompousness he always did around his impressive, dominant father. Some of us run like hell from them, others never budge from their shadow.

"Michael certainly knows what James and his own father did in the war," Susannah said, irritated at being interrupted. "Everyone in earshot has known for years."

"Does your father still remember?" the general asked slowly. One liver-spotted hand stroked his old cheek in a gesture of pleasure. "Does he still remember the money on the floor?"

I nodded. The office that the general directed had received a supply of counterfeit French francs to be used by Resistance groups, but the money looked so crisp and new that no German would have let them pass without suspicion. The general's solution, typically brilliant my father said, had been to lock the doors of the office in Grosvenor Street, scatter the counterfeit bills all over the floor, and have the staff walk on them as they went about their normal business. After a week, the bills looked as shopworn and genuine as the oldest ones in France.

"The forger was a man named Watt," the general said, half smiling and showing yellowed dentures. "An American from Iowa. He'd been a printer somewhere in the Middle West. When we got him, he became the greatest counterfeiter of the century. Used to forge Hitler's signature on false letters and paybooks. Couldn't read a damn word of German either. The war was the making of him, you know, the way it was for so many men. Released them from all the old taboos, taught them not to waste their lives."

"I'm sure Michael doesn't want to listen to war stories all night, James," Susannah said.

"The secrecy!" the old man cackled. "By God, we had the ultimate secrecy in our theatre. I worked it out and we used it all over southeast France. Those restaurants the French love with private rooms, you know. Take their mistresses to them." He swallowed more Scotch and looked from Magnus to me. We nodded. "The messages," he said, placing one brown hand confidentially on my knee for an instant, "the messages were carried from private room to private room by the waiters. The men in the field never set eyes on their partners. You could have gone the entire war without ever seeing your counterpart. Only the waiters saw them. Absolute utter security." Magnus and I nodded again in appreciation. "We had a chap in the OSS who taught our people how to kill with anything. Even a sheet of newspaper. You rolled it up into a six-inch stick, folded it into a point, and shoved it in the soft part under the chin."

"Dear God, not with the *Times,*" Susannah said.

"You were only a boy then," the general said to Magnus with some obscure satisfaction. To me: "You weren't even born until '45."

I shook out a cigarette and started to light it. The general frowned and I put it back. What I really wanted was to hear more about Angeletti.

"Oh, if it's the same one," the old man said. "And I think it was Carlo, yes. If it's the same one, he was just a boy. Eighteen or nineteen at the most." I calculated in my head. "There are a lot of Italians in southern France, you know, more then than now, I suppose. They came across the border in droves in the late '30s, when the Fascists started to take serious control of Italy, confiscating property and so on. Never did make the trains run on time. Carlo was an Italian, not a Frenchman. His surname means little angels, but we used to call him *diavolo,* I think. The devil. An utterly ruthless type, not particularly big physically, but hated the Nazis and the Fascists and loved to kill them."

Susannah passed a tray of cheese around the table. The general ignored her. "I remember one particular instance," he said. "I was in France myself for an especially long stay because we had just set up a new reseau between Marseilles and Bordeaux—"

"Reseau?" Susannah asked with a mouth full of brie.

"Network, reseau: a line of command in the Resistance. They all had code names. This one ran supplies from Marseilles, which was a very corrupt port—still is—in Free France to Bordeaux, which was in Vichy France. Ran supplies to Bordeaux, you see, refugees back to Marseilles. Very neat setup, if I say so. Angeletti had been extremely active in this one because he was so familiar with the Marseilles area. But we had a leak of some sort, serious one, that let the Nazis capture a carful of refugees and send them off to one of the labor camps. Someone had collaborated, you see, probably because of blackmail at home—that was the usual reason, that or money—and Angeletti simply took matters into his own hands and found the leak. So he said. Executed four men to stop it and set an example—lined them up and shot them in a cafe in Les Eyzies one morning—and one of them was a chap farther along in the reseau, in Toulouse, I think. The son came after Angeletti with a vengeance, I can tell you."

"Good God, James," Susannah said, "you sound as bad as the Nazis. Did this Angeletti kill the son too?"

"We often *were* as bad as the enemy," the general lectured. "That's the nature of guerilla warfare, which is what a lot of damn silly young people have ignored lately. It wasn't always idealistic work, driving some unsuspecting chap out somewhere one night and shooting him. But it had to be done. I did it. Many men did it. Some women too. There's still a true history to be written about the war."

"And the son?" I asked.

"Oh no, he wasn't killed. I stepped in, had to, you see. Can't have your own people quarreling in an operation like that. I transferred the boy to the north. Blanchard, something like that. Never saw him again. Surprised he didn't come back and do away with Angeletti after the war. That happened quite a lot, you know. Still goes on, in fact. Just last year, a chap in Lyons ran for mayor, was shot dead by someone who claimed he betrayed him in the Resistance. Another one was stoned to death in a casino outside Nice. He was a physiognomist—the casinos hire these chaps with amazing memories for faces—they're supposed to detect cardsharps—and he had worked for the Germans identifying Resistance people at gatherings. The French are long haters. Angeletti's in America now, you say?"

"I'm trying to trace his missing daughter-in-law."

The old man looked abruptly uninterested and began to pull himself out of his chair, ready to leave. The last question almost asked itself, the way the good ones do if you have any kind of luck at all in this business.

"General." I stood up too. Track lighting overhead gleamed a warm pink off the flesh of his scalp, flaky under the thin hair.

His eyes looked as fierce and clear as a hawk's. "Do you happen to remember the name of the reseau you set up with Angeletti? I'm just curious."

The old man snorted, half in amusement, half in affront. "Of course I do," he said. "You don't forget those things in the military. The code name was Marteau."

The man had sold me a Webbley, the standard pistol of the British officer class for 50 years and issued to every Army and RAF officer without exception during the Second World War, or simply "the war" as it is still called all over Europe. A Webbley-Fosbury eight-shot, .38 caliber gentleman's handgun. Spare parts and accessories from Harrods. I looked at its black chamber snapped open against the sky-blue bedspread. I should have gone back to Hamid, I thought, who would have scorned antique materiel. This way, I was beginning to feel trapped in a war that had ended six months before I was born.

The White Horse had sent up a bottle—anything but Scotch, I had said—but they didn't have ice on the premises, the bellman had sniffed, for purposes of drinking. For purposes of drinking, I poured an inch of Bombay Gin into a bathroom cup and clicked the chamber of the Webbley back in its frame just about five seconds before somebody knocked once on the door.

I stood up quietly. Room service had been closed for an hour, and the bellman had said he was going home. Roger? Caroline? The grip of the gun fit my hand like a rock. I released the safety and stood for a long moment listening to my pulse jump. Then I stepped to one side of the door and pulled the chain loose with a jerk.

"Michael dear, this is a perfectly squalid hotel."

Susannah breezed through the door untying the belt of

her raincoat and tossing her black hair in mock dismay as she looked around the room.

"Dear God, you've got a gun," she said with not much alarm. The raincoat flew off in a swirl and landed on the end of the bed like a fan. "Do put it away and pour me a drink. That lovely gin on the table will be super, if, of course, this palatial suite comes with an extra glass."

I rebolted the door while she circled the little room clucking over the furniture, slid my Webbley into its leather shoulder holster, and dropped them both in the nightstand drawer. She was standing a little unsteadily at the window and looking out at Bloomsbury Square when I brought her the drink.

"Thank you so very much," she said. "This is one of my favorite parts of London, you know. All those eighteenth-century buildings, and all those writers who used to live here when the Duke of Bedford had his great mansion up at the end and Boswell and Gibbon and the rest would trot up like stray dogs to the front door hoping to be patronized. There were the tedious Woolfs here too, of course, and their perverse, boring coterie. I know that she was a genius and a woman, not in that order, and a role model for the rising braless generation—though why they don't simply say 'example' I don't know—but I would truthfully rather be forced to read Nixon's memoirs or watch cricket for a week than plod through *Mrs. Dalloway* again. The only one of all of them that I ever admired at all was John Maynard Keynes, who really kept quite aloof from princess Virginia. I met him once when I was a girl—father brought him 'round to the house about some charitable foundation they were going to start and never did. He smelled terribly of cologne, which men rarely wore in those days, and he played with my cat. Father told me afterwards that I had met a great man."

"Most of us Californians never read anything longer than a tee-shirt," I said when she stopped for a breath.

She turned her long face to me, haggard and sexy, and smiled a high-voltage smile that had too much gin in it. "The reception was unbearable, naturally," she said. "And since Magnus and General James are likely to be still sitting at home reminiscing about old days on the Ardennes front, I thought I should come and see you."

"You're hard on him, Susannah."

"Oh bosh," she said. "You've still got a touch of hero-worship for Magnus. It's long past time you got over your boyhood idolizations. He's not the dashing young bachelor any more who took you in hand when you were a skinny 20-year-old dropout." She paused in her chatter while I splashed more gin into the outstretched glass. For some mysterious reason, the Bombay bottle had a picture of Queen Victoria on the label. "I'm assuming that you were skinny. You are now. Magnus, on the other hand, is turning into a slightly pot-bellied old geezer who snores and still takes an allowance from Daddy."

"Allowance?" I looked away from the window in genuine surprise.

"You certainly don't think we live on his income, do you? That pathetic fiddle he calls an architectural office doesn't draw two paying clients a year. We even had to sell the house in Sussex last summer. Magnus hasn't made any money to speak of in years, and I keep what precious little I make strictly to one side, like a good feminist. I wonder," she went on with the same forced gaiety, "if the opposite of feminist is masculinist."

"I always thought he was very prosperous," I said stupidly.

"General James gives us £10,000 a year to keep the wolf from the door." She put her hand on my wrist and curled her long fingers around my shirt sleeve. Susannah is a master at keeping the conversation off-balance. Or mistress. "Are you all right now, Michael, really? You looked very grim this evening at the house, and here you are carrying a pistol around your room and bolting your door. Are you actually in danger?" The fingers left my wrist, the glass flew up. "Or is this your usual bedtime routine?"

"I'm fine, Susannah. I'm perfectly safe."

"It's just that I never know whether to believe Magnus when he talks about other men's exciting lives. Touch of hero-worship the other way around now, I should say." She turned away from the window, cupping one breast for an instant in her hand, an automatic weighing gesture she must have been unaware of. "Are you going to start looking for this lost girl again?" she asked.

"I think so," I said. "I've been waiting for a call from her father-in-law's lawyer right now." Two hours overdue, I didn't bother to add.

"Magnus says you're a stalking horse, which is some bit of American slang he got from old Humphrey Bogart movies. He says you're being used."

I sighed. "Magnus may be right. I've certainly stirred up hornets all over London. And all I still seem to know is that the girl stole something from her father-in-law that he wants back, which is the real reason he hired me." Susannah said "ummm" in a low voice and licked the inside of the glass with her tongue, lapping gin from the bottom.

"And apparently somebody else wants whatever she stole, too," I said. "The police seem to think what's involved is heroin." Susannah raised one carefully plucked jet black eyebrow. "The new gold," I said. "Portable, convertible, infinitely in demand in a world of empty expectations. The philosopher's stone, converts reality into dreams. Civilization abhors a vacuum. Every emptiness must be filled." I filled my glass.

"Is the old man in California a drug dealer?"

I shrugged. "He has tankers that move around Europe. He has interest in banks with questionable dealings in large amounts of cash." I shrugged again. Don Corleone.

"Be serious. Why would he hire you to find her? Surely a man like that has people who work for him to do such things."

"Sometimes a crook has to hire an honest man."

She gave me a sly look, about two drinks away from drunken. "But why would you work for him?" she said. I didn't answer and she went on, slurring her words a little, shaking strands of black hair from her Florentine face. "You're not a stalking horse at all, are you? You knew what you were doing from the first. You're a spoiler. You've got the California tan and the whole casual laid-back mellow karma or whatever it is you people say—but underneath you're your father's son. I met him once, remember. Puritans both of you. Cold, blue, bedroom eyes of a Puritan afraid someone somewhere is breaking a rule. You took the job to turn the tables on the Italian and trip him up somehow, didn't you?" She stopped and a surprised look arrived on her face, like a late bus. "Or to rescue the innocent English girl who wandered by mistake into the real world." Her eyes widened. "The misguided, beautiful, English dolly."

"Room service is sending her up," I said, draining my glass.

"Don't you ever stop joking, Michael?" If I closed my eyes, I would still see the curve of her breasts and the swell of her hips in the tight blue dress. I left them open.

"You should hear my flip side," I said.

"Your parents may have loved England," she said, taking a step closer. It was hard to tell now if the slur came from booze or the natural languor of the British accent. "But you are the quintessential American. Underneath that tough-guy facade, you're about as cynical as Peter Rabbit. If you didn't live so much with mistrust and deceit and violence you'd put down your defenses once in a while, wouldn't you? And show us your soft underbelly." And in an astonishing gesture, she reached one hand forward and slowly began to knead the muscles just above my belt. They stiffened like a washboard. "I'd like to see the big, ruthless private detective in a spot where he couldn't just walk away and check into a hotel."

"Peter Rabbit?" I said, more hoarsely than I expected.

She put her glass down on top of the bureau. "A favorite furry friend." She wound her arms around the back of my neck, hands moving restlessly. Her breasts flattened against my chest with a whisper of fabric. "An unsuccessful member of the criminal classes. He tried to eat forbidden lettuce."

She covered my mouth with hers. Somehow my glass disappeared. Her tongue danced around mine, and I pulled her close, letting my hands rove over the warm slopes of her body. She moved and strained forward. Her dress slipped off one shoulder and I pushed the bra strap farther down and buried my face. She moaned again.

"Susannah," I whispered. And then louder. "Susannah."

On orders from somewhere, my hands clasped her shoulders, slipping the dress back up, and pushed her away a pace. She looked up at me blinking, her face starting to register surprise, then anger, then dissolving into a set of features without coherence or form.

Breathing hard, I put one hand gently against her cheek.

She took another step backward, out of reach, and ran her palms stiffly up and down her hips, straightening her dress. Her eyes were moist and unfocused, and her mouth was smeared with lipstick as if she'd been playing dress-up.

"Well, that's what a girl gets when she invites herself up to a man's hotel room, isn't it?" she said in a cracked voice. "It's quite all right, Michael. I didn't mean to frighten you. Thank heavens you have your great big gun."

"Susannah," I began. "You're a beautiful woman—"

"But the code of the Woosters won't let you bed down a friend's wife. A bit medieval, but quite right, Michael, quite right. Quite American, no doubt." She had the raincoat on and was tying the belt with trembling hands. "Magnus hasn't touched me in three years, but you still have your honor or whatnot, don't you?"

"Or whatnot." The word would have sounded just as hypocritical if I had said it. I stood there looking foolish. Queen Victoria stood on the bottle looking smug.

"Wife is still property, isn't it? One man's chattel." She finished tying the knot and raised her face to me again. There were tears running down from the corner of one eye, streaking mascara along her cheek. "I don't think masculinist will do after all, do you? Please don't bother to see me out. I'll find my way."

When the door had closed, not quietly, I glanced at my face in the yellowish mirror that the White Horse had provided over the bureau. Every day in every way I was getting better and better. But the lipstick smeared on my own mouth looked as if something had drawn blood.

CHAPTER 10

T HE CABBIE WANTED AN EXORBITANT £2 10 FOR THE RIDE
from the White Horse.

"Think of it as lend-lease, mate," he said in a cheerful
Cockney twang.

I got out of the most civilized form of transportation in the
world and leaned in the driver's window, holding out my pink
£5 note. When I didn't laugh at his joke, the driver shrugged
and looked away as he counted change. I didn't blame him. In
the mirror over the dashboard, I saw a face about as laid-back
and Californian as a set of brass knuckles. Around me on the
sidewalk, crowds of play-goers jostled and laughed, car engines
clattered, middle-aged Americans whooped it up as they filed
into a tour bus. *A Girl in My Soup* was letting out, and the
jolly after-theatre confusion of the Strand was at its peak. In
the mirror, studying the crowd for tag-alongs, I still looked like
Jonathan Edwards in the Combat Zone.

The cab launched itself into traffic again, and I crossed
the sidewalk and walked into the busy lobby of the theatre.
Merriman hadn't called at all, not even two hours late, and

I was taking the initiative, as the book recommends. I was repeating myself, as people do.

"Left my coat," I muttered at an usher and retraced my steps this morning down to the men's room in the basement, down to the unlocked fire door and the connecting tunnel to the hotel. One man observed me curiously from the almost empty intermission bar as I opened the door, but he was white-haired and 65 and supported his madras-jacketed belly on a walking cane. Even the cops don't dress like a 90-watt bulb when they want to shadow. The scowl on my face made him spin back to his gin rickey with a jerk like a puppet on a string.

The Webbley was a comfort. I kept my right fingers curled around its butt all the way across the tunnel and up the stairs, and they were still touching it lightly in the shoulder holster when I opened the metal door and peeked tentatively out at the third-floor corridor. Big, ruthless detective. My nostrils still twitched with Susannah's faint, powdery odor.

A bald man in a tuxedo stepped out of the nearest room, glanced at my wrinkled clothes, and walked on toward the el-evators. I followed him down the center of the red runner like a man with a key in his pocket, passed him at the elevators, and listened until the soft bell had sounded and doors had slid shut.

And at 312 I stopped with a bump.

From under the crack at the bottom of the door, light spilled in a narrow stream onto the parquet floor, stopping just before the runner. On the other side of the door, footsteps thumped, heavy on the Savoy's good carpet, heavy for a woman, and a door clicked shut.

I pulled out the Webbley, fingers tensed and shaking. But I didn't want a shootout in the Savoy, I told myself, and I would rather chat with Caroline alone than with some of the company I could imagine. I paused by the door a moment longer,

hearing another thump, and walked quickly back to the elevators and two doors beyond, halting at the door where the tuxedo had come out. I took a deep, shaky breath and hoped that
he hadn't left wife, child, manservant, or popsie in his room
while he stepped out for a six-pack. In the slight angle of the
corridor, I thought, the shadows would obscure my face while I
unsnapped my key from the White Horse, assumed the posture
of a slightly inebriated fumbler at the keyhole, and waited.

It was the Englishman, Roger.

He exited casually from Caroline Angeletti's room carrying
the small Vuitton suitcase I had seen that morning in the closet. I bent over my key, face hooded in shadow, and watched
while he pushed for an elevator. When the bell rang, he entered
the car without a peep in my direction. I shoved open the fire
door and sprinted down the service stairs two and three at a
time, trying to guess which turns would carry me closest to
the front door. Two mistakes, one upset laundry cart, and I
wrenched open the door marked "ground."

From there, about half a mile deep in the lobby, Roger was
nowhere to be seen.

"Sir?"

Ignoring the desk, I ran to the revolving doors and squeezed
through the squadron of retired major-generals who help you
in and out of the rain. Roger was walking up the driveway,
almost to the Strand. If he took a cab or had a car, I was in trouble. If he kept walking, I could follow at a distance for a time.

He walked. West on the Strand, against traffic, toward
Charing Cross. My breath was returning to normal. The book
says to follow on the opposite side of the street, lagging behind about half a block and wearing a false moustache and
funny glasses. To hell with the book. I crowded close to him,
no more than ten yards back, and watched his big shoulders

cut a wake through the late-evening pedestrians. Inches to our right, the midnight traffic chafed to get home and close the old town down, a pack of late buses roared by like hunted animals. Once, he stopped and looked around and I stepped into the doorway of a shop. He switched the suitcase to his other hand and walked on.

There were a tube stop, a train station, and a British Rail hotel at Charing Cross. You could lose a white rhino in its grubby British confusion. I closed in and he surprised me by crossing suddenly at flashing pedestrian lights and heading back and north. I danced through a chorus of horns and came up three feet behind him, in a line of people hurrying for a bus. He turned again on something called Agar Street, just before Trafalgar Square, and sped up.

Agar Street was short, narrow, and practically deserted. No stores, no restaurants, just a shortcut through the backs of buildings. At the head of it, I could see searchlights on the spire of St. Paul's church in Covent Garden and a stream of people going fast in both directions again. I was tired of people. I wanted to be alone with Roger. The Webbley jumped into my hand. I pushed my balance forward on the balls of my feet.

He turned left into an alleyway not 20 feet from the end of the street and the bustle of traffic. White paint on the dark brick walls announced that these parking spaces were reserved for physicians from King's Hospital. Under a sign that said reserved for Dr. Carnochan, Roger was opening the door of an Austin Mini. His back was to me. He was fitting the suitcase onto the passenger seat. I flipped the gun to my left hand and stepped forward just as he straightened and turned.

He whooshed when my fist slammed into his belly and his big moon face rocked like a ball when the barrel of the Webbley came down hard on his skull. Around the corner, a girl shrieked with laughter. Roger looked up at me from the pavement and blinked. I hit him again with the Webbley and when he was slumped flat I ran my right hand through his pockets.

The knife. I didn't forget the knife. I've never used a knife and I hate the sight of them. But Roger was a cutup by choice and kept his switchblade where most of them do in England, in a leather case down the small of his back. I looked at it with dislike and put it in my jacket pocket. The pistol *du jour* was a Beretta .22, long with a fat silencer, a simple padded barrel that looks like a television mike. Not much of a weapon, really; some people can spit harder. But its soft little bullets make ugly holes in human flesh. In northern New Jersey, the .22 long is much favored for close-up work. A pro's gun. I wondered if he had bought it from Hamid.

Roger started to cough. I slid the Webbley back under my shoulder and heaved him to his knees, then to his feet. Just a couple of guys trying to find the keys to the car, folks. Thirty seconds later, I had him propped in the driver's seat of the Austin, the suitcase in back, and I was sitting beside him, watching a snail's track of blood creep down his cheek toward his collar. In the strained light of the parking space, it had a rusty-green color, like swamp mud.

"What the hell . . ." His eyes fumbled from my face to his gun in my hand, back to my face. He started to sneer. Behind us, footsteps tapped south toward the Strand, vanished. I thought about good interpersonal relationships. Dale Carnegie didn't recommend starting with a gun in the hand, but Roger, even bleeding and dazed, was a professional tough guy, the kind of scar-faced ex-Teddy boy who would be unimpressed by polite questions and answers that put him at his ease, the kind of guy who would start his barbecue with a hand grenade.

"Where's the girl, Roger?"

"Bugger off, Yank."

The driver's window exploded into fragments of glass, most of them flying harmlessly into the alley. Some lightly raked the left side of his face and scalp, drawing thin rivulets of blood. A few slivers glinted in his hair like raindrops. The silencer had muffled the shot, but the car was acrid with smoke for a moment. Roger held one hand against his bleeding skin and looked at me with awe.

"Jesus Christ," he whispered.

I clicked the hammer of the Beretta back.

"I am a wild and crazy guy tonight, Roger. Where's Caroline Angeletti?"

"You're out of your friggin' mind, you are."

I raised the muzzle slightly. Most people, including the Rogers of the world, have never had a gun barrel two inches from their eyes. It looks bigger than the Holland Tunnel from that distance. It looks worse than a knife point or a razor blade or a filed-down ice pick. It looks like the last thing on earth.

"She's away from here, north London," Roger finally said.

"Drive me there."

"*Bloody* crazy. They'd kill me. . . ."

I pushed the key I had found in his jacket into the ignition slot and turned it. The battery light jumped on.

"When I shoot, Roger, I'm going to aim for your lap. If you're lucky, you'll bleed to death."

He licked his lips twice and his left hand, slick with blood, crawled down from his scalp. He pressed the accelerator and flicked the key until the motor purred into life.

"Drive nice and carefully," I said. "We don't want a ticket, do we?"

Roger steered in silence across the West End, making the tiny car shake as he rammed the gear stick sullenly forward and back, but otherwise behaving himself. I held the Beretta steady at hip level and watched him try to figure out how to jump me.

Twice we slowed for bottlenecks of traffic, at Regent Street and Oxford Circus. Cars wound around us in pale, orderly streams, in and out of neon lights, and a cold damp breeze blew in through the shattered window. On the sidewalks, people walked faster, leaning into the weather. Roger worked the muscles of his jaw but sat tight.

At the end of Oxford Street, we turned north onto Baker Street, and somewhere in the middle, about 221B probably, we passed the Sherlock Holmes Hotel. I looked at Roger's square, ugly head to see if he had noticed. Aside from the fact that he had recently cut his face shaving and wanted to dismember me, I could deduce nothing. At the dark squat mass of trees that was Regent's Park, we circled west, passing the American Ambassador's mansion and, next door to it, a huge new Moslem mosque, the only two private buildings in the whole park. The top of the minaret was brightly lit in orange and white and, far below it, dozens of men in caftans were hurrying in and out of green arched doors. Merrie England.

Fifteen minutes later and halfway through the dreary borough of Dollis Hill, Roger pulled down one side street, turned left at another, then slowed and stopped at the curb. Overhead, a single street light, sheathed in wire to protect it from rocks, gleamed off a red Watney's sign and the worn letters "Prince of Wales." The pub itself was dark and shuttered and, except for a few other parked cars, the street was empty. Paradise Court, the sign said.

"They'll kill you," Roger said in a guttural voice. "You'll do bugger-all by yourself."

"Which one is it?"

He didn't answer. The hammer of the Beretta made a clicking noise like a ratchet.

"Down there, then."

He pointed past the pub to a dead-end lane of attached row houses, monotonous and characterless as a box of pencils. They were made of gritty brown brick, three stories high, with tongues of concrete stairs leading down to the sidewalk from identical white wooden doors. The first two had boards across their windows. Trash barrels stood in disorderly groups in front of several houses, not a common sight in England, and the single street lamp halfway down was missing a bulb. The street ended in a brick parapet. Beyond it and over a low stone wall, I could see a lattice of wires and the spidery outline of an automatic signal tower. While we watched, a short passenger train, outward bound, rattled by and vanished.

"It's a wog place," Roger said. "Pakistani. West Indian. They all are."

"What's the number?"

"Twenty-two." It would be the fifth one from the pub. Roger twisted his damaged face toward me and sneered. "Marteau's going to 'ave your balls for this, you know. You should 'ave bolted when you could."

"Anybody in there with her?"

"Why don't you knock and find out?" He contorted his face into a smirk, puckering the congealed scratches across his cheek. Later, somebody would have to tell Roger about body language. Right now, he was rapidly losing his charm for me. I slipped the key out of the ignition with a sigh and dropped it into my jacket pocket.

"Sit tight," I said. "Don't go bye-bye." I walked quickly around the rear of the car and opened his door. "Get out. Walk in front of me to the trunk. Boot. This way. Now."

He did it ponderously, swinging his big hands loosely away from his legs like a gunfighter. The street light slid off the ripples of his brown plastic jacket and disappeared in shadows at his feet. He would jump me, I thought, watching his fingers clench and flex, not here, but near the entrance to the house, where somebody inside could help. He would want help this time.

"Stop now."

I could give him the chance, I thought. I could give him the chance and beat him bloody. Then march him up the stairs with the Beretta in his lumbar and knock on the door. Trick or treat, Caroline. How about a conference call with Carlo? Roger shuffled his feet impatiently beside the car and began to crane his head. Or I could be unsportsmanlike and continental. I flipped the gun over in my hand and swung it in a short arc, bouncing the butt off the fat occipital bulge behind his right ear, where they say you can hit hardest and risk the least possible damage to the brain. His occipital bulge made a sound like Borg's backhand and he sank into the shadows at my feet with a long, incoherent mutter. Nobody shouted, nobody ran to look. The wind kicked a few newspapers moodily down the sidewalk, the Prince of Wales stared regally from the sign on the pub. Otherwise, silence. I bent and heaved Roger head-first into the trunk and tucked his legs firmly against the spare tire. An unwholesome rattle came and went in his throat as he breathed. In the yellow light, his face looked like a jack-o'-lantern sleeping it off. What the hell, he could have it checked on the National Health. I slammed the lid of the trunk and turned the key.

An alleyway ran between the pub and the houses. I shoved the superfluous Webbley in the glove compartment and walked down it quickly, hearing nothing but my heels and heartbeat, and opened a flimsy wooden gate. At the other end of the Prince of Wales's beer garden rose a stone retaining wall for the train tracks, beside it half a dozen rusty oil drums used for trash.

I stepped on the nearest one and boosted myself with both hands to the top of the wall. Then a four-footed scramble up a gravelly bank and I was by the first of the tracks, crouched on a crosstie and skittish as a clay pigeon. What could go wrong was this, I thought: the Glasgow Express could rumble by and turn me into library paste. Somebody in one of the houses could look outside and see a man with a gun in his hand. A railroad cop could step out of the lighted shed three tracks away.

I took deep breaths and waited for one or two or all three to happen. From where I was, I had a view of the back doors of Paradise, straight down the line of fenced-in yards behind the houses. Overhead, thin grids of wires, curious, lowering clouds. Distant, unrecognizable noises came out of the night. The frumpy old city was turning in her sleep. I inhaled stale beer and burnt oil and began to duckwalk past the two boarded-up houses, past the first lighted one, all the way to the fourth.

Wog place, the man had said. From number 20 drifted exotic scents—kumin, turmeric, maybe—and the sound of calypso music on a phonograph. High voices laughed. I crept down closer to the top of the retaining wall. When Bloomsbury Square was brilliant with the silks and gold of Susannah's eighteenth-century dukes, all this miserable ghetto had been the pastures of dairy farmers and highwaymen. England's green and pleasant land. The farmers were long gone now. Swinging London was growing like an oil slick.

I got down on my belly and tried to stare in at number 22.

A tool shed of some kind stood in the far corner of the yard, its corrugated roof tilted at an angle and speckled with stray reflections. Then, ten, fifteen feet of shadow and a splintered, rickety wooden fence that wove its way to the back of the house. One light came from the door. Up above, another light glowed through a brown paper shade. Next door, where the music and the voices clinked, the whole bottom floor was lit. Upstairs, darkness. These would be tenements, one-family houses redivided into various-sized flats and crammed full of sleeping families. I would drop like a shadow into the darkness beside the shed, praying there was no doghouse against the wall, and pad across the yard on little cat's feet. From there . . . I would see. I put the pistol in my jacket pocket and leaned forward, bracing one hand against the wall, one against the wooden fence.

"Come on out, mon."

I sat like a stone man.

"Come on out, Derek."

"Who there?"

"Derek in the garden."

The two figures in the doorway of number 20 swayed in a drunken embrace, arms around shoulders, and stared in my direction. I was 20, maybe 30 feet away, against a background of black ground and shadow. They couldn't see me with radar. They could hear my heart beat in Brighton.

"Come on, mon."

"You too drunk. Go back in the house." A woman's voice. More movement in the doorway, a brief giggle. "Come back in," the woman's voice said again.

"I heard him out there in the garden," the man's voice said in a West Indian singsong.

"You heard a cat. Derek got mad and got drunk and got home."

"No, I heard—"

A British Railways train thundered over what he had heard, a huge diesel locomotive charging past, two tracks away, 50 feet behind me, hauling a string of heavy box cars west toward the Outer Hebrides. The whole wall vibrated with their weight and the wooden fence lurched under my hand.

"—cat," the woman said as it clattered away, fading. "Just an old tomcat in the garden."

Sullenly: "I heard him."

"Come on back in, tomcat."

Another round of giggles; and the door closed. I dropped to the soft ground beside the shed and exhaled a long, low sigh, like a man who was frightened. I was too old and tired for this job. My head hurt, my hands were raw, my breath clogged my throat. I was pulling 37 years uphill behind me, like boxcars on a train, and I was going to end up arrested as a Peeping Tom. I puffed into the chill black air. It's past midnight. Do you know where your detective is now? I could go home and go to bed and leave the Angeletti family problems to a suitable counseling service, like Interpol. I could go home and be a florist or a rewrite man for the *Sonoma Sun*. I think I could, I think I could, I think I could.

I scuttled across the little plot of garden—the English call two flowerpots a garden—and inched close to the ground-floor window, stooping just under it, still trembling far inside my belly. "You could no more give it up now," Dinah had once told me in one of those conversations that stick in the mind and replay themselves automatically, "you could no more give it up now than you could give up those self-defensive wise-cracks or Henry Weinhart beer."

"Or redheads."

She had been lounging in just my pajama top, the psy-chiatrist on the couch. I had been standing by the big French windows in the bedroom of my apartment, watching the lights on a freighter sail across the invisible water. "Or redheads. You were hooked by the first case you ever handled, when you brought back that girl to her parents. You had found a way to act that expressed something central about yourself better than anything you could write." And she had walked across the room to give me an oddly tender, maternal kiss. "You were always a better lover than a poet, lover," she said.

Like all the others in the row, the back window apparently opened into the kitchen, and like all the others I could see up and down the line, it was a casement window, swung open about six inches and fastened with an interior pin to let the night air in. I could peer through, past a counter and sink filled with dirty pans and grayish milk bottles, to the edge of the front hall. By stretching, I could see the lock on the back door, too, an ordinary throw-bolt with the knob straight up. My Visa card wouldn't reach the knob, would only rattle the lock, and this had to be done M.O.S., as they say in Hollywood, without a sound. I leaned against the building, then dropped as voices rose in front, shadows crossed the window, cleared. A few words came over clearly; the rest were drowned out by the sudden clatter of another train heading out of the city. Even with Roger's popgun, I thought, even with his switchblade and two bandoliers of bullets crossing my chest like Emilio Zapata, you do not gatecrash the bad guys. You do not swagger into an unfamiliar house and ask to see the deck. The only thing I had to fear was fear itself. That and getting shot with a gun.

I felt my way back across the black yard to the tool shed and started to explore. I could find a tommygun there, I could find smoke bombs, I could find Derek.

I found a mop. Someone had propped it against the outside, resting the head in a wooden fruit basket along with various corroding cans. I sat down quietly, back against the stone retaining wall, and began to work the handle free from the head. Then I rummaged through nearby cans and jars until I came up with a stray nail, a two-inch nail whose tiny bright point glinted like a star in a pool of water when I held it up.

Another train grumbled down the tracks, on the far side, and at the peak of the noise, I smacked the nail into the soft wood at the end of the handle with the butt of the gun. The train passed and I stood up again.

At the window voices could still be heard from the front. One sounded like a woman's. Another, male, rose briefly in nervous irritation, then sank to a drone. It was like trying to eavesdrop on mosquitoes. The mopstick would reach the throw-bolt with inches to spare. All I needed was another train.

Never there when you want them, of course. Five minutes passed. Somebody next door changed calypso to blues. Clouds sank lower and lower in the night sky, stringy and frazzled. My mind wandered over details. Had I locked the trunk? Yes. Would Roger have enough air? Only time would tell. Then the wall of the house vibrated gently and I heard the train coming, a close one this time, on the nearest track, and pulling a long line of flatbeds. In the rush of noise, I ran the mopstick through the window like a fishing pole, caught the knob with the nail, and pushed. The bolt slid an inch, resisted, slid all the way out. The door sagged open a fraction, and I was over the single wooden step and into the kitchen before the rhythmical boom of the train had died away. Behind me, the door swung a few inches over the threshold board, creaking, and stopped. I crouched instinctively beside a tired old refrigerator for cover and squeezed the grip of the Beretta as if I were strangling it. Down the hallway, still faint and intermittent, floated voices.

"No, goddamnit" was the first thing I made out clearly. "I don't care about a storm. He's not here yet, and I don't want to leave without . . ." There was a pause. Someone took a few paces in the room and the floorboard grunted in protest. "As much as that. All right, you should have said so. Just a minute."

It was an American voice, male, young, as free of personal-

ity and inflection as a lifetime of listening to electronic reproduction can make it. I had never heard it before.

He spoke to someone else in the room. Caroline? "He says
the weather pattern is changing very fast, and if we don't, we're
likely to be stuck here for another day. BEA has already can-
celed flights." A soft voice murmured a question I couldn't hear.
"How the hell do I know?" he answered. "The weather's so
screwed up there's no telling when they'll get there. Thursday
is the earliest possible. But we need to have at least one run-
through before they arrive, two if possible. So if we're going to
be in Bordeaux to supervise on Thursday, we're going to have
to leave now." Another indistinct question. "Bugger Roger,"
the man said. "We've called the hotel room twice. What else
can we do? If he's had a breakdown, he can catch up when the
weather clears—yes, hold on, I'll let you know in a minute."

There are only two people, I thought. He's on the phone,
waiting for Roger. There's no Caroline. I had taken two steps
from the refrigerator into the hallway when another voice spoke,
not the soft voice, but a male with a French accent, older.

"Marteau will be displeased with delay," he said. "You've
already bungled once. . . ." I lost the rest in the hum of the
old refrigerator as its motor kicked over and started to mutter. But I had heard that cool, assured voice before, in the dim
recesses of the London Underground. Monsieur Rampal. He
of the cigarette lighter, he of the whiskey neat, he of the knee
in the groin.

"I don't have my suitcase," a woman complained. Her
voice still had a coarse edge that kept her out of the Dame
Sybil Thorndike class, but with her face and shape, Caroline
Angeletti had probably never thought a lot about elocution. It
was impossible to tell from her tone if she was there voluntarily
or just sulking. I could walk in and ask, I thought, and just

maybe have a new player, one of Rampal's, come down the stairs behind me or through another door. Nobody wanted a shootout on Paradise Court, least of all me.

"All right then," the man said to the phone. He had picked up one or two British expressions, but they were no more than spots of flavor in a mellowspeak pudding. "We're coming right out. What gate is it? Special gate for charters, OK. Turn right. Number five, straight on through the hangar. Yes, I'll have her with me." Pause. "No, we'll leave it in the car park." Pause. "Yes, that's a guarantee. I'll have half in dollars. You just have the god-damn plane ready." He hung up. "Shit. I hate to leave a loose end."

"Roger is not a loose end," the Frenchman said. Like all of his countrymen, he used a negative whenever he could. "He has worked a long time for me. He is never a problem."

A long pause. I extended one foot back toward the kitchen. My palm grew slippery and I shifted the Beretta to the other hand for a moment.

"Haller is still in the hotel," the boy-voice said at last.

"Negligible," Rampal snapped. "Watched, warned, negligible."

"Some warning," the boy-voice began.

"Leave a note," he snapped. I wasn't at all sure any more that the smart thing to do was to barge in and play 20 questions. Or Family Feud. Caroline was unharmed as far as I could tell, whether kidnap victim or accomplice. But any sudden rescue attempt here might change that. If I found her in London, I could find her in Bordeaux. My shoulders hunched toward my ears in a protective shiver—body language. First I wanted to talk to Angeletti. First I wanted to get out of Paradise in one piece.

"Leave Roger a note," Rampal repeated impatiently. "He can close up this wretched safe house and do us all a favor."

Nobody spoke.

"I'll put it in the kitchen, where he'll see it," the American said.

"No," the Frenchman said authoritatively. "Place it on the mirror here. It will certainly be seen." My breath resumed.

Noises, rustling. Then the front door banged open and a damp, chilly breeze rushed straight through the house, sniffing down the hall, swinging the back door wide on its hinges. A door slammed, the breeze vanished, and after another minute I heard the faint whine of a car starting, pulling away. Would they see the Austin? Unlikely, I told myself, parked as it was in a line with other cars, on the wrong side of the street. Besides, over my heartbeat, I could hear the tattoo of rain beginning at last, brushing the windows, shaking the grass and shrubbery.

I stepped away from the refrigerator and into the narrow hallway, which smelled of mold, mildew, poverty. The calypso music followed me through the thin walls. I stopped. Upstairs the house had creaked loudly and gone silent. I waited. Only the natural settling of wood, as the weather changed and the old timber swelled.

The living room held a worn tan couch, a few glass-bellied lamps on end tables, an overstuffed mauve chair with a white lace doily pinned across the top. They hadn't emptied the ashtrays, little tin trivets from a pub. They had left the lamps on, for Roger I presumed, and streaks of light fell across a frayed, machine-woven oriental rug in a vague red and blue design, the kind of thing the British use to upholster subway benches and carpet pubs. Where they showed, the floorboards had been painted black years ago but now were the color of scuffed old shoes. I lowered the pistol and crossed to the mirror hanging above the gas fire. The note was on lined yellow paper and said: "Couldn't delay. M expects us in Bordeaux tomorrow noon. Call in report." It was signed "P."

I refolded it and placed it in an inside pocket.

Upstairs were two small bedrooms and a foul bath with

peeling linoleum on the floor and rust stains in the sink. I preferred the Savoy. Safe house, he had called it, using army intelligence slang from the war. Had I stepped into a time warp and come out in 1944, or had Caroline been mixing Le Carré with her Dorothy Parker? I stifled a yawn and poked through the shabby sticks of furniture. Nothing more sinister than a forgotten windbreaker in the closet, probably Roger's. They must have squirreled away here after the Underground misfire, in retreat, waiting to see what hares they had started. I listened to another period of creaking; when it had stopped, I walked slowly to the top of the stairs. It was pointless to look further; they had obviously planned their departure far in advance; Caroline had joined up with a well-organized outfit, using whatever she had taken from Angeletti as dues, joined up or been drafted, and they had left nothing for a sleepy, graying private detective to chew on. I thought I would leave by the front door, like regular folks.

"Bastard, bastard, bastard!" he screamed.

The glass lampbase shattered into jagged pieces as it hit my arm, the Beretta flew over the rug and under the couch. I fell back against the living room wall, scrambling, holding my numbed forearm in front of me like a man in an egg and spoon race. No feeling in it, no life at all.

Roger flourished the bottom of the lampbase over his head like a tomahawk, then flung it across the room where it smashed against the grating of the dead gas fire.

"Bastard!" he screamed again. His jaw worked soundlessly, his face swelled like a gourd, red with blood, shiny with rain. Along one cheek, the scratches from the car window had congealed into black lines of scab, like claw marks. Berserk, possessed—his body trembled with fury and his eyes danced madly, pupils rolling back and forth under frothy waves of white.

One of the milk bottles from the kitchen appeared in his hand and with a single swing, he smashed it against the doorjamb, a terrifying act of controlled destruction.

"Like to play with glass, do you, Yank?"

He jabbed the saw-tooth edges toward my face like a man poking into a cage. My left hand fumbled up for the Webbley as I dodged, as I remembered the glove compartment of the Austin where I had left it.

"Stand still!" he screamed and hit me a looping punch with a fist the size of a footlocker and I tumbled over the couch, landing hard on my shoulder, feeling my right arm dangle down my sleeve like a piece of string. The glass jumped at my face again, ripping the fabric of my jacket. My face would rip like that, my flesh, my eyes.

I got quickly to my feet, backing, my left hand reaching for my right jacket pocket.

"How'd you do it, Roger?" I gasped. My fingers closed on the switchblade, found the button.

"Tricked the fuckin' lock with my belt buckle, you flamin' sod!" He stood in the center of the rug, swaying. The jagged glass circled hypnotically in and out of shadow. His knees bent and he lunged at the same moment that I pulled the knife free. The glass ground into the right shoulder pad of my jacket. I ducked my head away and slammed one punch, the only punch I was going to get, a left hook knife first, into his belly, grunting with the impact, falling away to one side like a sack of clothes.

No one ever feels a knife going in, only the hot waves of pain a few seconds later as the shocked nerves sever and the flesh peels apart like shredded dough. Roger stood over me staring down at the stain of blood spreading over his shirt. In slow motion, he dropped the bottleneck and folded his arms across his middle. Bright arterial blood was gushing from his mouth. His eyes filmed slowly over, like scum rising to the top of a pond, and he sank to his knees, then toppled sideways toward the floor, dead long before he reached it.

# CHAPTER 11

"HOW DO YOU LIKE YOUR BLUEEYED BOY MISTER DEATH"
"What?"

"Nothing," I said. "Just a line from a poem."

Stock grunted and reached one big paw for the photograph I was holding, a Polaroid snapshot, taken with a flash and slightly underexposed. In it, Roger's face looked waxy and cold and his skin had the texture of dried cheese. Underneath him, the fake oriental rug had turned a shiny purple-black from the mixture of blood and cheap dye. I gave the picture back to Stock.

"Well?" he said. He sat far back in the chair and crossed one massive leg over the other, like tree trunks falling. The trouser cuff and brown shoe he showed me were soaked dark with rain. His teeth clenched the inevitable matchstick at a jaunty angle, like one of FDR's cigarette holders. He appeared to be in no hurry at all.

"It could be, sure. It looks like him. But I didn't sit down and make a sketch of him in the Underground. Don't ask me to swear to it."

"Finish your breakfast," he said almost genially.

I looked down at the tray the hotel had sent up. Another

recently fried egg, a thimble-sized glass of orange juice, coffee, white toast, pink bacon. The crust had been sliced from the toast with surgical precision, and the toast had then been halved and inserted in the slots of the wire cooling rack like tiny triangles of linoleum.

"Maybe just the coffee," I said. "You want some?"

He shook his head a fraction to the right.

"Why not?" I asked. "It's one of the perks."

He smiled briefly, still in his strange, friendly mood, and said, "Caffeine and cigarettes. Why do you do it to your body, Haller? That muck is just pure self-destruction."

"There's no pleasure," I announced, "without an element of self-destruction." You don't have a relationship with a psychiatrist and not pick up a few gags. I shoveled a couple of spoonfuls of refined white sugar into the coffee.

"Did you go out then, last night?" he said in the singsong rhythm of his working class accent. I sipped coffee and didn't answer. It tasted like car wax. "One of our people happened to see you down at the Savoy Theatre," he went on, sarcasm laid lightly over the accent like vinegar over cream. "You went there a bit late for the play. He thought you might be taking a shortcut to the hotel. There's a service tunnel, you know."

"Is there? London's a regular ant hill."

"He didn't see you come out, though, and everybody began to wonder if you maybe slipped out to Dollis Hill a little later in the evening."

"Is that where you found him?" I blew twin jets of smoke down my nostrils and watched them blend with the steam rising out of the coffee cup. Outside, the rain was falling hard on Bloomsbury Square, rattling the window panes. Rain was general all over England, the papers had said, general all over Ireland and France.

"Somebody ripped a knife up his belly," Stock said brutally. "In a dreary flat up in Dollis Hill. A Pakistani and West Indian neighborhood. One of the neighbors reported hearing a fight. When a car arrived, the place was pretty well picked clean—no lamps, no telly, no chairs, no food, just a few sticks of furniture too big to move. Picked clean, it was. The wogs went through and took what they wanted before they called us in. Nobody saw anything, naturally."

"You'd get a better class of murder in the Savoy, I guess." But remembering the knife, the impact of the blade on flesh, I was suddenly cold. I put down my cup and rubbed my hands together for warmth. "I'm not sorry he's been shivved," I said, "but I am surprised that an inspector for narcotics would take the morning off to tell me all about it."

"Funny situation," Stock said as if I hadn't spoken. "Apparently two men and a woman rented the flat, furnished, paid a month's rent and used it off and on for about a week. English men, the neighbors thought, except one sounded foreign."

"French?"

"American, they thought. But what do they know? Homicide called me because, as I told you, Henry and Roger and one or two others were known to us as working heroin distribution, mostly coming from France and Holland, mostly selling to black wogs in London and the Home Counties. Henry Dean and Roger Levet, they were." He turned his head to the right in his odd stiff-necked way and gazed out the window at the black rain. A narcotics cop who lived in a mildly paranoid world of wogs. A narcotics cop who didn't smoke tobacco or drink caffeine. Or let up. I wasn't the only Puritan in the room by a long shot.

"We're expecting another big influx of heroin in about three weeks," he resumed, still talking to the window. The matchstick wiggled in his mouth like a mouse's tail. Stock was up to something, I decided. He was far too chummy, too talkative. He was keeping his natural choleric impatience on a short leash. I took another drag of poisonous cigarette smoke. He was, I thought, setting me up.

"We keep a flow chart in the office," Stock said, "just like a bank or bloody IBM, and we use a few informers, one or two of the registered addicts, to do a little cloak and dagger for us. Dope is big business and it's usually as predictable as British Rail. But Marteau has been behind schedule this summer, and they haven't delivered at all this month. We know because we've got boffins who analyze the stuff we pick up on the streets and tell us who made it and when and what color knickers they were wearing. Everything except where. They say each lab's got its own signature, its own way of cooking the morphine that's as good as a fingerprint, just like wireless operators during the war had their special cadences." He shifted his bulk and looked at me again. "Now maybe the delay is because of their great respect and fear and awe of you and whatever the hell you're doing. Or, which is the way it usually happens, the suppliers are arranging a new routine for shipment."

"Why should that cause a delay? Surely your mysterious Charles Marteau—"

"Oh, I don't think the problem lies with Marteau," Stock interrupted. He picked up one of the pink strips of bacon from my plate and started to chew it. "He's a very well-organized bird, a regular tycoon. More than likely his partner—"

"Partner?"

"One man can't handle a drug network efficiently in Europe, Haller," he said, more brusquely than before. "Too many borders to cross, too much red tape. Marteau has at least two partners all right, somebody who provides transport from the

Middle East for the raw opium, and somebody else, maybe an Englishman, who gets the finished stuff into this country and starts passing it out after school. Marteau specializes in purchasing and refining. We know that much. He buys it in the Golden Crescent—that's Iran, or was, and Afghanistan and Pakistan—some chaps in the Foreign Office reckon it's the red Russians behind the whole heroin industry. He buys it from barns right there in the bloody poppy fields, where the wogs boil the pretty flowers down into a morphine base, and he takes it somewhere in the Mediterranean, like Sicily, and that's when the real labs make it into heroin. Dope isn't a vertical business. You want a lot of secrecy. There's a division of labor. Marteau makes it in Bordeaux, somebody else carries it out to Britain. That's the most common arrangement. But intermediaries do all the routine work, and they make bloody sure that nobody knows how to squeal on anybody else."

"Thanks for the lecture, Stock, but none of this has anything to do with me. I'm a skip tracer, not a narc."

He stood up and walked slowly to the window. Rain blew against it in angry blasts, like handfuls of sand. The trees in the square ducked, bobbed, and weaved as the wind came in swinging.

"You got a gun in here, Haller?" he said, turning around and crossing his big arms over his chest. "Or a knife?"

"No."

"Mind if I look, or shall I call downstairs for a warrant?"

I blew cigarette smoke toward the floor. I had left Paradise Court last night—this morning—loaded down with two guns, a knife, and Caroline Angeletti's swank suitcase. The suitcase and my ripped sport coat I had dumped in a trash barrel several blocks away. The guns I had wanted to think about. For ten minutes, I had walked through the soupy weather, shaking off the image of Roger's face each time it crowded into my mind, trying to guess the likelihood of somebody connecting me to him. Then I had started to look in parked cars. One out of every nine in the States has the keys still in it, and I didn't see why England would be different. It wasn't. On the 11th car, just off a street called Blenheim Terrace, I had found a blue Volvo with Danish plates, probably belonging to a businessman who had come to London expecting law and order. So had I. I had driven the Volvo through Maida Vale, along the Grand Union Canal, until I came to the boundaries of the zoo in Regent's Park. There I had walked 20 feet along the high metal fence and then lobbed the Beretta gently spinning over the top and into the black cane. The knife next. Chimpanzees or wolves had yapped at the splashes, and I had trudged on around the perimeter of the park, past the British Museum, and so to bed. The Webbley was still in the nightstand drawer beside the bed.

"Yeah, look all you want, Stock."

"To hell with it. You probably dumped the knife in bloody Buckingham Palace. You've got nerve, Haller. I give you that." He came around and sat down in the straight-backed chair again. Stock was somewhere in his early 50s, but up close his skin was still pale and smooth, like a piece of stiff white paper. When he was a boy, he could have had apple cheeks and cherubic blond hair but not the cold, black eyes that watched me the way a snake watches its shadow. Those come with what some of us overconfidently call the real world. In the small mirror behind him, my eyes had the same dead look. "I called San Francisco yesterday and had a chat about you," he said. "Know a Lieutenant Yetta?"

"We play chess together."

"He says you really are a skip tracer, whatever you call it. He says you have an instinct for it. He says you get obsessive and stubborn when you're working, and he says you're very quick to get rough, like you like it. He says he can't stand the sight of you."

"Maybe we go to the opera together. I forget."

He smiled unpleasantly, the odd, forced geniality back again, and inspected his palms with the confident air of a mountain man laying out traps for the small, dumb animals. "I had another telephone chat yesterday, too," he said mildly. "A chap named Russin called me from Cambridge. He's in charge of burglary, juveniles, and narcotics, the way they do in provincial stations. I met him once at a conference. He said a Yank private enquiries agent was looking,for a Cambridge student named Caroline Collin. She had a minor drug record, Russin said, and an interesting contact, so he wanted to call me. We're not computerized, Haller, but we're pretty good coppers in Britain. We stay in touch."

I watched the rain gust against the glass. Russin had held something back from the first, of course.

"She's your mark then?" Stock said.

I shrugged.

"You can help, Haller," he said. "I've got a daily check on the hotel records in London and Middlesex County, but that's as far as my budget runs. Do you know how many tourists come through London in a year? Seven million—almost the equal of half the population. My department hasn't got the manpower or the money to track her down, not without an arrest warrant, not on a hunch from a low-echelon copper about a runaway girl who might know something about somebody who knows Marteau. Especially not since your pal Lord bloody Jim made a few phone calls to my superiors to call off the hounds." I looked up, surprised. Magnus? "You can give me a push, Haller. You can help."

It was a curiously low-key appeal, as if he were going

through the motions and no more. My mistrust grew stronger every minute. "She's not involved," I said, stubbornly and obsessively.

He sat back and nodded as if he had expected that. One hand adjusted a new matchstick in the corner of his mouth. The weak light from the window washed him out and left him looking like a black and white photo of himself.

"She had a boyfriend was sent up to Dartmoor, according to Russin," he said. "For hard drug dealing. Cocaine, LSD, heroin. He got his stuff wholesale, so to say, from the Marteau group, the one you keep bumping into in all the tourist spots of London. He tried to kill a constable, our boy, and he was picked up for that too. Tried to do him in with the front end of a car, did you hear about that?"

"I heard."

Stock leaned forward, one hand on a thigh the size of a redwood, the other hand gripping the lapel of his suit coat as if he were holding himself down.

"His name is Robert Levet," Stock said. "The lad in Dart-moor. Roger and Robert Levet. Their mum must have liked that. They're brothers."

It was my turn to get up and walk to the window. Sheets of gray water covered Bloomsbury Square. Traffic crawled by under the window, lights on and wipers whipping. In San Francisco now, the sun would have burned off the fog and the city would be gleaming and preening like a newly washed pup. Dinah would be striding down the pastel corridors of her hospital, flouncing the pockets of her hospital whites with both hands and watching the patients come and go. Or she would be at lunch somewhere nearby, across the table from somebody and looking out at the bay. In fact, I supposed, it would be the middle of the night there and she would be asleep. It takes too much imagination to believe in time zones.

"So maybe you're not paranoid, Stock," I said wearily. "Maybe she is mixed up. But you don't make much of a case. A friend of a friend. I still don't buy it."

"Bugger," Stock said in disgust. He stood up and tossed the matchstick onto the breakfast tray and the fried egg quivered in fright.

"Narcotics cops are always the same," I said, as much to myself as to him. "You want to clean up the whole world at once, and you think everybody's dealing and everybody's connected. This is a missing girl, Stock, a kid, a new bride, not the rerun of the French Connection. I've got to protect my clients."

"You don't believe that, Haller," he said, picking up his raincoat from the unmade bed.

"Give me two days, Stock. Let me check this out my way."

He slipped the raincoat over his massive shoulders and came over to me. "See this, Haller?" He waved a blue booklet under my nose. "Your bloody passport. I got it downstairs. It's as far as the department will let me go, but it's far enough. I have plans for Marteau, you see. A change in routine brings everybody out in the open just for a bit, like rats sniffing new bait. The English contact will be vulnerable for a few hours, and maybe Marteau too. And what I don't want is any outsider sticking his boot in at the wrong time. You're confined to London, as a practical matter, to this hotel, in fact, until the magistrate's hearing."

"And when's that?"

"When I'm bloody ready!" he barked suddenly. He shoved my passport inside his jacket pocket and walked to the door. "You're not cocking this up, Haller, because you're going to be right here in front of your hotel telly while my lot are out doing their job. I can't prove you killed Roger Levet, and I don't bloody well care if you did. But that's the end of it, you're out, you had your chance."

I lit a new cigarette off the old one and watched him smirk. He didn't believe in his passport gimmick any more than I did. A streetwise cop like Stock would expect me to do what I was going to do, would have a second surprise in place. He buttoned the shabby coat and shook out his arms. Six-four, 230: he could have a bazooka up his sleeve.

"I might get to like you, Haller," he said, opening the door. "I repaired RAF planes during the war and I knew a lot of Yanks like you. You've got the soldier's eye. But if you think I'm about to let you muck this up, you're stark, staring bonkers."

After he slammed the door shut and his footsteps had died away in the corridor, I sat down by the telephone and listened to my fingers drum idly on the nightstand. The riff was either "England Swing Like a Pendulum Do" or "Come Fly with Me."

Come Fly with Me. I glanced at the windows where the rain was still drumming its own tune. Last night, according to the *Times,* the winds had been bad enough for a few hours to divert flights from Heathrow to Shannon; but the storm was due to blow past by early afternoon. My fingers did a slow roll over a box of matches. Without a passport, I wasn't going to get on a commercial flight anyway. I pulled the telephone over and dialed a familiar number. Magnus answered it on the third ring.

"How's the chap?" he asked heartily. "Find the missing heiress yet? Susannah wants to bet you won't." I grimaced. "Actually, I've got a lead, I think, Magnus. But I'm in a bit of a jam."

"Funny how we're always putting ourselves in food, aren't ye," he said. "In a jam, in the soup, in a stew. Sublimated cannibalism, what?"

"Up the creek."

"That's American," he said firmly.

"Are you busy at the consulting trade right now, Magnus? Or could you take a short holiday?" He hesitated, a long pause. "As a matter of fact," he said slowly, "things are—where were you going?"

"If I rent an airplane," I said carefully, "can you fly it to Bordeaux?"

Soaked, irritable, hungry, I stomped back into the White Horse three hours later and tossed my suitcase onto the bed. Still unmade, I noticed. Caroline and company had left in the morning hours for Bordeaux and unless they had been delayed by weather; I had already lost ten hours on them, thanks to the combination of Roger and Stock. I had lost ten days, to tell the truth, because I had tried to play white knight to a girl with a face like a renegade angel.

I lit a cigarette and packed my toothbrush and Tommy gun in the suitcase. Angeletti had dropped me, I thought, had used me like a point dog and dropped me flat. The only reason for going on now was a stubborn conviction that Caroline wasn't so far in that she couldn't be dragged out—that and Lieutenant Yetta's patently false character sketch. When the telephone rang, I was just telling myself that Angeletti had missed his last chance to call me.

I sat down in the armless chair Stock had used and looked at the phone on the nightstand. It rang again and I lit a fresh Players. When it rang the fourth time, I picked it up.

"Is that you, tiger?"

I stood up and sat down.

"Dinah?"

"Fred gave me the number of your hotel, Mr. Marlowe, and I've been trying to get you to come take this buzzard out of my living room."

"It's a falcon and the name is Spade."

"But is it still you?"

"Yeah, it still is."

"My dear boss Mendelsohn got a new international WATS line with her giant, and she said I could call for as long as I wanted."

"What does she use it for, to call Vienna?"

"Marin County," Dinah said. "She had a new telephone put in at the same time, a Snoopy phone about two feet high. He holds the mouthpiece in his hand and Woodstock stands on top of the dial. Her patients love it. How are you, Mike?"

"I'm OK. Engalund swing like a pendulum do." I looked out the window at the gusting rain. "No, I'm not. England is a tired old place, nothing like the way it was when I was 20. And the case has gotten turned on its head. I'm going to Bordeaux today. I feel as if I'm in a bad opera."

"Do you miss me?"

"I miss you," I said. And suddenly realized that I did, very much. "I miss you a lot."

"I can't hear you. There's terrible static at this end."

I laughed. I became graphic.

"My father," she said, "would tell you to walk five miles and take a cold shower."

"This is England. I can do both at once." Dinah's father, a retired mining engineer, runs what he calls an oyster ranch near Elko, Nevada, about 200 miles from freestanding water of any kind, let alone the ocean. "This must be costing you a fortune."

"It's all free. But it's a psychiatrist's phone, and it shuts off after 50 minutes."

I smiled. "Tell me the news." She would be sitting in Mendelsohn's office, which I had visited once or twice with her, a fifth-story corner with a view of Golden Gate Park to one side, a eucalyptus grove and part of a tea garden; from the other side, you could see the new towers of the Japanese trade center and the muggers pacing back and forth under the Coit Tower. Mendelsohn's jungle of plastic ferns, about three dozen of them, would be crowding the desk, and Dinah would have her shoes off and her feet tucked under her in the chair, fingers knotting and unknotting the telephone cord while she talked.

"Well, Fred bought a new car," she said. "With the raise he claims you owe him. He said it's a Buick Terrorist." I laughed again and three-quarters forgot the clan Angeletti, the image of Roger's face falling slowly toward the rug, the pain in my shoulder, and the water in my shoes. "And Mendelsohn is being sued by a patient who claims she's in a conspiracy to shorten his penis."

"They do call you shrinks."

"And I have a new patient, a stewardess with silicone implant breasts, who suddenly started to swell when the cabin pressure dropped over Denver—it's not funny, Mike, the poor thing almost doubled in size. And don't say a word about *Fear of Flying* or inflatable seat bottoms."

I watched the rain turn and blow hard against the window as if it wanted in; a chill draught rode across the room and made my shoulders hunch.

"Do you know when you're coming back, Mike?"

"I'm going to Bordeaux tonight. Really. I'll cable Fred the address when I get there."

"He wanted to tell you something about the boy." I heard paper crackle at her end of the line. "Something about Peter Angeletti." She read the name.

"I think I already guessed."

"He wants you to call him tomorrow anyway."

"OK."

"Mike?"

"Yeah?"

"I miss you too."

# CHAPTER 12

**M**ICHAEL, DARLING!"

Susannah was wearing a pale blue blouse, a long suede skirt, with Western fringes, and the chilly veneer that the English upper classes are dipped into at birth. The black hair made an oval frame around her face, free of makeup, free of expression. She looked sallow and ten years older, but she smiled in a perfectly ordinary way and asked me in. The mind has its watertight compartments, I thought, as I followed her tamely into the living room and greeted everyone like a friend of the family.

"The boys," Susannah said with a wave and her usual tone of ironic tolerance, "the boys, you see, are writing a book."

"My damn memoirs, Susannah." The general stayed seated on the couch by the butler's tray table and nodded his abrupt, not unfriendly welcome. From the other end of a stack of papers and battered cardboard files, Magnus rose, wiped his palms against his brown Norfolk jacket, and came over to shake hands.

"I've booked a plane from Peckenham," he said, "about an

hour's drive south of here, very small private airfield. I don't know why you won't use the firm's Cessna, but you must have your reasons."

I nodded and looked beyond him to the French doors, which showed a sky of slate gray and a garden still dancing with rain. "Is the weather a problem now?"

"Oh no," Magnus said, following my glance. "Wind's the big factor for flying. Rain hardly matters." He ran one hand through his thinning hair. Magnus is three inches taller than I am, but 50 had brought a stoop to his big shoulders. Our heads were almost level. I looked at him obliquely as he talked and noticed with surprise how many wrinkles an extra 15 years or so can add.

"With the wrong angle of wind," he was saying, holding his hands out flat like a plane banking, "even a big commercial jet can be blown sideways when it takes off, especially at Heathrow, where the damn fools laid out the two north-south runways over some of the least protected ground in England. No trees close by, no proper windbreak for miles, and you can't head into the prevailing east wind to neutralize it. That's why they shut down when the anemometer goes over force six from the east, which happens about twice a month in winter. Rarer in summer. Gatwick's much better designed, you know."

"But we're OK now?"

"I booked a Mitsubishi T-1," he said. From the coffee table, the general grunted in disapproval. "A nice two-engine machine with all the right radar and gear we need. But I'm afraid we'll have to stop once for fuel, old chap. I'd suggest Tours, which is about halfway down to Bordeaux. I've flown in there once or twice before, so that's a plus."

Susannah silently handed me a cup of tea and took her own cup to stand by the French doors. "How long should the whole trip take?" I took a sip of tea and watched her watch the rain.

"Two and a half or three hours to Tours; about the same again to Bordeaux. That is, if the winds aren't kicking the wrong way in France. But here's a difficulty, Michael." I looked at his hand smoothing the flight officer's moustache while he smiled apologetically beneath it. "The airport facilities in Tours are rather limited. The fuel office will likely be closed after six o'clock, and I'm afraid we'd have to stay over and take off again in the morning."

I looked at my watch and thought a moment. Susannah left the French doors and walked to the enormous bookcase that covered one wall. Caroline had gone to the airport at sometime past two that morning with her private escort service. It was almost three in the afternoon now. The trail, such as it was, had already turned as cold as an English August; an extra half day wouldn't matter. The whole enterprise was quixotic anyway, a tribute to Lieutenant Yetta's psychologizing. Susannah stooped and placed a record on a turntable installed among the books.

"That should still do," I said finally to Magnus, "if we can get off at dawn tomorrow from Tours."

"Are you still the great opera buff, Michael?" she asked in her mocking way from the bookcase. "Do you recognize this?" Music sprang out of cabinet speakers placed alongside the couch and the general frowned in annoyance.

"That's the overture to *Don Giovanni*" Magnus said, looking curiously from Susannah to me. "Even father knows that."

Susannah sipped tea.

"Would it be faster to rent a car in Tours and drive on to Bordeaux tonight?" I asked.

"Not really. I can have you in Bordeaux by eight tomorrow morning, fresh as a daisy, ready for whatever cloak and dagger this is all about. But I say, Michael, if the police have really taken your passport. You do know that French *douaniers* are rather martinets about that sort of thing, especially in the provinces."

I slipped the dark green booklet from my pocket like a magician extracting a rabbit, childishly proud of my trick.

"Canadian," he said, opening it.

"It's the only accent I do."

"In the name of Edmund Spenser?"

"A contemporary of Marlowe's," I said.

Magnus wrinkled his brow thoughtfully and Susannah took the passport from him. The general watched us with interest.

"Where on earth did you get it?" she asked.

"Cecil's Court, the West End, ma'am."

"Dear God, Cecil's Court," she repeated. "That's by Leicester Square, Magnus, the little pedestrian mall with all the antiquarian book and print shops, where I bought you the Daumier last year. You do make London seem like the most awful place, Michael."

"We're off then," Magnus said, clapping his hands once. "I'll just run upstairs and get my gear and call the charter office that we're coming." He started for the door, followed by Susannah.

"I've got your shirts to put in," she said, then paused and looked back at me. "I assume you're paying for this airplane charter." I nodded and she turned on her heel and vanished with a swish of fringe.

The record had gone into Leporello's aria *"Notte e giomo faticar."* I walked over and snapped it off.

Magnus's father looked up from the stack of papers while I poured myself more tea and then sat down in a wingback chair across the table from him. He was wearing a black pinstripe suit today with the same decorative gold button in the lapel. At 75, his shoulders still had less stoop in them than Magnus's and his eyes far less warmth. He cleared his throat of phlegm.

"You sleeping with her?"

I leaned back slowly in the chair, observed that the floral pattern on it was becoming faded, pulled out a cigarette, remembered, and put it back. It was foolish ever to think the young were more shocking than the old.

"No," I said in what I imagined to be a normal conversational tone. "No, I'm not," I added.

"Somebody is." He cleared his throat again. "And it isn't the boy. He's too busy throwing what little money he has down every casino and bar in London. And don't sit there looking all stiff and pompous," he said. "I'm too old to have any feelings about other people's sex lives. Even my son's."

I took a swallow of tea and he looked back down at his papers.

"Sometimes I think he never properly grew up," the general said after a moment, staring at a piece of yellowed paper as if he were reading it. "Never got properly tested in life. I've made it too easy for him, and this has turned into a bad marriage, soured right from the start. Not like mine. Some kind of center missing from the boy." He glanced up from the sheet of paper and held me with the glacial blue eyes. "You were how old when I met you, when your father was so worried about you? Twenty-one?"

"Nineteen," I said.

"Hmmmph. You never set the world on fire either, did you?"

I finished the tea and put the cup down on the table as muted voices drifted from the hallway.

"Susannah thought there might be some interest in my memoirs," he said, "from a publisher's point of view, so I brought out the first box of records."

The question that had been tottering on the back shelf of my mind for two days suddenly fell off. "Do you remember the name of the man who tried to kill Carlo Angeletti?" I asked.

He snorted and pulled a tea cup from under a manilla folder. "You jogged my memory on that whole operation, young man. Name of Blanchard it was. Henri Blanchard. Haven't the slightest idea what became of him."

Magnus and Susannah returned—he was carrying a pigskin suitcase and wearing a spotless Burberry's trenchcoat—and looked at me expectantly.

"Better hurry now, Michael, lad. The traffic begins to pile up just after four, you know, especially in this miserable rain."

I nodded and got up. I had been ready to go for about a generation.

"I'll call from Bordeaux," he told Susannah and pecked her on the cheek. "Father."

"You were wrong about one thing, young Haller," the general said brusquely as we started to leave. He was pouring himself more tea from the elegant Georgian service. We waited.

"Carlo Angeletti couldn't have a son," he told us. "He had mumps when he was 19 or 20—your age—and swelled up down there like two bloody balloons. I know. I saw him and talked to the doctor, who was British and knew his medicine. He said the man was permanently sterile."

Anybody who isn't afraid to fly, Dinah says, lacks courage. I looked down from 5,000 feet at the oily black hole in the twilight that was the English Channel, an immense long bruise on the landscape.

"'Murderous innocence of the sea,'" Magnus said, quoting. "Right on."

"Yeats," he said.

"If man were meant to fly," I said, noticing again that only two inches of metal skin kept us from tumbling out like a pair of ball bearings, "he would have been given free booze. Don't you have a stewardess on this boat?"

He laughed and adjusted a knob on the instrument panel. Around us, the storm had blown swiftly away, leaving scraps of gray clouds that floated like crumpled balls of paper across the horizon.

"Relax, old man. Flying is safer than crossing the street. Flying one of these is safer than being in a commercial jet. Do you know what the most significant danger in a 747 is?"

"Muzak." I didn't tell him about Dinah's patient.

"The seats come loose at the base on any kind of impact. Aircraft manufacturers use weaker bolts than automobile makers to hold them down. Heavy bolts cost fuel and space. Most people die in crashes because their seats break free and slam into the others."

"Just fly the plane, Magnus."

"Weren't you in a helicopter crash?" he asked suddenly, turning his face toward me. "In the army?"

"One," I said. One helicopter crash that had left me stunned and broken-legged on the floor of a Texas canyon, about ten feet away from the face of my sergeant who was trapped under a section of fuselage. Whose back was broken. Who took two hours to die, ten feet from me, while the party from Fort Hood was searching for us. "I didn't like flying before that."

"When I was a boy," Magnus said, "well, teenager, at the end of the war, I went once with Father to Richmond airfield, where the B-17s were based. That day, they had come back from a terrible flak bombardment in Germany. They had to hose out the body of the turret gunner from the plastic turret ball in back of one of the planes. Used a high power hose from a fire truck. I'll never forget it."

"No."

Magnus checked another instrument and banked the plane gently to the left. You never know, never, what is real to other people.

"I'm sorry if I caused trouble," he said, "by calling the CID, old boy. Just wanted to be helpful. Take them off your back."

"No harm done."

"And you're sure we weren't followed to Peckenham?"

"If we were, they were wearing invisible ink."

He snorted like his father and righted the plane. Somewhere ahead, below, France lay spread out like a dark green blanket. Two hours more to Tours, Bordeaux by nine the next morning.

"Father says it's a permissive society," Magnus said in the odd, unconnected way he sometimes had. "Drugs, runaway wives."

I closed my eyes for a moment. Four hours of sleep since Roger. The hum and vibration of the plane shook my concentration loose.

"At least it's a free one," I said. In California, I thought, letting my mind find its own disconnections, a juvenile is permitted three murders by the state before he can be sent to prison. One 16-year-old I tracked down for grieving parents had been killed in Santa Monica, shot point blank on the beach near the pier because another 16-year-old thought he was diluting his cocaine. Since it was his second homicide, the kid got six months in the reformatory, was out in two. A lot of mob killings in California are actually carried out by juveniles, cheap labor with quick turn-around time.

"Yeah," I said. "It's a permissive society."

"Do you think father is right about Angeletti being sterile, not having a son?"

I shifted my torso and rested the side of my head against the plane window. Cold. Magnus had one fat plastic earphone twisted up, like a spare cheek, so that he could hear me; in the fading light his face looked smoother, younger. He glanced quickly at me before returning his gaze straight ahead toward the French horizon. A confident pilot, unalarmed. But no center, his father had said. I didn't know about that. Magnus had sustained an elder-brother image a long time in my particular world, a kindly, urbane man who had . . . not set the world on fire either.

"The general is no fool," I said finally. "It explains something about the girl's behavior. I'm going to call San Francisco when we land, to check."

"She's running away from him, from the old man," Magnus said firmly. I was relieved that he didn't ask me what it explained.

"She's running to something else," I said, barely stifling a yawn. "They always are."

"I understand," Magnus said with surprising intensity. "Both the *from* and the *to*. I feel a little that way myself today, liberated you know, a mile high on one of your adventures." He paused, letting his tongue lick his lips, and uncharacteristically looked for a word. "Like one of your rabbits," he said.

The hotel Metropole in Tours was gloomy and expensive, but the restaurant had one star from Michelin, so Magnus dug both hands into my expense account, ordered the *speciality—aiguilettes de canard aux pruneaux—*and sat back with the bright air of a man on an adventure. I poked at the food briefly, still tired, still sore in my shoulder, and excused myself to search out the hotel switchboard.

Merriman didn't answer, but his tape gadget oozed prerecorded cordiality and told me that in an emergency, he could be reached at the following number in New York City. Or at the tone, I could leave a message. I swore and hung up, the way I always do, and lit my third Cauloise of the evening with my plastic lighter. Through the doors of the telephone booth, I could see that Magnus had come into the hotel lounge and sat down with a large whiskey, gesturing expansively to the waiter, thoroughly enjoying himself. He was beginning to remind me in fact of a flower in California called the whispering bell, which only blooms after a forest fire has swept over a piece of ground. I slid the doors of the booth closed again. What the hell. It's difficult most of the time to telephone across the street in France, much less overseas, but maybe I'd be twice lucky. I beckoned to the woman personning the switchboard.

Not Merriman, but Angeletti answered in New York, and I told him *bon soir*.

"Haller, yeah," he said in his thick godfather accent. "So what's up? Why you calling me here?"

"Merriman's machine gave me the number. I thought somebody ought to know that I've left London. I'm calling from France. And it just crossed my mind that I might have heard from one of you before now."

"Yeah, Merriman told me you called. We had to come East on business, in a hurry." His high-pitched voice seemed to dissipate over the wire. I held the phone closer and strained to hear. "He told me you found her, then lost her. Sloppy, Haller. I pay for results."

"Is that all he told you?"

His manner softened slightly. "All right. There was a fast shuffle, I admit it. Piero was in a little hot water, and we had a few other things happening that don't concern you. So we dressed it up. You didn't think you were buying Girl Scout cookies, Haller. You're supposed to be good at finding people. So find her."

If I were hinting for an apology or an explanation, it would be a long wait. I exhaled a cloud of bluish Gauloise smoke. "I expect to catch up to her tomorrow," I said, "in Bordeaux."

"Bordeaux?"

"Maybe you ought to think about coming over, Angeletti, and seeing her yourself. You're close enough to make it in a day from New York."

"Why should I do that?" The voice was a disembodied hiss.

I remembered the voice of the American in the other room of Paradise Court—young, bland, male—and I took my time answering his question. "Because the last time I saw her," I said deliberately, "I think your son was with her."

I don't know quite what I expected—yelps of surprise, maybe, cartwheels, applause. He said very calmly, "Yeah, maybe I should, Hunter and me. You got an address in Bordeaux?"

"I'm planning on the Normandie Hotel, under the name Spenser."

"I'll call your hotel if I decide to fly over," he said. And hung up.

I woke up long before dawn.

The luminous dial on my wrist read 4:15. I blinked in that information and rolled over to go back to sleep. At 4:30, I got up and walked to the window. On the other side of the curtain, the sky still hovered cloudless and black over the dark umbrella of a foreign tree. Maybe today I would realize that this was France, that I was back again.

I yawned, rubbed the grit from my eyes, and felt again the sensation of nervous gray clarity that envelops your head when you're 20 years old and on your own and doing what everybody warned you not to do. What you knew was dangerous.

Then I dressed and padded through the silent hotel until I found the kitchen and a busboy, too sleepy to be surly yet, and came back to my room with a cup of coffee and a stale croissant.

The sky was still black and bitter, but I drew the curtains and sprawled in a chair, my feet propped on the cold radiator, and watched nothing at all.

Thursday morning. The American voice on the telephone had said two days for setup and rehearsals, if the contact had good weather. That made it tonight at the soonest, or tomorrow. We would reach Bordeaux before breakfast, Magnus calculated, and I would have one day to find her before whatever rehearsal they had planned was over and whatever real thing they had planned began. I wiped crumbs off my lap and sipped the strong coffee. What kind of person would be delayed by bad weather?

The top of the window lightened and the first streaks of green appeared on the tree. I had come to France from London when I was 19, after my stay with Magnus, dropping out of college on hands and knees and sprinting like crazy from home. I had last been here on vacation five years ago, two months before I had met Dinah.

I put the cup on the bedside stand and picked up the envelope with Caroline Angeletti's picture. Still the same sad eyes, the same downward curve of the mouth so typically British. So sexy. She smiled out of the California sunshine as if she'd never heard of drug traffic or boys who carried knives or Charles Marteau. Or maybe the picture was just underexposed. I slipped it back into the stiff brown envelope. I had met Dinah in the basement of the San Francisco city morgue, I remembered, reaching for the coffee cup and gulping one last lukewarm swallow. The crown of the sky was golden now. In the distance, beyond the black outlines of buildings across the square, something glinted and moved hungrily: that would be the River Loire. A chilly white concrete building, the city morgue, on a corner of Franklin Street not far from the Hall of Justice and backed under a freeway like an abandoned truck. I had gone there to check a John Doe to see if he was somebody I had been hired to find—he wasn't—and she had gone there, I learned later, to identify the body of one of her patients, a 20-year-old girl with anorexia nervosa who had rented a room in a Tenderloin hotel, piled the furniture against the door, taken off her clothes, and stepped out the window.

Dinah was the one in need of comforting, in fact, but she had spoken to me first, while we waited for the elevator, because my eyes looked desperate and wounded, she said later, as if I were ready to cry. And I had answered because, under the mop of red hair and over the small, plump figure, she had the most wonderful face I had ever seen.

Outside my door, somebody wheeled a cart with a squeaky wheel down the corridor. On the street, something banged twice. If I opened my eyes, I would see a freshening summer sky, brighter, golden like a crust of bread. If I opened my eyes, I would begin to look for Caroline Angeletti. I crossed my arms on my chest and lowered my chin. Over dinner that night, at an Italian place called Trattoria Venetia that hires only Chinese cooks and has a balcony with a view of the Golden Gate, she had told me about growing up in the Sierra, about her father in Elko, about medical school and divorce, about . . . We made love exactly one week and six dates later, moral fossils by San Francisco standards, on the brand new waterbed she had installed in her apartment and forgotten to seal. I had just reached a greedy hand for one small, perfect breast when the seams of the bed exploded and dumped me along with 75 gallons of distilled water onto the floor. And as I looked up in stark masculine bewilderment, her red head had peered over the soggy sheets, giggling, "Was it good for you too?"

Through the thin walls, I heard Magnus's travel alarm begin to ring.

We were airborne before seven, tank brimming with gas-oil, which is what the French call diesel, thermos brimming with hotel coffee, and by 7:30, we were flying low over a patchwork of spiny mountains and green farmland, across the curve of a perfect August morning.

"The Dordogne Valley," Magnus announced through a croissant. "The only undiscovered part of France." He broke off for a moment and said, *"Neuf-cent, trente-trois, bey, bey, tay,"* into his microphone with the easy patrician accent they teach at Oxford. *"D'accord,"* he said after a moment and rattled off another set of numbers. If anything, his French was smoother, more idiomatic than mine, and I had spent two years working in the damn country once upon a time.

"Those hills," he told me as he pointed one gloved hand downward and resumed his lecture, "are all limestone. Water runs through it like a piece of cheese, makes all those woolly-looking valleys and underneath them makes more caves than almost anywhere in the world. Has done for millennia." He banked and let me look down one white Mitsubishi wing. "No industry or big cities because of the limestone," he said, "and the only tourists who ever come are Frenchmen dedicated to le camping and Englishmen dedicated to truffles." He brought the wing up slowly and I blinked at the strong early-morning glare.

"And the cave enthusiasts," he said.

"Yeah." That much I knew myself, but Magnus was in his elder-brother/schoolmaster mood and, short of sitting on the wing for the rest of the flight, I would hear what he wanted to say. I sipped more of the strong black coffee that they will hand out at the pearly gates.

"Did you ever see them, Michael?"

"My assignments were mostly in Provence and the Riviera," I said, remembering my early 20s and the tedium of writing mindless tourist features for UPI, of border checks later in my nine months with Interpol. What you go through at 20 or 22 you would never put up with later, which is of course the principle behind early engagements and the draft. "I never traveled in western France."

"We're about over Les Eyzies," Magnus said. "Little village, should be just beyond those hills on a river. The cave capital of France. It's where they discovered Cro-Magnon man, and there's a hotel built on the actual spot now."

I watched the landscape revolve under me like a painted backdrop turning on rollers.

"Most of the caves are concentrated right there," Magnus said. "Some of them covered with prehistoric paintings, which are quite fun to see, really—bison with spears chucked in them, fertility goddesses, the outline of a hand with four fingers— quite the Victoria and Albert of cavemen."

"I thought the French government closed the caves."

"You're thinking of Lascaux, the famous one Andre Malraux wrote about." I must have been. "Many, many more caves down there, Michael. The tourists were breathing carbon dioxide on the Lascaux paintings, making a mold grow, so the government sealed it off. But there are caves on practically every farm, and the owners show them to the odd tourist in their spare time—some of them are enormous caverns too. One ancient peasant woman, dressed completely in black, snaggle-toothed and wrinkled like the devil, took Susannah and me down through a cave on her goose farm and illuminated the paintings with a blowtorch that she waved around like a candle in the dark—a grotesque sight half a mile underground. I thought I had stepped into a scene out of *Macbeth*."

"A far cry from Bordeaux," I said, thinking ahead to the business of finding Caroline, hearing the steady tick of time running out. The cave country below looked as unfriendly and as unpopulated as the Delta.

"Oh Bordeaux," Magnus said, flipping a hand. "Since they dredged the Gironde estuary, Bordeaux is in a fair way to becoming one of the major oil ports of Europe."

# CHAPTER 13

**W**E DID IT WITH RENTED CARS.

While Magnus had checked us into the Hotel Normandie downtown, I had stayed at the airport canvassing all the cab ranks and the car counters, following the only idea I had come up with in a day and a half, an idea I could have clipped from Dick Tracy in the Sunday papers. But it had worked.

"Yes, but how did you know they weren't using their own car?" Magnus protested, following me across the room. "Or a limousine from Marteau? Something?"

I bent over my open suitcase and pulled out the shoulder holster and the Webbley. The customs officer in Tours had hardly looked up from his Asterix comic when he had waved us through. "I didn't," I said. "I guessed. I depended on the fanatical secrecy the good Inspector Stock talked about. These people use code names and safe houses and paid thugs. They aren't going to send limousines for each other." The fat holster fit under my arm like a brick.

"You do believe him then, that she's mixed up in drugs voluntarily?"

I lit another Gauloise and paced from the bed to the window, exhaling bluish hydrocarbons like a six-wheel diesel. In California, somebody would have checked my muffler. Magnus remained by the bed, arms folded across his brown Norfolk jacket: the elegant farmer from Saville Row with the missing center. In contrast, the decor of the Normandie was cruelly modem according to the new French manner—taut synthetic fabrics stretched between rigid lines of chrome, squares of black leather and polished stone everywhere, abstract prints framed in aluminum and screwed into the precise center of each wall. There had been less metal in the Mitsubishi. I pushed open the window. My nerves were tapping their feet in impatience, my synapses were going off like a string of firecrackers. Outside, barely two miles away in the Hotel Sofitel, using the name Christine Audra, Caroline Angeletti was presumably rehearsing whatever had brought her from the Sacramento Delta to Bordeaux. I glanced at my wrist. Twelve-fifty. In five minutes, I was going to leave Magnus and start for the Sofitel. Below the window, indifferent to my impatience, the Garonne River swept effortlessly along toward the deep water anchorage just outside the city and the green Atlantic beyond.

"What she does voluntarily," I said, watching the river and taking the long way around his question, "is part of the mystery. I figured that they would split up when they arrived, that the girl would go a different way. They kept apart in London, too. If they had stayed together here, we would be padding from hotel to hotel this minute."

Magnus would want to go with me, I thought, would expect to be in on the end of the adventure, after all he had done. But from here on, amateur night was over.

"You look absolutely pale, Michael," he said, "absolutely tense. What story did you invent this time?"

"Canadian lawyer," I said, grinding out the Gauloise in a pure white ashtray shaped like a kidney. The butt of the Webbley dug a trench in my ribs. My stomach had contracted into a slipknot. "Trying to find a young woman who's just inherited a sum of money from her estranged husband. I put Caroline's picture on top of an envelope of hundred franc notes. In France, you can't go wrong by appealing to romance or greed. Or both. Avis was number two, naturally. Hertz never heard of her."

Magnus shook his arms out straight. "I'd hate to have you after me," he said. "You are an intensely stubborn man. Let's go get her now, for God's sake, before something happens."

"Magnus—"

"What's that?"

The knock at the door had been almost inaudible. Magnus looked at me. I nodded and he took three steps across the carpet and jerked the door wide.

"Hello, Haller," Stock said as he walked in. "Close the door, Mister Harpe. Close the bloody goddamn door and lock it."

"I set you up." Stock's big, permanently angry face was built wrong for smiling, but today he made an exception. One hand rolled the matchstick into place in the corner of his mouth, tugging the lips upward and showing yellow teeth and gums the color of a used eraser. The crow's-feet around his eyes crinkled and joined the network of crimson and purple capillaries that rose like a freeway map from the base of his nose. He stirred his bulk in the severe modem chair, all canvas and wood, and smirked from me to Magnus and back to me. He looked like a bear in a peach crate.

"I set you up, Haller. There are only four established dealers in stolen passports in central London—we have people who make it their business to know—and I had all four staked out five minutes after you left your hotel. Your visitor's entry number came across my desk from the *douane* in Tours about an hour after you landed, and lord cock-up's flight plan, which he conveniently filed last night, was there 20 minutes later. I came to Bordeaux on an Air Inter night flight, with a legitimate passport and a police welcome. You ought to try it sometime."

"You can't do a thing here," Magnus said, but the old haughtiness was missing from his accent: there was nothing but patrician bluster. "This is foreign soil and he's an American citizen."

"Mister 'arpe," Stock said in exaggerated Cockney. "The man with friends in 'igh places." He took out the matchstick and appeared to inspect the tip, then replaced it carefully, enjoying his little charade. "Do you know, Mister 'arpe, the penalty for being accessory after the fact to a felony? Leaving the United Kingdom under false pretenses and against police orders? I'd say six months, maybe with probation, maybe not. And no more pilot's license for weekend trips to the race meets or the charity shoots."

"Lay off, Stock. He didn't know about police orders or passports."

"You, cocky," he said, propping the grin back in place with the matchstick, "you should do two to four in bloody jail before the magistrate even gets around to the business with the Underground. Not to mention the chap with the bleedin' belly over in Dollis Hill."

"If this were a collar," I told Magnus, who still stood openmouthed beside the door, "the Inspector wouldn't be sitting with his legs crossed and his mouth running."

"I want her, Haller." He stood up quickly for so big a man and lurched toward me, smile wiped away like condensation on a mirror. "I want the girl you came to find." He planted himself in front of me and stared down at the bridge of my nose. "I want you to hand over what you've got, photos, names, places, all of it. That or you and his 'ighness take the next bloody flight to London, guests of the city."

If he ever hit me, I thought, with his 50-pound advantage I would crumple like a tin can under a tire. I shook another Gauloise from the pack and lit it. You can get the same flavor by smoking a shoetree, but I had remembered them as tasting much better. "Her married name is Caroline Angeletti," I said. By the bed, Magnus's jaw snapped shut. "You can have her picture if you want it, but she's not what you're really after at all, is she, Stock?"

"Show me the picture."

I took one of the photos from the brown envelope I carried in my jacket pocket and handed it over. Stock framed it with the pudgy white fingers of both hands and squinted at Caroline posed beside the swimming pool in the bright summer glare of the Delta, half a planet, half a year away.

"She ran away from her husband in California," Stock said after a moment. I nodded. "She came back to Cambridge and went straight to the mate of the lad who's in Dartmoor for heavy-class dealing. From there, she came to London. From there, she came to Bordeaux. The very time and place where Charles Marteau is going to crawl out on his rock while his supply system gets overhauled. Why don't I want her, Haller? I forget. Is it because she's your client and you got something to trade?"

"You want him," I said and pulled the other photograph out of my pocket, the folded piece of UPI paper with the grainy likeness of Peter Anthony Angeletti on it.

"The husband she ran away from. That's your trade?"

"He was in London," I said. "In Dollis Hill. And now he's in Bordeaux."

Stock folded the picture again, being careful to follow the original lines; then he tapped it into his front pocket like a dress handkerchief and walked around me to the window.

"I hate Europe," he said fiercely, staring popeyed at the river and the city that stretched along it. His hands gripped the window sill at either end and the muscles on the back of them stood out like cables, as if he were going to lift and heave the wall out. "Bloody, fucking Europe. You're too young to have been in the war, Haller, and Lord 'arpe there probably saw it through from Eton. I was 15, big like now, lied to say I was 18, and got myself into the RAF repairing the miserable pieces of wood and baling wire the lads took up every day to fly at Jerry. Richmond Field in Kent, it was, and I saw every kind of carnage that could be done to young men's bodies. I did it because I believed that godawful rot about Free France and the end of civilization and the bloody Hun." He turned around and glared at Magnus. "My dad was a milkman," he said. Magnus never changed expression. "My dad was a milkman in South London, the finest man I ever knew. He was killed by a Jerry bomb in '42 while he sat in his lorry under Waterloo Bridge, where the old Southwark road used to run." Magnus made a barely preceptible nod. "I joined up two weeks later," Stock said, redfaced, "and kept the planes flying till they made bloody Germany a fucking rubble. I wish they'd bombed bloody France as well. The greediest, most immoral nation in Europe. Fifty million pimps. To hear them tell it now, they were every one of them part of a Resistance group sabotaging the wicked Huns as the day was long. I could tell you stories about collaboration would curl your blond Yank hair, Haller." He spat the matchstick into one big paw and looked at it for a moment as if it were a vile memory tumbling out of the war. "There aren't heroin factories in Bonn," he said. "Or Madrid or Glasgow. Bloody French *wogs*." Then in a sagging voice, half-exhausted, half self-mocking, as if all the energy had suddenly drained from his face and shoulders, he muttered to his shoes, "What the hell. Me mum didn't intend me to turn into a sour old man." He walked his mountainous body back to the canvas chair and sat down.

"Do you know why most heroin is made in French industrial cities?" he asked.

"Chemicals?" Magnus said tentatively. He had moved to a straight-backed chair by the bed.

"You need one of two kinds of protection to make heroin," Stock said. "Purifying a morphine base is smelly work and bloody noisy if the vacuum pumps aren't tightly muffled. So a heroin factory needs to be in a place like this—" he pointed a new matchstick toward the open window and the chimneys and oil tanks silhouetted on the horizon—"or it needs to be in deep isolation, like parts of Sicily where there's nobody to notice smells and noise."

"So complicated?" Magnus said. He made his voice ingratiating, to hold Stock in the unexpected tame mood. Magnus's world existed only in social intonations, I realized. He would try to charm an earthquake. "I thought people just smuggled it in raw from Turkey."

Stock looked at him with weary eyes. "What's brought in from Turkey," he lectured, "is just raw opium—you call it brown sugar, your dealers do—which is heavy and bulky. To make heroin out of it, you need a laboratory and a chemist who can work with hydrochloric acid and butane heaters. It takes 17 steps in all, some of them dangerous—you get the odd explosion—but no unusual skill beyond what a good industrial chemist has. They get paid per kilo of heroin they produce, and paid a lot. When they get through processing the opium, nothing's left but a small bit of white powder, about an ounce from a pound. And smart chemists, the kind Marteau uses, repeat the refining several times—one run a day—and get a purity rate of 70 or 80 percent per kilo. And every time they do it, there are more fumes, more noises, more chances of discovery. But the purity is what your junkie in Dollis Hill or Soho pays for, what he wants to squirt up his arm, what he wants to turn his brain to shit with. And the smaller amounts just make it that much easier to smuggle in through Heathrow." He glowered at Magnus, then me. "The other kind of protection you need," he said, "is police indifference."

"So all those petrochemical plants in Marseilles . . ." Magnus began.

"Marseilles is shut down," Stock grunted. "The Yanks did that, and they're doing the same to Sicily—what they used to call the Godfather Run from Palermo to Kennedy. But there are almost as many oil refineries in Bordeaux, north up along the Gironde estuary. You could cook morphine in your bloody hotel room up there and nobody would notice, not where the goddamn tankers unload."

Magnus started to say something else, but the big man ignored him and turned his head ponderously toward me, like a giant sea turtle blinking.

"You're right, Haller. I don't give a damn about your missing bird. What I want is for her to lead me to Marteau, or the next man down. We can arrest small fry all year, you can throw one a week under the bloody tube, or maybe knife them when you get the fancy, but Marteau will stay in business and his killer crap will keep pushing straight along up the arm of England, about as hard to buy as bloody French wine." The red-ness began to swell his face again and his shoulders stiffened in the rumpled suit. "But now, this week, this month, the transporter's got to bring him out. They're changing over, I know it—there's tremendous quantities of opium out there since Sicily started to feel the pressure, tons of it waiting to land. And Marteau has got to look at the new system, just once, or else the troops will rob him blind. One look, routine set, and he'll crawl back under the rock and I'll spend the rest of my career picking up scum like Levet."

He stood up and shook his massive torso vigorously, shedding whatever lassitude had held him.

"What you're trying to tell me, Haller, is that the girl's husband is linked to Marteau and the girl just runs his errands."

I rubbed out my Gauloise beside the other. It would be foolish to underestimate Stock, either the range of his various angers or the quickness of his mind.

"Besides cooking heroin," I said, "the other hard part would be bringing in the bulky opium."

He rolled the matchstick around his teeth. "That's fair," he said. "You can smuggle anything smaller than a bloody beer mug through any big airport in the world. But the raw opium takes up space. That's why freighters smuggle most of it, to port towns, where there's lots of sailors and confusion and lots of crates nobody wants to reopen."

"The girl's father-in-law owns three oil tankers," I said, "that run between the Arab Gulf States and northern Europe."

He glowered at me for half a second, working his mouth around the matchstick like a woodchuck gnawing a sponge. "If you're trying to finesse me, boyo, you'll end up pissing down both legs."

"He's at the Bristol Grande," I said. "They split up when they arrived. The girl is at the Sofitel, under the name of Audra.

The boy was bringing money or information or both. He called it a rehearsal. If you're right, it's about the transport."

He reached for the telephone on the writing desk, picked it up, put it back.

"Why the hell should I trust you, Haller?"

"You should trust me as much as you trust all the French cops I don't see you calling. But I want the girl."

"This is *my* case," he snarled. An old man, shaking with rage: his jowls quivered and his yellow teeth clenched the matchstick stub where he had bitten it through. "I've been after Marteau for five bloody years," he hissed, and his breath rolled up like sewer gas from his belly. "And he's never stirred, never come out in the open. Nothing but a bloody name in a file."

He pushed me away like a sack of lint and turned for the door. "You can go after the girl, Haller. I'm doing this without the goddamn French. But don't try another thing unless you want to rot in the bottom of Old Bailey."

Magnus was up from his chair and striding forward, arms slightly open as if he were pleading. "I want—"

"No, bloody no!" Stock roared. "No lords and ladies!"

And the door jumped on its hinges as he slammed it.

Before Magnus had turned completely around, I was back at my suitcase, ripping through layers of clothes for the second box of ammunition.

"Michael . . . ?"

"The opium supplier and the refiner have probably never laid eyes on each other," I said. The box was the size of a throat lozenge carton and held 16 bullets. It was under my other necktie. "According to Stock, they could have worked together for years without ever seeing each other or knowing each other's name." I was at the door, holding it open, watching Magnus stand bewildered in the center of the bright modern room. "You stay here," I said. "There's a phone call coming." And before I closed the door I added more gently, as much to myself as to him, "It's just possible that Caroline Angeletti brought Marteau information she didn't know she had."

# CHAPTER 14

THE ELDERLY DESK MAN HAD IMPRESSIVELY FORMAL manners and spoke very slowly, as if his lips were sore.

"*Oui, Madame Audra,*" he said, giving Caroline's Avis name. "*Une Anglaise.*" The young clerk behind him looked up at me and winked. "*Elle a suite numiro deux cent cinq.*"

They both turned around to look at the row of pigeonholes behind them. Her key was on the hook. "Would you like me to ring her suite, Monsieur?" he said, switching politely to English.

"*Merci, non.*" I didn't think Caroline would take the call. "I'll leave her a message."

He slid a pad over with "Sofitel" printed in capital letters and went back to sorting mail. I took a sheet from the pad and strolled across the lobby, apparently looking for a chair and a writing table. A party in dinner jackets, diamonds, and summerweight furs burst in through the entrance and crowded around the front desk, chattering about a limousine. I stepped quickly past the two elevator doors and started up an open staircase to the second floor.

Two-hundred-five faced east, toward the river. I waited until two French matrons dressed in floor-length gowns had sailed past and into the elevator, then knocked loudly three times on the paneled door.

Her voice was muffled behind it. "Who's there?"

"*C'est l'administrateur d'hôtel, Madame Audra,*" I said, lowering my voice. "*On vous a envoyé un télégramme.*"

The door slipped open a fraction. I dropped my shoulder and bulled straight in. Franco Harris.

"You!" Caroline stepped back, whirled, looked at me again, and raised both hands to her mouth like a poster of a woman about to scream.

I snapped the lock on the door and tugged to make sure it held.

"Where's your husband?"

"*Get out of here!*" But it came out like a hiss instead of a scream. She retreated two steps with the hands still in place. I strode past her and slapped the bedroom door back. Empty. Bathroom steamed up but empty. End of suite. Caroline stood in the middle of the living room dressed in a yellow terry cloth bathrobe and dark slippers, revolving like a mannikin on a turntable as I paced the room. In one corner, beside another brutal modern sofa, a new Vuitton suitcase stood closed. I hefted it. Full. On the floor beside it was an overnight bag, open, with a silver toilet kit grinning out. I glanced through the curtain and saw nothing but the Garonne shining in the late afternoon light, no fire escape. I crossed to the chair nearest the door and sat down and leaned back. She continued to stand in the center, trembling with fright. She had a pink hairbrush in one hand, like a little girl.

"Where's your husband?" I asked again. She didn't answer, so I extracted a Gauloise from the pack in my shirt pocket, brushing the butt of the Webbley with my knuckles. "I know that he flew down with you," I said through a cloud of smoke. "Roger told me, before his accident." Her eyes widened, but she said nothing. "Maybe you'd rather talk to somebody else," I said. "Your father-in-law flew into town this morning, for example." For all I knew it was true. She turned abruptly and went to the sofa and sat down.

"What do you want?" she asked in a tiny voice.

"A little straight talk for a change."

"How do I know Carlo is in Bordeaux?"

"I can pick up the phone and dial him. Would you like that?"

"No, don't," she said more loudly. "Let me think a minute, won't you?"

She crossed her legs; the terry cloth robe slipped off her knee and exposed a few inches of thigh. I blew smoke through my nostrils. Even from halfway across the room, her eyes had a green, Pacific look. Her blond hair, short and stylish, still shone with moisture at the temples. There was no denying it. I had gone to Angeletti's houseboat out of curiosity, not expecting to work for a man like that but intrigued. And I had seen the picture of wide-eyed, innocent Caroline, as fragile and lovely as a fawn. How much of this chase was white knightery, Haller to the usual rescue, empathizing with the dropout in trouble? And how much was incipient mid-life doldrums, like Magnus's middle-aged bleatings?

Be honest, I told myself. He had called it a middle-aged letch. From where I sat, she looked about 16. I felt about 50.

"Give me a cigarette," she said after a moment.

I got up, walked over to the couch, and sat down beside her. She took a Gauloise in two trembling fingers and lit it herself with paper matches from the coffee table.

"You told him I was here," she said finally, calmer, like a bright yellow cat lifting its head.

"What you stole from Angeletti," I said, "besides pocket money, in our friend Merriman's fine phrase, was information. You stole information that was useful to Charles Marteau, information that he wanted very much. Information that had to do with the transportation of heroin from Bordeaux to London."

She leaned forward to rub her cigarette ash slowly against an ashtray on the table, a gesture I remembered from the restaurant on St. Martin's Lane. The robe rode a little higher up her thigh and billowed forward at the shoulder. Shadows from the metal table lamp behind me disappeared into the folds. I didn't see a bra strap. What is the first thing you notice when you are introduced to a new person? somebody once asked the actor Jeff Chandler. Whether the person is a man or a woman, Chandler said.

"You've been a busy man," she said with the same mixture of bravado and attempted sexiness she had tried before. She had Magnus's emotional agility, I noticed, the capacity to leap from mood to mood in an instant. By contrast, I seemed ponderous, obsessive.

"Angeletti didn't care about the money," I said.

"No." She took a deep breath. I didn't look away. "When I got back to England, I made inquiries in Cambridge, people I knew from university. Horse—heroin—has been in short supply in Britain for almost a year, since the Americans started putting so much pressure on Sicily and the Middle East went completely to pieces. Carlo had been in the business of transport, but only as a sideline, a few kilos of morphine in some Lebanese sailor's footlocker, and the poor devil got caught half the time. But he's arranged to increase his shipments soon from a new supply, because of the shortage. I thought the market would drop if he did, and I was selling that information."

I stood up and walked to the wet bar that the Sofitel had

installed on the side of the room by the window. Over a full-sized sink and hot plate counter, there was a small refrigerator, two cubic feet maybe, built into the wall, and when I opened it, I found an assortment of miniature airline bottles and a couple of splits of champagne. Caroline followed me to the bar and stood very close, so that I smelled the flowery bath soap she had just used, something French and sophisticated and a light-year away from guns in shoulder holsters and heroin in kilos. I poured us each one of the bottles of Beefeater's gin and dropped in ice cubes for dilution. Magnus had told me at the Blue Boar in Cambridge that gin literally attacks the nervous system, like the venom of the coral snake, and makes a mean drunk.

"Caroline, honey," I said, handing her a glass, "Marteau could have read about the supply of heroin in the *Financial Times*. You're a liar."

She flushed and chewed the rim of her glass. "Rampal believed us, in London."

"Rampal's the Frenchman with the sunglasses who wanted me to ride the Underground."

She turned redder and took a step away, then back. "I didn't know about that," she wailed. "Really I didn't. They were following me all the time Peter and I were in London, and I didn't know it. They made us stay apart. They didn't trust me, they said, and then they saw you take me from the hotel. . . . Rampal is in charge for the Marteau group in England. My Cambridge friends helped me contact him."

I sipped the bitter gin. "'Contact' isn't a verb," I said. The stuff was already making me meaner. "Why would Marteau want to know about Carlo's drug running?" I braced my hips against the bar and looked at the sad, sensual mouth, at the line of shadow that curved along each cheekbone. "What difference would it make to him?" I said.

She waited a long time before answering, so that I had plenty of time to study the cheekbones, the hair, the downcast eyes, and the gin had plenty of time to wrap its fists around my neurons.

"Rampal told me they were desperately short of money in the Marteau group," she said at last, and it began to sound like the truth. "Because of the short supply. They needed cash." She licked her bottom lip with the end of her tongue. "They would raid the shipment before it was unloaded and sell it themselves. I was supposed to get ten percent. Peter and I. Almost £50,000, Boyer thought."

"Nice business you're in," I said flatly.

"Look, Michael." Her hand rested on my forearm for an instant. The gin tumbled down my throat like a wildcat. "I didn't owe Carlo anything," she said. "It was an impossible situation. Haven't you ever wanted to be free of something, to run away and start over? I thought I had got free when I married Peter, but that house, that miserable valley—"

"If this is the I-get-so-bored-in-the-provinces speech, I heard it in London."

"Don't be awful," she said with that disarming bravado. "I like you."

"I remember."

"Carlo is a horrible man, and Peter—listen, I know what you're thinking, I know that heroin is a terrible thing. I never should have got close to these people. But I can't stop the world. I just acted, I just did it—it was like breaking out of jail. I'm too young to be trapped like that. I didn't want to waste my life."

"You wanted the money."

"Not just the money," she said.

She put down the glass. I placed my hands carefully around

her face, framing it, and leaned forward. Her mouth fluttered against mine. Her tongue dove. My right hand slipped the cord belt loose and her robe spilled open and I ran my fingers down, thumbs digging inside the hip bones. She curved into me and I felt her legs move apart.

"There's only one thing," I said, breathing the scent of soap, the scent of warm, slick skin. The robe curled off her shoulders and onto the floor. My hand grazed her cheek and throat on its way down.

She moaned a question. I drew my fingers lightly upward. The telephone rang.

"Marteau and Angeletti are partners," I said.

She took a step backward, green eyes wide with surprise. I wheeled and walked to the phone like an automaton.

"*Oui.*" I looked back across the room. She was still standing by the bar, the robe crumpled around her ankles, shadows clutched to her breasts and belly. I felt a thousand years old.

"Is that you, Michael? Thank God."

Magnus.

"Yeah, what is it?"

"I'm sorry, Michael. I wasn't going to call, but there've been two telephone messages in the last five minutes. I thought I'd better—"

"What are they?"

"A man named Merriman called. He said Carlo Angeletti is here in Bordeaux, and he gave the number, not the address."

"And the other?"

"Stock just called and wanted to know where you were. He wants you to pick him up. His car broke down on road D-10 at a curve just past the sign for Bassens, he said. He was following Peter Angeletti to the docks."

"Stay there." I hung up and walked slowly back to the bar, picked up my gin and drained it. Caroline licked her lips.

There was a second Beefeater's in the refrigerator and I dumped it into the glass, skipping the ice cubes this time. Some guys like to whisper "vermouth" from the next room and add an olive. I take it just the way it comes from the snake. "Where's your husband?" I asked in a voice so hoarse I could have been drinking Drano.

I could barely hear her elegant English accent. "I don't know."

She was two feet away, small breasts lightly swaying, blond hair shining. She might as well have been clipped from the back of a cereal box.

"You can tell me, sweet Caroline, or I'll pick up the phone and tell Carlo where to pick you up and then go home myself to a nice cold shower. Either way, I don't care."

"Michael, no," she said softly. Good, Haller, good. Bully the girl, scare her to death because the white knight fell into the tar pit. Dinah would call it overcompensation, or neurotic projection.

I swallowed half the gin. No, she wouldn't. She would call it infidelity and browbeating. "I've been set up more times than a ten-pin," I said less roughly. "Carlo didn't hire me to find you. He wanted me to find you because he thought his son was close behind. Or ahead. You were a dodge, a stalking horse." The wrong kind of horse, I thought, and finished the gin. Why the hell did they name something horse that turns your brains to egg white? "Shit" is what the kids in San Francisco call it. "Peter ran away first, didn't he?" She nodded and bit her lip. "And you met him in New York, and you both flew on to London, where you could look up old school chums and strike a deal with his information." She bent her knees and picked up the robe. "*He* was selling out his old man," I said. "You were just along for the ride."

"He's not his real father," Caroline said dully. "Peter was adopted years ago, after the war, when he was ten."

"Fathers and sons," I said mechanically, my mind somewhere else.

"Peter *hates* Carlo," she said. "He always has. Carlo tries to mold him into a gangster—he dominates everybody—and Peter hates him for it. This was for just the once, and poor Peter's no good at it, no good at all. He couldn't even find anybody to deal with in New York. That's why we came to England, to my friends."

"Clear as a bell, Caroline," I said, "clear from start to finish. Put on your clothes. I don't have any more questions." I pulled a cigarette from the pack in my pocket and started it toward my mouth, sick of the taste of them, sick of myself. She draped the robe around her shoulders and held it close, her face fixed on the floor. I looked at her and thought about myself, naturally, and wondered why she should look more guilty and furtive than I did. And then the penny dropped.

"Or is that all of it?" I asked suddenly.

She whirled and bolted for the bedroom. I jumped two steps and smacked the door shut an instant ahead of her. She turned wildly and I grabbed both her hands together tight, neck high.

"*What are they doing out there tonight?*"

She twisted and shook and I gripped harder.

"Me or Carlo?" I said between my teeth.

"I don't know!" she cried. "I don't know!" Then: "I think they're going to kill him!" She wrenched free and stumbled around me toward the couch.

"Peter? Who's going to kill Peter?"

"Rampal and Marteau," she sobbed, flinging herself face down across the cushions. "Rampal and Marteau. Dear God,

I never really thought—I never really admitted—they're supposed to be cleaning the empty oil tanks now. That's how the dope gets in, that's the new way. Peter worked it out. But it's dangerous in the tanks, something about gases." She pressed her face against the couch, muffling her voice, and I jerked her hair up to raise her head. "Oh God, I never thought it would be like this," she whined. The gorgeous child's face was distorted with tears, ugly flushes. "I never really thought."

"And they'll come back for you when they're done, you dim-witted little bitch. What's the name of the ship? Where is it?"

"*The Luchon,*" she sniffed. "At the docks on D-10."

I dropped her hair and started for the door.

"What are you doing?"

"Lock the door," I said as I began to slam it. "Lock it now!"

# CHAPTER 15

I COULD HAVE BEEN SET UP, I THOUGHT, AS I ROUNDED A CURVE on D-10 and slowed. In the distance, beside a parked car on the shoulder, a figure waved one arm. She could have set me up for Marteau and Rampal the way she had half set up Piero. My rented Peugeot rolled to a stop ten yards back of the parked car. But I didn't see how I could change that now. If it were a trap . . .

Stock clambered through the door like an irascible bear.

"Bloody camshaft," he growled over the whine of the motor as I spun back onto D-10. "I had him three cars back like a—slow down!" The speedometer of the Peugeot had already jumped to 90 kilometers, and I kept the accelerator floored, swinging wide around a lumbering diesel truck and spraying gravel off the shoulder of the road. "Slow down, goddamnit!" he shouted, bracing himself with one arm against the dashboard as the little car tossed us back to the right. "What's the goddamn hurry?"

I told him, in five or six clipped sentences, and rocked the car past another slow-footed truck, horn blaring.

"We're not calling the bloody frogs," he shouted over the

motor. I nodded. He had one hand still braced on the dash while the other hand pulled out 'a snub-nosed service revolver. "This is my pinch," he shouted again, face red and frowning. "Five trips here in four years, and all the frogs give me is a desk by the loo and a map of Bordeaux—have you got a gun?"

I nodded again and kicked the horn with the heel of my hand. The Webbley was warm under my arm, like an egg in a nest.

"I bloody thought you did," he muttered and stared straight ahead, big jaws working like pistons.

We roared through a village—six or seven stone houses, an ELF gas-oil station—and followed D-10 as it curved in the twilight alongside the marshy Gironde estuary, the big seaway that flows out of the Garonne and Dordogne. Rain began to smear the windshield and I punched the wiper button. Thirty-two kilometers from Bordeaux to the tanker docks, and Stock had gone almost halfway before his car had tripped and fallen.

"Watch the signs," he snapped.

I slowed to 100 kilometers and saw a cluster of road signs and billboards flipping toward us on the right: Ambres, ten kilometers north. Fort Lajard-Raffinerie de Petrol, straight ahead. Through the streaks of rain, lights began to crown dim structures on the horizon.

"They unload the supertankers out in the channel," Stock said, his voice barely audible. The motor kicked into passing gear, and his head swayed in the odd, stiff-necked way. "Special platforms and pipes. Regular tankers come into dock and unload into trains." We skidded for an instant on the slippery pavement and fishtailed straight.

"Slow *down*, goddamnit! We'll be picking the transmission out of our bloody teeth before we ever see them."

I dragged out a cigarette and lit it from the dash. It wasn't going to help Peter A. if I ran the car up the tailpipe of an oil truck. I pulled back to 80 and the road slowed down and straightened. Stock rumbled a sigh.

"Tell me about gases on a tanker," I said through the cigarette. "How can they be dangerous?"

"When they flush the hull," Stock said promptly. To our left, the Gironde was steadily widening. A sign and a one-lane bridge pointed to Pauillac and the famous vineyards of Bordeaux. "The crude is flammable," he said, "but they pipe it off in big flexible hoses like fire hoses. It'll burn if you flip one of your poisonous cigarettes in it, but it's not gas. That comes when they hose down the empty oil tanks inside with hydraulic pressure. Great corking nozzles built into the hull. They run filtered seawater on it for two or three hours, then they fill the whole hull with inert gas they pipe up from the ship's engine. That's why smokestacks on your tankers have a cylinder on top, to block the smoke."

"You're a right bloody wonder, Stock."

"You got to know your homework, ducky. The inert gas chokes off the oxygen that hangs around hydrocarbon residue, the tar patches that stick to the metal. That's the muck you find in the water when they flush at sea. But the dangerous gas is when they go inside."

The Gironde had reached almost half a mile in breadth now, and scattered brown islands bobbed in its current. I held the Peugeot at 80 in the middle of the empty road. "When do they go inside?" I asked. Caroline could have skipped the Sofitel by now. I should have called Magnus.

"Visual inspection," Stock said, fitting a new matchstick into his teeth. "When they flush the hull, a crew has to go down inside and inspect all the metal fittings for damage. You've had 100,000 gallons of oil in there; it's not like bloody tea sloshing around a cup. If the girders are broken or bent, the whole ship can break up under the next load or in a storm. The crew all wear wet suits and oxygen masks and tanks of compressed air, like scuba divers, because there can still be pockets of hydrocarbon gas clinging to the hull. Envelops your head like a bubble. Irreversible brain damage if you breathe it 30 seconds, fatal in a minute." He rolled the matchstick to the corner of his mouth and spun the chamber of his pistol one position. "That's one way to kill your gangster lad," he said.

In another mile, the marshy banks of the estuary began to surrender, first to occasional buildings and stretches of unfinished sidewalk or driveway, then to cinder-block warehouses, cranes, oil tanks, an impenetrable clutter of trucks and heavy equipment that looked as if a factory had been dumped helter-skelter from a box. And suddenly a ship rode up out of the brown wet haze on our left, a tanker almost the length of a football field, separated from the highway by only a cyclone fence. The first two-thirds of its length was a long flat platform, low in the water, dotted with valves and pipes and about as nautical as a subway car. At its stern, a bony superstructure climbed 30 or 40 feet above the deck and ended in a smokestack and a bristle of antennas. Its black iron sides looked close enough to reach out and touch. Behind and over it, where the river curved west, strings of lights and columns of smoke outlined the storage tanks of the refinery. In front, suspended from the fence, we read a black and white sign—"Quai 97"—and a huge chalkboard with the Exxon logo and the handwritten words "*S.S. Maid of Derby.*"

"Drive on up," Stock said. "Stay on the main road. I *know* the bastard's here—this is the only way in from Bordeaux."

"What was Peter Angeletti driving?" I concentrated on the cluttered road, dodged some kind of delivery van parked to one side. *The Maid of Derby* slipped behind us.

"Green Peugeot," he grunted. "Same as this."

"Alone?"

He didn't answer but thrust his big head in front of me, blocking the windshield. "There, goddamnit," he whispered. A Shell truck rolled past in the other direction, and then I saw the sign—"Quai 95"—the locked cyclone gate, and beyond it, over our heads and streaky in the drizzle, the white letters on the great rusty bow: *Luchon*.

I wrenched the car left, rattling over train tracks, and slid to a stop beside the fence. A shabby two-story shed, roofed in tin and sided with green shingles, blocked the ship from the road.

"Not the main gate," Stock hissed, and was scrambling ahead of the car before it had stopped. Ahead of us, ten yards past the shed, the snout of a railroad tank car poked through to the road. Stock was already kneeling beside it when I caught up, his snub-nosed pistol buried like a toy in one giant fist.

"Look at how high she rides," Stock said. "They've already emptied the oil. See the water line." He squeezed between the tank car and the fence and followed the rails onto the dock itself, coming out at a point just opposite the smokestack. At the other end of the ship, voices called; a motor complained and coughed. We ducked into shadow behind the tank car.

"Is this the customs house?" I whispered and gestured with my left hand at the shed. Except for the men at the other end, the quai looked deserted. No lights in the shed, no movement, no noise.

"Warehouse," he grunted. He was staring intensely into the drizzle. Twenty feet from us, at the end of the railroad siding, a rickety wooden gangplank slanted up into the murky light. Another gangplank ran down from the bow almost 40 yards away. "Customs comes on board with the harbor pilot, out in the deep water channel," he whispered. "They inspect the crew's quarters and gear and the cargo manifest out there. If you're looking for help, forget it. There's nobody on this quai but Marteau's people."

I started to ask another question, but he was gone, waddling to the end of the tank car in an infantryman's crouch. When I caught up, he had shoved the pistol somewhere back in the soggy folds of his suit and was bracing both hands against the coupling, about to push off.

"See that sedan?" I followed his finger to the main gate, saw the low black car and two figures standing beside it, and nodded. Voices called down to them from the bow, and Stock tensed. Rain drummed across the concrete in squalls. "You go along the shed," he said, pointing again, "back there and up. I'm going on board to find your friend."

"I'm coming."

"Don't be a bloody fool!" he spat. "I've been on these tubs before. You don't know a sail from a bleedin' rudder. You get the license of the car, that's all—but *do it!*"

And he was gone, clumping across the open space of the dock, bouncing up the gangplank with both hands working the white guide ropes, about as inconspicuous as a tuna in a fishbowl. I pulled the Webbley and aimed it after him into the rain. Water spilled off my forehead and eyebrows, blurring. Nobody shouted at Stock or shot, and when I blinked my eyes clear again, he had vanished.

The shed took me five minutes to cover.

By the time I had reached its far end, under a yellow and black "*Defense de fumer*" sign, Stock could have navigated half the deck, I figured, could almost have gained the point on the bow where two more figures stood in a huddle, looking down. At the gate in front of me, the sedan glistened, a black Mercedes 280 SL, license plate invisible, engine murmuring urbanely.

Next to it, in a jumble of crates and barrels, squatted an ugly green Peugeot. The two men we had seen were gone.

"Three minutes," I thought and looked at my watch again. "I'll give him three minutes." The driver's door of the Mercedes opened and a man in a yellow slicker stepped out, hunched his shoulders against the rain, unlocked the gate, and swung it open. As he scurried back to the car, someone in the front seat shifted, a shadow. "He's an old man," I thought angrily. "Almost old enough to be my father. Old men fighting my wars. Two more minutes and I go up."

I crept a few feet out into the open, dodging broken-field fashion, and my feet slipped and sank two inches into a puddle slicked blue and green with oil. I scraped and sprawled to a kneeling position beside a trio of stacked oil drums. I needed Magnus's father, I thought, to direct the battle. I needed Magnus, I needed half a platoon and a cannon, I needed a pair of galoshes. The two figures on the bow were men in black wet suits and air tanks, like inspectors of hulls. As I watched, they stooped and one of them twirled a valve wheel on top of a stubby pipe. One minute. Behind them a shadow moved in the rain. The sky lightened, then fell, as if taking a breath. I stood up.

"Stop! Police!" Stock shouted.

Guns slammed twice like doors in a house. The man closest to the edge took two steps back clutching his belly, caught the safety cable with the inside of his knees and plunged backward, his body flipping once slowly as he fell, so that he landed spread-eagle on the concrete, face down, making a sound like a brick dropped on an egg.

The driver of the Mercedes opened his door. The second man on the ship tumbled and rolled down the gangplank, staggered and ran. Stock appeared on the deck, ducking toward the gangplank, and the man by the Mercedes raised a pistol over his slicker. I placed my right hand across the oil drums and balanced his head on the barrel of the Webbley. My heart boomed in my ears, my mouth filled with cotton. Squeeze a trigger, never pull. My fingers felt half a mile down my arm. Squeeze. A bright blossom of red exploded on a field of yellow, and the man turned wet, incredulous eyes in my direction and sat down in the rain. The Mercedes began to move.

"Haller!"

Stock was halfway along the gangplank, one arm wrapped around his middle as if he were cradling a baby. The Peugeot started. Somebody shot once more and kicked a geyser of splinters into the air from the edge of the gangplank. Stock doubled and slid. I fired the Webbley into the blur of rain and ran through the water to Stock.

"Them!" he roared from 20 feet. The taillights of the Peugeot bounced and sank.

"I'm all right!" he shouted fiercely. "Bloody in and out, it's nothing." His left hand was clenched in a fist against his abdomen, dripping rainwater and blood onto the soggy suit, and miraculously the stub of his matchstick wiggled from tooth to tooth.

"Angeletti?"

"No hope—he's at the bottom of the ship. Did you get the license?"

For an answer, I twisted and stared. In the distance, two sets of red taillights climbed and dropped on the road to Bordeaux.

"Bloody hell!" Stock roared again. "Leave this lot to me. The frog coppers will keep you here all night."

I looked at the man in the wet suit, motionless, ten feet away. The car lights accelerated. Ten miles away, I had left Caroline, face down on her couch.

"Go, goddamnit!" Stock bellowed, and I sprinted like a colt for the car.

But I lost them all the same.

Halfway to Bordeaux I knew it. Two big oil rigs, nudging each other and wheezing like cows, pulled out onto the road near the bridge for Pauillac, and more than a mile passed while I bobbed out and back, then finally blew the Peugeot past them like a bullet.

Too late. My suburban roadster was no match for a Mercedes with a clear track, and the other Peugeot could have turned off anywhere by now. The road to Bordeaux stretched ahead, wet, narrow, and utterly empty.

At the sign for Ambres, I danced on the brakes and skidded to a stop in the driveway of the ELF station, next to the only telephone booth I had seen on D-10.

Magnus answered on the first ring and I told him in three words where to find Caroline in the Sofitel, what to bring me. Then while the ELF man changed my 50-franc note with maddening slowness, counting the coins twice and waiting to see if I would buy a little something—I grabbed two packs of cigarettes and left the change—ambulances flashed past in the rain, drowning us for a moment in the caterwaul they use for sirens in France. I dialed, got nothing; dialed again. Caroline answered with a jump and I told her where to meet Magnus, nothing more.

When I reached the Sofitel, they were both standing in the lobby as I had instructed, in plain sight of the desk and 50 people, an awkward, ill-matched couple. No Boyer in sight, nobody interested in them at all. I shook off a doorman and led them down the front steps into the car and headed toward the center of the city.

"The cab driver made it in four minutes," Magnus began, obeying his usual impulse to disarm any situation by talking it into unreality.

"Look for a telephone kiosk," I snapped. Caroline cowered in the back, legs drawn up on the seat.

"You'll do better at a cafe," he said in a grieved tone. He was right. I swung the car down the busy Avenue Clemenceau and stopped at the first cafe I saw, a brightly lit Tabac de Paris.

"Wait here, doors locked," I muttered, took the slip of paper he handed me, and trotted under the dripping awning and into the restaurant. The patron at the cash register sold me a *jeton de téléphone* and pointed to a three-sided booth in the back, beside an espresso machine. I lit one of my new Gauloises, took a deep breath of coffee fumes, and dropped the *jeton* in the slot. Nothing. I tried again. Steady noises like a phonograph needle stuck at the end of a record side. French philosophy, they say, concerns the problem of noncommunication in the modern world. You could see why. I cursed in French and English, tried a third time, and heard ringing at last, then an American voice: "Hello."

"This is Haller. I want to speak to Mr. Angeletti." My voice sounded bruised and weary even to me. I switched the phone to the other ear.

"This is Hunter Merriman, Haller. It's damn late for us. We got in this afternoon and Mr. Angeletti is sick with jet lag. What do you want with him?"

"I want to ask his opinion of the Common Market, Merriman—get him, for Christ's sake, and fast."

He put down the receiver and I waited. Outside the cafe, Magnus was leaning over the seat and speaking to Caroline. Inside, by the door, two old men in berets were sitting in front of a carafe of red wine and smoking slowly, as if nothing were left to hurry about in this world. The patron polished a glass and stared at me. I turned my back to him and the telephone crackled.

"Yeah."

"I want to see you right now. This is Haller. What's the address?"

"Call me tomorrow. I just got off the plane. I'm an old man."

"Me tonight or French narcotics tomorrow morning, my friend."

There was a pause, long enough to inspect my cracked and muddy shoes and look out again at passing traffic. The old men in berets hadn't moved. Goddamn old men.

"Take this down." He gave me an address in the northwest corner of town, near the Parc Bordelais. "Third floor," he said and hung up.

In the car, Magnus looked up at me with sad, wide eyes, his long face mottled and pale under the street lights and the shadows of drizzle.

"Stock's been shot," I said bluntly. "At the docks." The engine snorted to life and the wipers jumped.

"Oh my God—dead?"

"A lot of bloody blood," I said, almost smiling, "but only a flesh wound, he said. He still had his matchstick. He wanted me to leave because the French police would tie us both down for days with this. We missed Marteau. We missed them all."

"The boy?" Magnus said, half mouthing the words and letting his eyes stray to Caroline, still huddled and silent in the back.

"You'd better take her and get to the airport, Magnus, back to London. Call the police there. Call her father."

"You need me here," he said. "I'll stick. There's a lot at stake."

I nodded without quite understanding and let out the clutch.

Angeletti was staying in a handsome nineteenth-century townhouse, each floor apparently given over to a single tenant, like the luxury service flats in England. Magnus and Caroline waited in the car, a block away from the door and away from street lights, while I went through the lobby, spoke to the concierge, and entered an elevator.

Merriman opened the door. "This had better be good," he said by way of greeting.

"Ever been disbarred before?" I asked pleasantly and walked past. Angeletti was sitting in a wing-back chair beside a dead fireplace. He was wearing a bright red dressing gown over white silk pajamas. His bony horseface was propped back against the upholstery, and his jaw hung slack, showing the toothless gum and the black pulp of his tongue. His legs splayed on either side of the chair and disappeared into wool ankle warmers and leather slippers. He looked as if somebody passing through the room had simply tossed him into the chair like a pile of laundry. Beside him, hand and elbow on the white wooden mantel, a tall man in a nautical jacket of some kind—dark blue with maroon stripes at the cuffs—stared at me through tinted plastic glasses. Around them both, I saw expensive bric-a-brac, a good oriental carpet, tables and chairs in muted stripes and woods. A handsome furnished apartment for businessmen who avoided hotels.

Angeletti didn't get up to shake hands. He raised a cocktail glass to his mouth, took in a piece of ice, and chewed it with a sound like two bones knocking. Then he spat it back in the glass.

"I'm here," he whispered. "I flew the goddamn Concorde from New York to Paris, then flew to this dump on a charter. I'm ten hours behind time, Haller, and at my age, I can't afford to lose ten hours. Like the man says, this better be good."

"Listen, Carlo," Merriman yapped from behind me. "You're tired, you don't have to deal with this gumshoe any more. We've got enough—"

"Make your yoyo pipe down," I said to Angeletti.

He squeezed out half an inch of smile. "I thought you were too goddamn polite when you come to my place, Haller," he said in his soupy French-Italian accent. "I heard you were a real smart-ass before I hired you."

"I thought we were all too goddamn polite," I said. He let the smile fade very slowly, like a spark dying. I pulled out a new Gauloise. "You're smuggling opium into Bordeaux," I said.

"Hey!" Merriman squawked.

"Maybe Captain Bligh there hauls it through on your oil tankers," I said. "Maybe on the one sitting at quai 95 right now. The *Luchon*."

"Listen here—" Merriman began.

"Shut up, Merriman," Angeletti said. "Haller is all heated up. He's mad. He wants to talk. Haller didn't drop by to play patty-cake."

"You set me up, Carlo." I lit the cigarette and flipped the burnt match into an ash tray shaped like an oak leaf; then I sat down in a chair on the other side of the cold fireplace. The nautical chap followed me with his eyes but kept his elbow on the mantel. Merriman took bird steps around Angeletti and stood behind his chair, hands on each corner, chin peeping over the top like a frightened kid. He might have skipped this class in law school.

"You set me up," I repeated. "You hired me to find the girl, but you really wanted to find your son. Peter A., the Stanford boy who skipped out on dad's business. Find the girl and the boy will be in the next room, you figured, and some of your people can take it from there. You wouldn't cross the street to find the girl, would you, Carlo?"

"No," he said, drawing it out. "I don't give a shit about the girl."

"But you'd give an arm for the boy, I guess. You had me followed all over London because of him, didn't you? New York, Cambridge, the works, and all for an adopted son who ran out on you."

"He's my son close enough," Angeletti said calmly. "Legally. But it never worked out. It never worked out for 15 years. You don't know him, Haller, you don't know him and me. A bad match, but I took him in for my wife, I told him after she died. I took him in, I could turn him out. I put him through the good schools, I sent him off to Stanford with the sports car, the good clothes, I told him enjoy yourself, then come back and help papa with the business, all of the business, the way a son does for a father. I'm the old school, Haller, I told you that before." He paused and took a sip of whatever he had in the cocktail glass. "You want to know the truth," he said, swallowing. "I hate the little son of a bitch. I hate him just as much as if he was my real son."

I rubbed out the cigarette and looked over Angeletti's bald head at Merriman. He had gone pale as the old man's silk pajamas.

"I don't have the organization you think, Haller," Angeletti said. "I don't have goons follow a guy all over the country. That's why I hire you, because they tell me you're the best. I got a couple of good friends in New York. The rest of that crap's in your head."

"Part of it wasn't, Carlo. You made a mistake." I got out of the chair and walked across the oriental carpet to an imitation Louis the someteenth cabinet filled with bottles and glasses. There was nothing but Scotch in front. The whole world drinks nothing but Scotch. They must ship it in tankers, like oil. I reached back and grabbed a bottle of Courvoisier by the neck and poured myself a lethal dose into a whiskey glass.

"Have a drink," Angeletti said from the chair. He was as jumpy as a block of ice.

"What you didn't know, Carlo," I said, "was that somebody else got interested in the runaway kids, and they figured out I was working for you when they saw me talking to the girl in London." I turned around. His head had straightened away from the chair and one hand was holding out the empty glass for Merriman. "Humor me a little, Carlo. What's your new way of getting opium into Bordeaux? Just for the hell of it."

Nobody said anything while Merriman bustled over to the cabinet beside me and refilled Angeletti's glass with Dewar's. Angeletti took it from him and said something very fast in French to the sea captain.

"We take it out in oil drums," the Captain said. "In the Middle Eastern port, we wrap it in waterproof plastic doughnuts and plaster them to the hull inside before we take on oil." His accent was lazy and urbane and he could just as easily have been talking about polo ponies or the price of wine. "When the hull inspectors go through, they unstick the packets and hide them in their wet suits. Then they put the packets inside the residue drums." I raised my eyebrows in a question. "The oil drums you flush the tar into," the captain explained. "Every tanker has perhaps two dozen oil drums of unusable, worthless tar that's flushed from the hull. Nobody inspects it. You can't throw it in the harbor without a fine. So most companies simply pay someone to haul it away and burn it or stick it in an old mine. In this case, our buyer hauls it away and unpacks the opium where he needs it."

"And you bring in double the amount you used to sneak through in sailors' footlockers."

"Ten times," Angeletti said. Merriman mumbled objections from behind the chair.

"You ever think about where the opium ends up, Carlo?"

"A preacher," the captain said in his lazy English.

"I don't give a shit about that either," Angeletti said. "You can't change the world. Get to it, Haller."

"How long have you been trading in Bordeaux?"

"Eight, nine years." He spread one hand wide in a gesture of impatience. When I was younger, I used to think that anybody with long, graceful fingers was meant to be a pianist. "Who cares?" he said.

"Ever see Charles Marteau?"

"Never. We don't do business that way. Nobody does. I'm getting tired now, Haller. I'm nice and polite so far, because I think you know where my boy is. But don't strain it."

"How's your memory for Henri Blanchard?"

"Never heard of him." Like most people with power, Angeletti had fallen into the habit of answering questions instantly, decisively. But his face started to work as I stood silently, twirling the brandy in the oversized glass, and he suddenly pulled the red robe tighter around his chest, as if a chill wind had entered the room. I took a dose of brandy.

"Marteau's a code name from the war, isn't it?"

"Yeah, I like that. It gave me a kick." He stood up and looked vaguely around the room. Merriman moved uneasily. Angeletti looked old and frail, as if he would collapse into a bundle of bones and empty clothing.

"There was a guy named Blanchard," he whispered finally.

"Marteau and Blanchard are the same guy," I said. Angeletti turned his face away from me. His eyes swept the shelves of bric-a-brac, looking for something.

"What's all this?" Merriman barked, getting his voice back.

I ignored him. "I like it, Carlo," I said. "It gives me a kick. You and Blanchard working together all these years, smuggling dope and selling it to the kids and not changing the world." I remembered the girl on the floor in Cambridge, named Michelle, the cop had said, like in the Beatles' song. I finished the brandy in one gulp and put the glass down on the cabinet. I wanted both hands free. "Just one of history's little ironies," I said. Angeletti wandered another step or two. "One of the war's skirmishes that never got resolved, you killing his father like that and his coming after you. Some sons do carry a grudge. But there was no problem for you—you'd disappeared into California and your oil tankers work under a corporate name buried ten feet deep in some Liberian registry. No problem, unless one of you found out about the other. And Blanchard found out. Peter A. and your new daughter-in-law stumbled right into his hands when they came to sell information in London. Only, they didn't know what information he was really buying. They thought the Marteau group was going to raid your first shipment on the *Luchon*"—the sailor stiffened and I held up a warning palm—"raid it and cut them in. But Blanchard had a better idea." I put my right hand on my jacket lapel, near the butt of the Webbley. "I imagine Blanchard thought he could finish the girl later. He didn't know all about you and Peter A. and modern parenthood. I imagine he just wanted to send your son's corpse home to you floating in a tank of oil aboard the good ship *Luchon*."

Angeletti started for the bedroom door. "Get out of my way, Haller. I got to make a call."

"Where's Blanchard now?" I blocked his way.

"Take care of him, Merriman." Merriman took two steps toward us before I had the pistol out. The sailor started, then stopped. Everybody stopped. I backed around Angeletti toward the hallway door.

"Where's Blanchard?" I said again.

The sailor looked at the pistol and shrugged. "The truck is always a farm truck," he said in his lazy accent. "With Perigord digits on the license plate. It could be from anywhere in a radius of a hundred miles. We were always very careful."

"I was at the ship an hour ago," I said, moving away. "The girl is gone. We were too late to help your boy."

Angeletti broke for the bedroom with a growl, I slipped through the door and headed for the elevator. Nobody bothered to follow.

# CHAPTER 16

"Y OU CAN QUIT NOW," MAGNUS SAID.

I twisted in the car and stared at him. He touched his flight officer's moustache nervously with two fingers, let his right hand creep an inch along the seat top.

"You can quit," he repeated. "You've found the girl. The boy's dead. You're not going to get any fee from Angeletti, Michael. Let Stock do it, Stock and the police."

I lit a cigarette and rolled down the window for ventilation. The warm summer rain continued to splatter on the street like grease in a skillet. Caroline leaned forward in the back seat.

"I'm a little like Stock," I told Magnus, keeping my voice mild. His brown eyes clouded in puzzlement. Occasionally in San Francisco, I point out a man to Dinah and ask if he's handsome—always Magnus's type, I realized now, tall, graceful, expensively groomed, sensitive about the eyes and mouth like a mouse or a deer—and she always shakes her head in amusement. Sensitive plants, she calls them. "I don't think the whole world's divided into wogs and good guys the way Stock does," I said, "and I don't think all the wogs are dealing drugs. But I see too much of it. I see too many kids going belly up in San Francisco because they think they can puncture their troubles with a needle. I see too many kids with brains turned to Twinkies and livers turned to wood pulp. I pick them up in alleys in Berkeley and Oakland where they slink off to have the shakes. I pick them up in hospital wards and free clinics, after their friends have driven up and opened the car door and dumped them onto the sidewalk. And sometimes I pick them up in morgues, where a guy with pimples and a dirty white lab smock wheels out a metal cabinet that looks like a breadbox and lifts a green sheet and reads a tag on the toe and asks me if that's the kid I wanted. I could tell you I want to go after Blanchard because, if I don't, his hoodlums are going to come after me. But that's probably not true. Blanchard's people probably don't give a damn whether I stay or go, as long as I don't stir my fingers in the almighty cash flow. I'm going after Blanchard because Stock is right about that one thing: the small fry don't count. I hate the big bastards and I want to shut one of them down."

I threw the cigarette butt out the window and watched the red spark hiss and go out as it hit the pavement. Upstairs a block away, Angeletti would be on the telephone calling whoever he still knew to call in the old country. Down on the street, I was making speeches and pounding my chest.

"Caroline?"

"Yes."

"Did you see Blanchard at any point or was it all through Rampal?"

She was quiet a long moment. Then: "Blanchard came to the airport," she said in a soft voice. "He met us in the coffee shop. For just three minutes."

"What did he say? What did he look like?"

Her clothes made a rustling sound in the back seat. "He just looked—old. He's an old man, like Carlo, in his 60s. Gray-haired, ordinary looking. He was very soft-spoken, joking."

"What did he joke about?" My voice grated even to my ears. I must have plowed up my throat with cigarettes in the last 24 hours.

"He joked about the weather. He said an English girl must be glad to see the sunshine."

"Yeah, terrific. What was he wearing?"

"Just a business suit, dark blue. Blue tie."

"Don't you think you'd better call Stock or the police?" Magnus said.

I glowered through the window at the rainy night.

"I remember something else he said," Caroline whispered.

"What was that?"

"I asked him what he was going to market the horse in, you know, kilo bags or tubes, and he said he would mark them '*mis en bouteilles dans mes caves.*'" I sat very still. Magnus inhaled sharply. "That's a wine term, isn't it?" she added.

I closed my eyes and leaned back in the seat, shutting down my brain, wrinkling my memory into a frown. "Not if it was a joke," I said after a long time. "Not if it was a joke."

I sat up and leaned across to the glove compartment, opened it, and took out the oil company road maps that Hertz still puts in their cars in France. Magnus flipped on the overhead light. According to my watch, it was 20 minutes to nine.

"I want Les Eyzies," I said. He nodded and pulled out a map marked *Department de Dordogne.* 'The cave capital of France. I've never played a crazier hunch," I said. He nodded again and pointed one long finger successively at Bordeaux on the map, at one of the main bridges, at a blue meandering line, like a vein in an arm, that was labeled N-136. "Look for signs to Bergerac," I said and started the car.

It was past 11 when we got there. After a stop somewhere along the Dordogne river for gas and three ham sandwiches that a vending machine spat angrily at us, Magnus and Caroline had slept most of the way. As we slowed for the bridge over the Dordogne and rattled on the cobblestones of the old part of town, he sat straight and rubbed his eyes.

"Bergerac," I told him. He looked out the window for half a minute, twisted, and went back to sleep. The sound of Caroline's regular breathing rose from the back. I lit another cigarette I didn't want and twirled the radio button, hunting for news. All I got was big band music from the '30s—another French fad—and a weather report for southwest France: rain diminishing. I switched off the radio and concentrated on the road, driving the rain before us.

At a little river town called Le Bugue, I turned north and followed a narrow departmental road along one of the Dordogne's tributaries toward Les Eyzies. And at ten minutes past midnight, I braked us into the driveway of the modern, brightly lit Hotel Centenaire at the head of the town's main street. Full. Try the Cro-Magnon, the clerk said. At the Hotel Cro-Magnon, I took a space in the half-empty parking lot and woke my passengers.

The desk clerk, a sleepy middle-aged man in a turtleneck sweater and a green blazer, looked at us unhappily as we entered.

"'sieurs et 'dame," he said curtly, as if he were in training for the Savoy. Our damp clothes, my mud and petroleum aroma were not Michelin-sent. Caroline was only slightly more presentable in rumpled blouse and skirt. I guided her forward, hand on elbow.

"We have just driven all night from Nice," I said apologetically. "We would like three rooms with private baths if you have them. I know it's late . . ." He opened his reservation book and pretended to study. "The car ran very poorly," I added. He bowed his head with sympathy. In France, one struggles with one's liver or one's car.

"I have a single with bath and also a suite," he said at last. "They are free now." He looked at me, at Caroline, at Magnus with frank curiosity.

"The gentleman and I will take the suite, the lady the single," I said.

"Your passports, please," he said, swiveling a registration book on the desk.

"In the morning." I slipped out my wallet and placed a pair of 1,000-franc notes on the glass top of the desk. "I insist on paying for two days in advance." He smiled slightly and, like everybody in France, took my money.

I came downstairs before seven, cleaner and neater, leaving Magnus asleep in our suite, and went into the silent lobby. You have to try, because sometimes overlooking the obvious is a good way to fall flat on your face, but there was no Charles Marteau or Henri Blanchard in the telephone book. Nor was there a Mercedes dealer. I took a cup of cafe au lait and a croissant in the empty hotel dining room and then walked out into the bleak, sleepy morning.

At the end of the main street, bordered on one side by high limestone cliffs and on the other by a narrow green river, the Vézérc, I found the garage that I had seen when we had driven past the night before. The mechanic on duty, a thin, swarthy man in greasy coveralls, slid out from under a dusty *deux chevaux*, sat up, and asked me in horrible French what the hell I wanted so early.

Did he work on Mercedes? He took the Gauloise I offered, stuck it behind his ear, and looked me over. I lit my cigarette. Sometimes he worked on little things for tourists, he said, spark plugs, fan belts. Nothing big like a tune-up or a fuel pump. Who did the big things? He tugged the cigarette out of his brown hair and got it going with my plastic lighter. Brombert et Fille would handle my Mercedes, he finally decided. In Sarlat, the next town over. He leaned back and disappeared under the *deux chevaux*, cigarette and all, and I walked back to the Cro-Magnon parking lot. Over the street, on the ridge of a white limestone cliff and just under a sign that said "Musée Préhistorique," a 30-foot-tall statue of a caveman stared after me with a scowl.

Mademoiselle Brombert turned out to be in her mid-50s, with cropped white hair, cheeks like withered brown apples, and a collection of foul-smelling briar pipes on her cluttered desk. Not at all prehistoric. Her father had died two years ago, she told me and sucked noisily on one of the pipes; but she was at my service.

"I'm considering buying a house near Les Eyzies." I tried to make my French ponderous and German and sounded instead like a duck gargling. "A summer home when I vacation from Bonn. But I want to determine if my Mercedes 280 SL can be properly cared for here." She inclined her head toward the window, through which my Peugeot could be seen blocking traffic on the sidewalk.

"Rented," I said.

"*Une vache*," she said and dropped her jaw so that a cloud of smoke could float out. "A cow."

"But you do service Mercedes?"

"*Bien sûr*. We receive parts directly from Bordeaux. My chief mechanic has been to the service school in Munchen for a course."

I pursed my lips like the Nazi colonel in *Casablanca*. If I had a Mercedes to service—and of course I did, 9,000 miles away and old enough for college—Mademoiselle Brombert would put up with my act. "May I ask—you will excuse my thoroughness—do you have a list of customers whom I may consult for recommendations?"

"In Sarlat?"

"Les Eyzies would be preferable."

She looked through a cylindrical file of cards, muttering to herself in French so fast and low that I couldn't follow. While she made occasional notations on an old Esso pad and belched smoke, I glanced around the office. A row of triangular bronze deer hunting plaques sat on a shelf above the inevitable plastic-bound service manuals. When I looked closely, I saw that all the plaques were inscribed to Marie-Rose Brombert. At the end of the shelf, in a filigreed silver frame that should have gone around a wedding portrait, stood a color photograph of her clutching a rifle barrel in one hand and the limp head of a buck in the other.

She tore off the sheet with a flourish and handed it to me across the desk.

"*Voila,* four names in the area of Les Eyzies. I am certain you will find these satisfactory, Herr Hoffman."

I thanked her and left, roaming the little town until I found a sporting goods store with a trim modern look. There I bought a Peronnier 16 gauge pump-action shotgun and two boxes of cartridges. Then, armed to the eyebrows, I flogged the *vache* back, past tourist signs for caves to visit and more prehistoric museums, past the turn-off for the closed Lascaux caves, and on in light showers toward Les Eyzies. From time to time, thunder rolled out of the old earth's belly.

"Yes, I think I have the kind of list you want, Monsieur. If you will follow me into my office . . ."

I stepped behind the counter and threaded my way through several filing cabinets and some dusty display cases with bits of rock and bone in them. The teenaged girl unpacking cartons looked at me appraisingly. I winked and she turned away blushing.

"We haven't much call for these lately." The assistant director of the Museum of Prehistory spoke a clear, educated French with a slight Parisian lilt. A well-dressed, affable man in his mid-40s, he carried thick black hornrim glasses on a big nose as if he were wearing a Groucho Marx mask. He seemed happy enough to believe that I was a visiting amateur archeologist from America.

I accepted the packet he pulled from a cabinet—three sheets of yellow paper, mimeographed and stapled at one corner.

"This list was revised two years ago," he said, "but it should still be helpful. Ours is not a fast-paced field"—with a smile. "If you could give me a precise idea of what you need . . ."

I looked up from the list of names and places and smiled politely back. "I'm really just searching at random," I said truthfully. "As I told you, I've come to Les Eyzies several times to look at paintings—I've seen the well-advertised ones—but I felt there must be a complete list of caves with prehistoric paintings on private property as well, ones not usually open to the public."

He sat behind his desk and waved me to the straight-backed wooden chair in front of it. Outside, the teenaged girl answered the telephone. "Most of the caves not actually listed in the guidebook don't have paintings, I'm afraid, Monsieur"—he glanced at the plain printed card I had given him—"Haller."

"I'm equally interested in cave formations," I said. "Limestone sometimes forms very unusual stalagmites, and we don't see those much in the American West."

"No," he murmured. "You speak very good French."

I smiled again. It costs a Frenchman an effort to say that. "What do these asterisks mean beside a name?"

"Those are for caves that are formally closed. Some of the owners have grown tired of giving tours, even for a fee. Others value their privacy."

"This one, owned by Victor Brossiere, interests me very much," I said after a moment. He took the sheet of paper and pushed the heavy glasses back up his nose with one finger.

"Yes, there are one or two paintings of interest there, chiefly of large animals. Buffalo. I saw it long ago when I was a student. It belonged to someone else then. Brossiere bought it about ten years ago. I don't know him. As you see, it's quite a deep cave, about four kilometers long altogether, counting its two main branches; about one and a half kilometers below the surface at the deepest point. This one was actually a popular tourist spot in the late nineteenth century, when there was a wave of interest in simply exploring deep caverns. One of the former owners built a little railroad track with an electric train all the way down, to ferry tourists around more easily."

"Is that still in place?"

"Oh yes, I suppose so. Not worth the trouble to take it out, eh? But probably quite rusty. Funny, isn't it?" he said, warming up to his subject. "I remember that cave because of the immense number of graffiti all over the walls, put there by the nineteenth-century tourists, names and slogans scrawled everywhere, even over the paintings. Nobody back then cared in the least about prehistoric paintings, you know; they were actually thought to be rather ugly." He smiled with the Frenchman's relish of an irony. "Now"—he spread his hands to indicate the museum—"the government spends millions just to keep them intact."

I took back the list. "Obviously, tourists were as bad-mannered then as now," I said meaninglessly.

"I don't think so," he said leaning forward. The glasses slid down the big nose again, and he pushed them back. "I have a theory. It was really quite adventurous to go down in a cavern then, you know, without proper illumination, guides, and so forth. Even that electric train for the lady tourists was exciting. To go down into a deep cave always disturbs people strangely—there you are, wrapped inside the earth itself, in complete darkness, complete silence. It's like a stone womb, cold, silent, enclosing. To go down into a cave like that always releases primitive instincts, primitive fears. And I think anyone who reaches the farthest point of a dangerous trip wants to leave evidence that he made the journey—that's why paleolithic man made most of his paintings at the very bottom of caves, why the tourist wrote his name with charcoal. Look at you Americans, leaving a marker on the moon with the astronauts' names. Same thing exactly."

I stood up and extended my hand. "Thank you very much," I said. "This list will be most helpful. I may even try to talk some of these owners into reopening their caves for me."

He frowned. "Some of them might. But I don't think M. Brossiere will be interested. He keeps to himself."

I folded the sheet and patted them into my inner jacket pocket, beside the scrap of paper from the Mercedes dealer in Sarlat. Brossiere's name was third on her list. "It can't hurt to try," I said politely.

It can't hurt to try, I thought as I entered the lobby of the Cro-Magnon, unless I'm right. Behind the clerk's head, a polished grandfather clock read 12:15. In my note for Magnus, I had said I would be back for lunch. The clerk himself turned around and handed me my key.

"Did you miss your friends?" he asked. "They said they would wait for you in the parking lot." When I looked blank, he added, "By the archeological exhibits."

I thanked him and walked back into the drizzle. The hotel's main building had been built squarely against the cliffs, which towered 90–100 feet above its second story, so that the back wall was actually rough limestone and boulder with masonry fitted around. And at one end of the parking lot, under a dark canopy of vines, the hotel had laid out a small exhibit of prehistoric artifacts found on the site. I walked to the end of the lot, almost deserted except for some delivery vehicles, found no Magnus or Caroline and walked back to the Peugeot. The windows were already steamed again from the moisture. I stopped and bent to look through the driver's side. The shadow that I had thought was Magnus turned out to be only the seat back. But the shotgun that I had left stretched across the rear seat was gone. When I straightened in a hurry and started to turn, something round and hard and probably 38 millimeters across pressed into my kidney, and Rampal's cool voice spoke in my ear.

"Get in the car slowly, Monsieur Haller. Then drive exactly where I say. Otherwise, I shall kill you now instead of later."

He jabbed me once with the gun barrel, and as I opened the door and got in, he began to laugh.

I DIDN'T THINK WE WOULD STOP AT THE FARMHOUSE.

"*Tout droit,*" Rampal murmured behind me. I craned my head and looked back at him, and on down the slope of hill toward Caroline and Magnus, who were trudging wearily up. Below them, where the path curved around a stand of beeches, you could see through the drizzle to a neat gray stone farmhouse, two-storied, with a red tile roof: according to the mailbox, the official residence of one Victor Brossiere. In the driveway by one corner of the house poked the back third of the delivery van that Rampal had kept in the parking lot of the Cro-Magnon until Caroline and Magnus had strolled out after breakfast. And then me.

Wonderful work, Haller. The mechanic, the Mercedes dealer, the museum director—I could have sat in the lobby of the hotel sipping cafe au lait and found Blanchard twice as fast, at no expense. What had they been doing since Bordeaux? Watching Angeletti's townhouse, maybe. Watching the local hotels. Bribing folks like the doorman at the Sofitel for the license of my car. Any of the obvious, easy ways to snap up an excitable, slow-thinking private eye.

"*Vite, vite,*" Rampal puffed and swung the pistol through the air. He kept a healthy distance from me as we walked, remembering our other meeting in the subway, I suppose. But there were two extra reasons for me to behave this time, one on my left, a pig-faced man wearing a brown anorak and carrying my new shotgun, the other directly behind Magnus and Caroline, about 20 yards back and carrying a rifle.

We left the open spaces of the farm's meadow and entered a light forest, coming very close now to the base of the limestone cliff. Under the puffy trees, the drizzle slackened to no more than a mist, and wisps of gray fog roamed silently through the upper branches. The trail wound parallel to the cliff, which reached 50 or 60 feet above us, like a gigantic forehead and brow rising out of the mist; and I could imagine prehistoric hunters climbing the same way, over the same landscape of black trees, limestone, and mud, to their cave homes. Alley Oop and Ogg. I felt like a carcass slung over somebody's shoulder. Deer droppings littered the ground for a few yards, then we passed a weathered sign that read "*Chasse Interdit*" and walked right up to the door of Blanchard's private cave.

You had to look for it. Two heavy plank panels behind a curtain of shoulder-high forsythia bushes, secured with fallbeams crossed in an X and a length of padlocked chain. Rampal waved me closer. The Grotte de Gradignan—to use its official title—was bolted tighter than a bank vault. The pig-faced man came around me and started to unlock the chain.

"Who are these?" the new man asked in rapid French, and Rampal stepped deferentially to one side to let him through.

Brossiere. Blanchard. Whatever he called himself. The kid Resistance fighter from the war. The middle man in a prosperous drug network—reseau—that stretched from Lebanon to

London. The man at the end of the long string that I'd been following all the way from the Sacramento Delta. He looked slowly from Caroline to Magnus and me, all three of us backed against the wall of the cave just inside the padlocked entrance. His eyes were as expressionless as stones.

"Is one of these the lawyer?"

Rampal muttered something too low for me to hear, and Blanchard nodded once curtly. Then he walked the two paces it took to plant himself directly in front of me. To my right, the pig-faced man slammed the two heavy panels of the door and lowered another fall-beam.

"Haller," Blanchard said quietly. He didn't look scared to death. He looked as if he were deciding whether to step on me with the heel of one of his polished workboots and twist. In his late 50s, I guessed. Medium height, long jaw, thick black eyebrows like two caterpillars crossing his face. Thin, narrow nose, doughy skin, extremely white, setting off the coal black eyes and making him look like Frosty the Snowman, if Frosty needed a shave. He was dressed in a crisp checked shirt of red and brown, baggy corduroy trousers, and a light yellow windbreaker zipped halfway up his chest for the chill of the cave. The prosperous gentleman farmer. Prize truffles in the front yard, a heroin lab in the back 40. His head was nearly bald except for three or four strands of dark hair that had been carefully positioned across his scalp, positioned and then plastered down with pomade or penguin fat, like lichen clinging to a boulder. You might take the gloppy strands of hair as a sign of vanity, of weakness, if you didn't look closely at the eyes. He wore a gold chain and medallion around his neck, the way a lot of Frenchmen do. He was built like a crowbar.

He had his look at me, glanced at Magnus—his lips curved up at one corner in a smile of contempt—and moved to Caro-

line. The light cast from a line of low-wattage light bulbs overhead, their connecting wire encased in clear plastic tubing,
glistened on his doughy scalp as he walked and threw his face
in shadow for a moment. To his right, Rampal waited stolidly
with the pistol in his hand. A few feet beyond him the rough
walls of the cave—here about 15 feet high, 30 feet wide—
abruptly turned, and I could see nothing.

"Mademoiselle Collin," Blanchard said. He stood very
close, jacket just touching the white fabric of her blouse, and
placed his right hand lightly on her jaw, turning her profile to
him, her eyes toward me. "How do you come to be with these
sad people?" he asked in English.

Caroline rolled her eyes back toward him. The cords in her
neck stiffened as the pressure of his hand increased.

"You were to wait in your hotel until Jean returned,"
Blanchard said. "Until Jean returned with your money."

"Yes," Caroline whispered.

His fingers gripped her chin and wagged her head gently
back and forth. "But you left with them," he said in his mild,
hypnotic voice. "Why didn't you wait?"

"I was afraid," Caroline said with difficulty. Her wide green
eyes stared at me as Blanchard's fingers pressed harder, hard
enough to bruise. Magnus made some indistinct sound. My
fists tightened uselessly at my side. Near me, the pig-faced man
stirred, and the shadow of his shotgun crept across the dirt
floor of the cave.

"Jean, what do they say in Bordeaux?" Blanchard asked,
continuing to hold Caroline's jaw in his stubby fingers.

"They called from Bergerac an hour ago, Monsieur. They're
bringing him up now. No trouble. The lawyer was nowhere near."

"Angeletti," Blanchard crooned in a low voice to no one in
particular. "*Enfin*. They should be here at any moment then.

You had good reason to be afraid, Mademoiselle. But possibly we would have set you free. Possibly we would have given you some money."

"I was afraid," Caroline said more loudly, urgently. Her eyes moved in desperation.

"Now we shall have to find another use for you," Blanchard continued as if she hadn't spoken. Then he slapped her hard with the palm of his left hand. She gasped, more in surprise than pain, and he walked away toward the rear of the cave without looking back.

"Bring them in here," he said over his shoulder.

Rampal stepped back and waved the pistol at Magnus.

"In there," he said in French. Behind me, the pig-faced man spat on the floor.

We shuffled single-file around the corner and along a passage no wider than a big man, no higher than six or six and a half feet. Gray limestone pressed all around us and bore down from above; it felt as if we were squeezing through a fist. After perhaps two minutes, stooping, we entered an oval chamber almost 50 feet long and half that wide, with a jagged ceiling that reached 15 feet in places. All around us, huge knobs of smooth stone, pink or gray or white, rose from the floor like drip castles on a beach. Behind the knobs ran curtains of limestone, rippled and corrugated into immobility. The stone overhead was also rippled, but odd pustules of dirty white spotted the ceiling in many places. And around the edges of the entire oval, suspended from pink stone like giant incisors in a gum, hung narrow, pointed stalactites, glistening. Tourist trap, I thought. No paintings.

Rampal hustled us forward. The stalactites in the center of the ceiling had been sawed off to leave headroom, and through their stumps, more wires in clear plastic tubing had been woven.

From these, on short, small-link chains, swayed two rows of fluorescent lamps. And underneath the lamps were three long tables with collapsible metal legs, arranged in a U and crowded with all the usual apparatus of a school chemical laboratory—large glass retorts and receivers, white pharmaceutical trays and test tubes. At the end of the nearest table stood a stack of blue enamel boxes, and underneath the table, in a disorderly heap, heavy brown sacks with the word "Acide" printed diagonally across their corners. Beside them two black jugs with the label "Eau oxygénée." Hydrogen peroxide. Two men wearing sunglasses and orange-stained white smocks were bent over a tray in the center of the U, while a butane tank fueled a ring flame about a foot in diameter beneath another tray to their left. A wide-mouthed flexible rubber tube stretched from the center table across the cavern floor to a small gasoline-powered engine that ran what looked like an air compressor. Several dozen cardboard boxes had been stacked at the far end of the oval, flanked by two olive-drab footlockers and a jet black Cummins safe. On top of the boxes, someone had placed an assortment of cylinder flashlights and battery lamps; on top of the footlockers several neat plastic pouches of the sort you keep pipe tobacco in. These were stuffed with white powder that looked like sugar. I guessed it wasn't. I didn't see a miniature railroad track.

Blanchard conferred with one of the men behind the tables, who rubbed his hands across his smock and smiled, showing a middle-aged, nondescript face and a few spectacularly black teeth. His facial skin was chapped red and pitted badly, corroded by acid fumes, I supposed, if he spent his days bent over trays of steaming morphine. The other man dropped a metal rod with a dial at one end like a meat thermometer into the tray. Blanchard looked at his watch and asked something in a low voice.

"That's a vacuum pump," I said to Magnus. He turned his long face to me, looking more wrinkled than ever in the fluorescent glare, and worked his lips. "The small copper tubes go right up to the roof and probably out through the rock, like little chimneys," I said.

Blanchard looked up from his conference. "What are they talking about, Jean?"

Rampal shrugged and moved the pistol barrel an inch toward me. "They spoke too fast," he apologized.

"We were admiring your vacuum pump and chimneys," I said.

Blanchard walked slowly around one of the drip castles and stopped in front of me, appraising. The black eyebrows crawled closer together in a frown. I wondered if I would get the chin-wagging treatment too, or if that were just for women. Maybe if I told him we were both Mercedes owners . . .

"So you understand about heroin, eh?"

"Chiefly at the other end. I see a lot of dying junkies."

"I had this chamber enlarged to hold my equipment," he said. "Those pipes carry hydrochloric acid fumes through ten feet of limestone and diffuse them harmlessly in the forest. No one can hear us, no one can see us. Before I bought this land, I had to work out of an old plastics factory in Bordeaux. Before that out of a warehouse in Marseilles."

"*Mis en bouteilles dans mes caves.* Too bad your secret's blown then, isn't it?" It was getting cold in Blanchard's cave. I wanted to reach for a cigarette. Except that lighting one in a roomful of boiling peroxide might just blow pieces of us half-way to Les Eyzies.

Blanchard curved his lip in a bigger version of the contemptuous smile he had given Magnus. He needed Magnus's dentist. "I knew Americans like you in the war," he said. "Big

physically, resourceful. Childishly flippant. A crude combination of cynical and innocent. Many Europeans are inclined
to look down on Americans like you, because you display no
breeding or culture. Jean made that mistake in London, I believe, and you managed to eliminate two of his handiest men.
I am not likely to make the same mistake at all." He turned his
head and began to speak to Rampal. I interrupted.

"You were in the Resistance in the southwest, Blanchard.
With the English. Did you find out about Americans when you
were ordered north, after Angeletti killed your father?"

He turned back to me, surprise wrinkling his face. I was
sick to death of old men. My next case would be runaway tod-
dlers. If I had a next case.

"I haven't used that name in 20 years," he said. "Blanchard.
Do you hear this, Jean?" I considered mentioning Magnus's father, decided against it. "A private detective who even detects in
the past." His doughy face looked elongated, misshapen under
the fluorescent lights, as if somebody had kneaded the skin into
lumps. "Yes, I met Americans when I went north to Normandy
as Henri Blanchard, when the English put me to work with
the American 101st paratroopers, as far from Carlo Angeletti
as they could send me. But after the war, I came south again;
I worked my way up and down the Mediterranean coast from
Nice to Barcelona looking for him. I spent five years working
in the docks, the waterfront cafes looking for him, before I
stopped. But I never forgot."

"That was 35 years ago, Blanchard."

"Europe is not held together by ribbons of concrete like
your country, Monsieur Haller," he hissed. "Our memories
hold us together. I never forgot how my father died, not for
one day."

"You forgot something about chemistry," I said. "You're

running your opium through a solvent of hydrochloric acid and hydrogen peroxide. That's not cooking sherry. That's a highly explosive combination." Caroline took a step backward, and Magnus looked sharply up.

"That is why we are so unusually careful," Blanchard said sardonically. He turned his head toward Rampal. "These two are ciphers. The American makes me uneasy. Take them below and dispose of them." He turned his gaze to Caroline and slowly zipped the yellow windbreaker the rest of the way up. "Leave the girl."

Rampal took one step toward me, and my arms and shoulders clenched in tension to meet him.

"They're here!" the pig-faced man cried behind me. Blanchard whirled toward the cave entrance and clapped his hands once in a gesture halfway between command and impulse. Scraping noises, the thud of the fall-bar carried in from the first chamber. Swinging his arms, Blanchard walked a few paces in a semi-circle and looked around like an actor checking a set.

"*Enfin*," he said softly from the center of the U, gesturing the two lab men to one side of the chamber with impatient flips of his hand. Rampal looked from the trembling white face of his boss to me, back to Blanchard. Caroline and Magnus moved with me to the right a few steps, closer to the tables, leaving the entrance to the chamber completely clear. The stalactites grinned. After a long, silent pause, broken only by the bubbling of liquid in the big tray over the flame ring, we heard footsteps grinding. Then shadows leaped suddenly onto the far wall, long, grotesque shapes that shinnied their way up the rough folds of stone and over the pink gums. Feet shuffled in the dirt close by. Angeletti stumbled in.

Blanchard took a deep, loud breath. Angeletti stepped a

foot more into the chamber, stopped, eyes narrowing at the sudden light. Behind him came another of Blanchard's henchmen, dressed in denim workclothes, a flat automatic pistol of some sort poking like a snout from his fist. The pig-faced man had disappeared.

"A long time, Carlo," Blanchard said in French.

Angeletti lifted his chin an inch and blinked rain out of his eyes. He was wearing a light-weave brown suit, a white shirt, no tie, shoes caked with mud. The wreath of gray hair around his skull, soaked by the rain, had shrunk to a narrow black line, penciled and smeared. His jaw hung loosely open, exposing the black tongue, the toothless gum. Inside the suit, his frame was all angles and points, as if children had been removing bones at random, dismantling a stick man.

"You know me, Carlo," Blanchard said after a moment. Angeletti continued to stare his old man's vacant stare. He looked like a marionette about to tumble unstrung to the floor. Revenge would lose its taste for Blanchard if Angeletti was too dazed to know him. "Don't pretend you've forgotten," he said more sharply.

But the old man's hands flexed once and bunched into loose fists. "I have nothing to say to you," he whispered at last in French. The lip slapped the gum with a wet noise. He shivered violently in the chill of the cave. "After 30 years," he said, still shaking, "even a vendetta should die. You've wasted your time, Henri. You've wasted your life hating."

I glanced toward the laboratory table just behind Blanchard. The liquid over the flame ring was turning rusty and brown and a chain of fat bubbles stood up in one corner. Heated peroxide can blow up in your face. Ask any teenage girl who wants to dye her hair. Like everyone else in the room, the chemists were intent upon Angeletti's face, watching its stringy muscles jump in abrupt, nervous twitches. I slid my feet a few inches to the right.

"Did you see the corpse of your son?" Blanchard asked in the same tone of voice you might ask for a light. Angeletti jerked his shoulders.

"They picked him up outside the hospital in Bordeaux," Rampal volunteered.

"I thought I had a great deal to say to you," Blanchard went on, ignoring Rampal. His hands fluttered restlessly up and down the yellow windbreaker like birds against a window. "Every time I have visited my father's grave in Marseilles, I have sworn that one day I would have you in my hands, that one day I would act with the same summary justice that you used on him. I wanted to send you the mangled body of your son in one of your tankers. I wanted to let him die at my pace, smothered to death in his father's oil. But I see you now—" he flicked his hand in an untranslatable Gallic gesture.

Angeletti ignored him. His eyes found Caroline, then me, and moved on, giving no sign of recognition. Blanchard puffed his white cheeks in a quick scowl of irritation. This was like taking your revenge on a two-by-four. He rubbed his hands together and resumed the patter.

"That was how I planned it, Carlo," he said briskly. "But there are other ways. Get the needle, Jean."

Rampal began to rummage in the equipment on the farthest table. I slid another step to my right and looked across to find Caroline watching me. Blanchard took one more survey of Angeletti's bony face and walked across the chamber to the stalactites and the Cummins safe. The two lab men moved to one side as he took a key out of his trouser pocket and knelt in front of the lock. Caroline kept her eyes on me as my right hand finally reached the edge of the table and gripped it.

"The average packet sold on the street is only four percent heroin," Blanchard said as he got up from the safe, closed it with a snap, and returned to us. "Only four percent. The richest addict in the world never gets the pure thing, 100 percent perfect, because the best a chemist can do is about 90 percent." He swept his eyes our way to make sure we were impressed. "We usually make the best and then cut it with sugar or caffeine down to less than 4 percent, to increase our profit. But this is what I want for you, Carlo." He opened the kind of square plastic container I keep old hamburger in and showed Angeletti the powder. The Tupperware lady making a sale.

Rampal gingerly held up the tube of a hypodermic needle while he spooned in a measure of heroin. "Fresh from our table, Carlo," he said. "There are ten kilos of heroin like this in the safe, stored up over six months, worth about $3,000,000 on the street, ready to be cut and sold. Five cubic centimeters at this purity would send most men to the hospital." He capped the needle and shook it until the mixture turned milky. "I've put water in here, Carlo. Water and 30 ccs of nearly perfect heroin. The water will dilute it so that your respiratory system won't simply close down. That way you should take about an hour to die. The first five or ten minutes may possibly be very pleasant." He squirted a tiny jet from the needle into the air. Angeletti shook his head as drops fell across his face. His raw old mouth worked soundlessly. Blanchard was beginning to get the effect he wanted. I lifted the finger of my right hand into my jacket pocket and closed them around the tubular shape of my cigarette lighter.

"Pull up his sleeve, Jean. It doesn't matter where we start. Why not the wrist veins?" Rampal tucked his pistol away and grabbed Angeletti's left arm. Blanchard leaned toward the trembling old man. "We'll skip the alcohol swab," he mocked.

"And not worry about infection. After the first ten minutes, Carlo, I'm afraid you will find your death truly terrifying. I want you to think of my father as the heroin begins to hit your nervous system. Try to remember him as he was when you took him into the Cafe Central in Les Eyzies. Think of him then, a strong man, in the prime of life, a little older than your boy was, but not much. When the heroin begins to tear your brain apart, like millions of tiny scratching fingers, think of how you lined him against the wall with the others. No trial, no mercy. And how you emptied your pistol into his back. For as long as you can, try to remember that morning. I shall be here beside you, comfortably watching. Afterwards, we shall toss your body back in the cave along with these quite stupid employees of yours."

Rampal shoved the sleeve up, and Blanchard positioned the needle over the old man's broom handle of a wrist. The chemists and Blanchard's henchman stepped closer, staring, in perfect position for what I had to do. Caroline threw a frightened glance at me. They were in perfect position, but she was still too close to the table—Magnus was safer, three steps farther back and staring the other way in horror. I clenched my fists. There wasn't going to be a second chance to arrange the cast, not a second chance for anything. As she looked; I made my lips form the word "scream" very slowly. Angeletti grunted. Her eyes went from me to the table, back again, and her lips parted.

"Down!" I shouted as she began to shriek. Blanchard looked up. I bumped Magnus with my left hand; with my right hand pulled out the lighter, flicked it, and tossed. The flame sputtered but held as it sailed the six feet to the bubbling tray. The chemists shouted, and in the instant before the peroxide exploded, I saw Rampal fling himself toward the table. Then the cave crashed over me like a runaway truck. Magnus or somebody scrambled beneath me, arms, legs —and a second blast thumped the room and shook down a shower of rock and metal and glass. Then silence.

A minute of silence, maybe two. My cheek was bleeding into the cold dirt of the floor. Splinters of glass and wood balanced crazily on my back. I raised my head into the darkness and took a shallow breath of gaseous air, thick enough to make me cough for a moment like a broken ratchet. Above me, sparks were spitting along the roof of the cave, probably from shorted light fixtures, and disappearing in billows of dark dust. Groans rose softly from somewhere on my right. Wherever the hell my right was. I wobbled to my hands and knees, pushed aside the metal edge of one of the tables, and began to crawl, one hand waving in the darkness ahead of me like a crippled ant.

A gallon mixture of peroxide and hydrochloric acid would have had the explosive power of a stick and a half of TNT, if my memory of high school chemistry was anything like right. In the constricted stone mouth of the chamber, the force was probably doubled. Redoubled. I had either closed down Blanchard or I had killed everybody in the room. Everybody I wanted to save. My mouth filled with bile and I hawked and spat. At the far end of the darkness, in a swirl of black and brown, a flashlight beam went on, tilting at unsteady angles.

"Magnus?"

The flashlight beam lurched, rose. I crouched. It moved away to my right and disappeared.

"Michael." Behind me. I craned my head, wincing at the pain along my cheek. Another flashlight beam hung in the dust. Over it, just inside the glow of light, Magnus's face hovered. "You're all right," he said.

"I'm all right. Where's Caroline?"

"That wasn't you with the torch?"

"Where's Caroline?"

The light floated up, wavered, and Magnus began to play it across the room. The tables and laboratory equipment lay in shambles, steam and little tongues of flame flickering at random. One shoeless foot poked at an unnatural angle from beneath debris. The flashlight traveled up: Rampal. The light went higher and touched what was left of his face, a scarlet pulp like a shattered fruit. Magnus moved the beam quickly away. Nearby he picked out the two chemists, huddled motionless against a wall.

"Peter?" Caroline was whimpering far to my left. Magnus picked his way through the dust and jumble, past the still body of the man with the automatic, and reached her, sitting up now and holding one hand tight around her shoulder.

"She's in shock," he said.

"Put the light on Rampal again." He hesitated, then moved it slowly back to the right. I spat more bile and crawled toward him. The pistol was still where I had seen him put it, hours ago at the parking lot of the Cro-Magnon, in the outside pocket of his suit jacket, now ripped down one side and sprinkled with bits of glass like sugar. The Webbley I had brought from London, the officer's issue pistol from the war that wouldn't stop. I curled my fingers around its butt and got to my feet. Magnus was sitting beside Caroline and shining his flashlight over her face. Scratches, dirt, terror were all there, but nothing worse, nothing anyway that I could fix.

"She's in shock," Magnus repeated. "I found this other torch right beside her. She's got a bad cut on her face. She needs to see a doctor." He handed a glowing five-cell flashlight up, and I took it with my left hand. My right hand was still busy with the Webbley. I moved the light carefully up and down the oval chamber, measuring in halves, then quarters, then eighths, the way you're taught to search a space in the army. Magnus kept talking as I looked, the dust kept billowing and shifting as various small fires licked and hissed.

"Get her outside," I said finally, in the middle of one of his sentences. I aimed the flashlight. "The corridor there will take you out."

"Michael," he began.

"That wasn't me with the torch," I said. I stumbled clumsily and stepped away, to my right again. "Blanchard bolted into the cave." I stepped past the last debris and pushed around a corner into absolute, impenetrable darkness.

# CHAPTER 18

A LIMESTONE GULLET. A STONE THROAT. I WAS BEING SWAL-
LOWED by the throat of the cave in a long, noisy gulp. I
moved my shoulders and scraped wall on either side. I tilted my
head a fraction of an inch and bumped my forehead against a
knobby ceiling. I was inside a snake, inside a coffin. My feet grew
cold at the toes, on the soles, up my ankles where the cave's chill
breath crept and squeezed. Not silent, as I had expected. There
were noises everywhere, plumbing noises like the noises that must
go on in the center of your body, dripping sounds above me,
around me, tiny metallic plinks of water striking stone, eroding
stone, building up or wearing down the cave's irregular floor and
walls. Sounds everywhere, but no sounds of footsteps ahead, no
glimmer of light whatsoever.

I moved forward a step or two at a time, pistol in my right
hand, long tubular flashlight ready in my left. Panic flapped
against my face like icy wings. In the utter blackness, my mind
began to sway, without sense of balance or direction. Primitive
fears, the museum director had said. Just to go down into a cave
stirs up the lowest level of human fear, pries open the basement of

the civilized brain and lets the caveman's demons out. It was that all right, that or the thought of Blanchard waiting around the next curve with his own pistol out and pointing.

I stopped and pushed at an unseen obstruction with my shoe. A small rock slid to one side and tumbled into something with a splash. I resumed my paces, stopped again at another obstruction, and pushed. The walls of the cave lay farther on each side than I could reach. I knelt and patted the ground with the heel of my right hand and touched the cold metal curve of a train rail, and memories of the Holborn Underground suddenly began to percolate through the back corners of my skull.

I placed the flashlight on the ground beside my foot and leaned forward, following the track with my left hand. Evidently the system began here, where the cave widened and rose. I leaned another inch or two and put my ear to the rail like an Indian on the prairie. Vibrations pounded like angry waves, and I swallowed, unable to tell if I heard my own pulse or Blanchard's movements somewhere far ahead. Or somewhere close by. Sooner or later I would have to risk the flashlight. I knelt by the track. Sooner or later I would have to take the chance and see where I was, what lay around me.

I poised my thumb over the flashlight button and waited for half a minute. Pushed.

The beam sprang across a black sheet and bounced into a ripple of cream-colored wall some ten or 12 feet away. The empty train tracks, maybe two feet apart, mud brown with rust, ran forward ten or 15 yards in the darkness, through sawed-off stalactites, and then swung out of sight as the cave wound and descended. I stared until my eyes watered, searching, memorizing, and finally let my thumb slide back along the switch.

"Michael."

I jumped and flipped the light into Magnus's eyes—he yelped and stopped, one hand raised to block the beam.

The light went black.

"Get back there," I whispered furiously. "Leave this to me."

I heard him creeping closer, across the little track.

"It's all right, Michael," he whispered. I could barely hear him, couldn't see him. "Caroline is better. I took her outside. There's nobody left in the farmhouse. The noise must have driven them away."

"Did you call the police?"

He paused a long moment. "No," he said at last. "Sorry, no. I didn't think of it."

Our voices now were wisps of sound in the black rock, carrying no more than a foot or two.

"I've got a flashlight," he said. "You need my help here."

I chewed my lip. The cave put cold hands down my back and made me shiver. The hand with the flashlight slowly rubbed the thin cloth of my jacket. "OK," I said. "Stay behind me. I'm going to follow this track on in. He may have a second exit built somewhere. Or he may plan to wait us out."

"He's got the key to the safe, hasn't he?"

"He's also got a gun."

I turned and began to work my way inward, shuffling my left foot along the outside rail. Behind me Magnus scuffed. His breath mingled with the incessant plinks of the dripping water, and once when I looked back, a gauze of white condensation drifted somewhere near where his head should be. Not exactly a picnic for a 52-year-old man, out of condition, out of a center. Not exactly a picnic for an aging youth of a private eye out of his league. I shuffled directly into an upright metal rod and reopened the painful cut on my cheek. Magnus bumped gently into me and stopped. I tucked the flashlight under my arm and began cautiously feeling, a blind man touching an elephant. It was a switching mechanism for the defunct railway, I decided after a minute of chilly groping along lines of metal, wood, dirt. I knelt and touched the track, which seemed to be multiplying or coming loose beneath me. Silence everywhere except for the drips. I inhaled deeply through my nose and flipped on the flashlight for a count of three and flipped it off again. The cave branched sharply to our left, through rippled columns of gray-white stone, and also continued straight ahead. The little train tracks went both ways.

"What do you think?" I breathed to Magnus, trying to remember the map I had glimpsed in the museum director's office.

"The one on the left looks a lot steeper," he whispered, invisible behind me. "Bigger angle, quicker descent."

"Yeah."

"What was all that on the walls?" he asked after a moment. "It looked like writing."

It looked like the subway cars in New York, in fact, hundreds of looping scrawls in black and red paint, names, numbers. "Graffiti from the nineteenth century," I said. "Tourists' names. Jolly slogans. I say we keep going straight."

"What about going separately?"

"No."

He didn't argue. We resumed our progress along the track. Still no sounds except the constant plinking, the occasional faint scrape of our shoes against moldy earth or the whisper of cloth against stone where the cave walls jutted out or narrowed. The temperature was dropping rapidly. In the blackness, my knuckles gripping the pistol banged again and again against the dank stone of the walls and started bleeding lightly down my wrist and into my palm. The pain was sharp and annoying, but the little rivulets of blood were the only warm thing about me.

After what might have been five minutes, or fifty, I halted and pressed my elbow backward to signal Magnus. The track had stopped.

"Stay there," I whispered. I knelt gingerly to the cold floor. A few inches past the end of the rail stood some sort of bumper, formed by several planks bolted horizontally and vertically. My fingers brushed wet shredded cloth like burlap in the center of the bumper. I stepped one pace around it and stretched out my hand. Cold air. Cold black air. Another step and my fingers grazed stone. I leaned forward and patted carefully, higher, lower, both sides. We were at the end of the tunnel.

"Magnus?" I spoke in the faintest possible whisper.

"Here."

I winced. His voice came from the left, nowhere near the direction I had expected.

"I'm turning on the light," I said and placed my left hand over the glass lens. Light wriggled between my fingers and to the gray floor of the cave. I kept my gaze high, avoiding a direct glance into it.

We were in a rounded chamber, perhaps a dozen feet wide, but it was hard to be sure in the splinters of light falling from my hand. As far as I could see, more graffiti covered the walls, and water ran glistening down the frozen limestone curtains. The black ceiling hung above me, ready to fall.

Magnus touched my elbow and guided the flashlight toward the near wall. Long furrows crisscrossed yellow stone in short neat rows.

"Bear claws," I guessed. "Prehistoric bears. Come on, we took the wrong branch."

I stepped ahead of him, waved the light for an instant on the twin rails, then snapped it off. The blackness rushed back, rolling about us in invisible clouds, taunting with false glimmers of color as my retinas relaxed and readjusted. I began to step back along the track. Behind me, Magnus picked up the rhythm—pause, shuffle, pause, shuffle—and we moved back toward the fork, on a slight ascent, breathing the chill.

The fork came sooner than I expected. First, a draft of even colder air brushed over our faces from the right, and in a moment

I felt the metal confusion of the switch. I knelt again, found the rail running left, and without a word we started down it.

After several minutes of tentative stepping, I paused again. The cave seemed wider. Some primitive radar made me bend and grope with my pistol hand beside the edge of the track, and I felt the earth slope away quickly toward a ditch, maybe two or three feet deeper than the rails. Another ditch ran parallel on the opposite side. I tried to reconstruct it in my mind, tried not to think of Blanchard somewhere ahead or of deeper ditches that my radar might not find until I had stepped off into them. The builders had laid the rails on a molded bed in the center of the cave, I decided, a fat platform raised above the natural floor. Probably because of water and mud. The dripping was louder now and everywhere, rolling and spraying downward into the Dordogne Valley's center. I took another deep breath of dank air and started forward.

"Damn."

Magnus' mutter died on his breath. His hand reached, found mine, and pulled it to one side, and then I felt what he had stumbled against—the edge of a carriage. I touched high and low with my flashlight, trying to picture it.

"Turn on the light," Magnus whispered.

"No." Blanchard had not been down the first branch. The whole cave ran almost three kilometers underground, the museum director had said, but there were only two branches. I worked my hands over the carriage, straining my eyes to paint the blackness. We seemed to be in a loading space, and the carriage seemed about seven feet long, four-wheeled, with a metal frame at the base and rotted wooden seats mounted on top. The old owners would have removed the motor and left the worthless carriage when they sold the farm. My hand pressed the top of one of the backrests and it slipped forward with a creak. I waited, pawed the mechanism again. They would be reversible seatbacks, to be shifted for the return ride so the passengers would always face forward. There was-nothing in front of the carriage except more track, more cave. Again I knelt and did my Indian listening pose, this time keeping my ear just above the rail.

The slightest imaginable sound.

A scrape, not a plink. Metal against metal.

I listened.

Nothing, nothing but my heart pounding, nothing but visions of Roger and Henry and the Underground tumbling over my eyes. I forced my nerves to steady and thought of Magnus behind me, relying on me, thought of Dinah. Thought that at least there was no third rail here.

I stood and took one step forward. Another. The Webbley sat in my right hand like a piece of ice. My index finger closed around the trigger. I took another step.

"Michael!"

Blanchard's light exploded into my eyes—I leaped wildly to my right and tumbled into the ditch—his pistol shot ricocheted into the darkness, booming like artillery.

Magnus flashed his light for an instant from the carriage. Blanchard shot again, and I raised the Webbley toward the sound, firing twice quickly, firing again. Water splattered my face, gunshot echoes slapped my ears silly in the contracted space of the cave. I fired a fourth time, and footsteps stumbled away on my right, deeper into the cave, and Magnus shouted my name again.

I scrambled out of the swampy ditch and crashed my face into the side of the train carriage. Metal squealed against metal farther down the blackness, a rocking sound.

"He's in another car!" Magnus yelled somewhere behind me.

I yanked the flashlight forward and beamed it toward the noises. Twenty feet or more away, Blanchard's yellow windbreaker was shoving a second train carriage down the track, picking up speed.

I heard Magnus's puffs at my side, and then Blanchard was gone, vanished around a cluster of pink stalactites and rippled wall.

"Push the damn thing—push it!" I set my shoulder against the metal frame and shoved the carriage into motion. Magnus grunted. The carriage groaned and tilted, moved and stopped. I braced my knees, feeling the water from the ditch slosh in one shoe, feeling the soppy cloth of my trousers clutching both calves.

"Push again."

The wheels slipped across something—moss, dirt—and began to roll slowly downhill, sending up their own dull clatter to match that of Blanchard's car far ahead in the darkness. Magnus's puffing breaths fell behind. I heaved again with my shoulder and swung one hip high, then sat on the metal corner as the carnage rattled on its own, pulled by gravity downward to the bottom. I was going maybe three miles an hour, maybe twenty—in the suffocating darkness, it was impossible to know. Magnus's flashlight beam suddenly rifled past my head, drilling the black cave open, and from the wall just beside me, two feet away, a gigantic buffalo sprang—yellow and orange and outlined in red and black like the strokes of a cartoonist's pen. I flinched and ducked as the painting rolled past me and disappeared again, a prehistoric ghost. Who knew what other animals were sliding past me, down the throat of the cave?

Behind me Magnus's footsteps thumped, ahead the clatter of Blanchard's carriage.

Three kilometers, the man had said. Three kilometers long. The end of the cave had to be close. I gripped the Webbley harder, dropped one heel into the muddy bed to slow the carriage. Somewhere nearby Blanchard's clatter had stopped, leaving only me, a ponderous, noisy target. With a single deep breath, I dropped full-length from the metal frame and slid and rolled again up to my knees in cold, foul water. Ahead, the carriage creaked and squealed and collapsed into the other carriage with a thunderous smash of metal and wood. Somewhere along the track, a piece of stone clumped once against wood, and then there was silence. I lay sprawled across the rail bed, fighting the cold in my legs and the pain in my neck and ribs from the jump, listening for any sound, any movement.

Nobody stirred.

Magnus was somewhere back along the track, Blanchard somewhere farther down. Or back. Or beside me.

Nothing but the tom-tom of blood in my ears and the chorus of water drops. Nothing but blackness so cold, so complete that it settled around my ears and eyes like the muffling folds of a cloth, of a shroud.

Three of us lay or stood in the blackness, waiting. Two of us had guns.

I hurt in every crevice and joint of my body, I realized. Face frozen into wax by the cave's fetid air. Cheek bleeding. Legs and feet soaked and ready to be hung like slabs of beef from refrigerator hooks. Like slabs of sacrificial lamb. Why the hell had I let myself run ahead of Magnus and his flashlight? Why the hell had I come this far after a man I had only seen once? Resourceful. You are the most resourceful man I know, Dinah had said once, surprising me with the serious compliment. Resourceful, my army sergeant had written on my OCS evaluation form. Resourceful, compulsive, and obsessive, he had added.

The silence crouched beside me in the darkness. On the walls around us would be crude paintings, tens of thousands years old, of strong, cruel, predatory animals, watching this primitive hunt, still as stone. And names. The names of all the travelers who had made a dangerous journey.

I eased my left hand up the tube of the flashlight and let my thumb rest on the slide-switch. No sound around me but the chorus of running water. Slowly, millimeters at a time, I extended my left hand until my arm was rigid and the flashlight was as far away as I could hold it. I pointed the lens one way, moved my body and my hand with the gun at an angle. If he saw the light come on, he would shoot at it. I would. And if he missed, I could shoot back. If he missed.

I took a long breath and counted three booms of my pulse.

I flipped on a golden explosion of light, followed in an instant by the explosion of Blanchard's pistol ten feet away. One shot much too high, careening off glassy rock. I fired twice at the spot where his gun had flared. One shot went wild, skipping across the cave walls like a rock across water. One shot made the dull thud of a fist into sand that a bullet makes when it hits flesh. Blanchard yelled, and I heard thrashing noises, a scramble, and I was on my feet and running toward him, playing the beam back and forth while Magnus' light jumped down the blackness 20 feet or more away.

"Michael!"

His light caught Blanchard first, a writhing mass of yellow and brown twisting in and out of the beam.

"The gun, Magnus!"

Closer by five feet, Magnus spotted the silver pistol inches from Blanchard's outstretched hand and scooped it up, showing me for an instant his familiar patrician face as he moved into my light, the thin hair and wrinkled features, the ludicrous Norfolk jacket covered with dust and stains: a completely gorgeous sight.

Blanchard groaned and stopped. Magnus cautiously approached. He was sitting beside one of the rusty brown rails, arms folded across his chest in a shivering hug. The yellow windbreaker showed a spot of dark red as big as my palm, slowly spreading and blotting under his right shoulder. Not the frothy, gushing arterial blood loaded with oxygen, but the dull blood running from muscle and fat. His eyes ate me with fury.

"Look there, Michael."

I turned and saw on the wall behind me, inches away, a large painting, six feet across, of another brown and orange buffalo. Scrawls of graffiti swirled over most of him, but underneath them you could see dozens of straight lines like spears converging in his torso, and from each spear little red lines of blood running away in all directions.

"I know how he feels," I said wearily.

Magnus waved the beam back to Blanchard so that our lights crisscrossed him. All the shadows crowded closer around us to look.

"We have to get him back up," I said. "That's not arterial blood. He's not hurt bad. But we have to get him up."

"He has the key to the safe, the one in the laboratory, hasn't he?" Magnus said, not moving.

"He had it back there," I said. I stooped to adjust one slippery shoe. If we figured out a sling, we could carry Blanchard up. If my groaning muscles held out. The two carriages appeared shattered into firewood. Or we could leave him here and send the cops down. Or one of us could stay and stand guard while the other went up. I shivered, not altogether from the cold, and looked again at Blanchard's sitting figure. The stain of blood on the jacket had stopped spreading, his eyes glistened under the black brows with feverish intensity. If the bullet had hit the lung, he would be hemorrhaging internally now and almost dead. But he still probably felt as if he had sat down under a bus.

"We can take the key," Magnus said. In the insane blackness of the cave, only a sliver of light reached his face from his hand, touching his chin in an inverted crescent. His voice was slow, dragged out, and disembodied. I didn't believe he had said it. "We can take the key and the heroin," he said. "There's more than a million dollars for us each in it."

I stood and waited. Clumps of mud slid down my coat and shirt and plopped to the floor of the cave.

"I can't go back," he said. Pain cracked across the surface of his beautiful accent. "I can't go back," he repeated, in a whisper. "I don't want to. I can't. I'm one of your rabbits, Michael. My life has been spilling between my fingers for years, no marriage, no work, no point. I missed my war. I'm too old to go back. But I can go away. We can take the heroin and go away and find some means to sell it—that part should be easy—you would know how—and then I can . . ." He stopped. "Then I can obliterate myself, so to speak." He barked a high-pitched, nervous laugh that stopped abruptly. The waters of the cave dripped on inexorably.

"No, Magnus."

"'Leave not a rack behind,'" he said, quoting and pleading. "Leave Susannah and the general and the whole dreary English coffin."

"No."

There was a rustle of cloth. The crescent of light dropped from his chin, and I saw only a bright circle lowering.

"I thought you would say that." Harsh intake of breath. "After your righteous speech about heroin. But you can't change the world, Michael."

"It's not just that, Magnus." The light moved lower. My mind turned slowly, as if frozen, unable to come up with words for him, unable to answer my old friend. In the beam of my light, Blanchard had stopped trembling and now sat tense as a wire, watching. I strained to see Magnus. The darkness rustled behind Blanchard like heavy curtains moving.

"Will you stay here then?" he said finally. "While I go up? Will you give me time?"

"Magnus."

"Michael." Bitterness strangled his voice. "Michael the self-reliant. Michael the damned cocksure."

I took a step forward and stopped as the hammer on the silver automatic clicked.

"I would do it, Michael," he whispered out of the darkness. "I would shoot you."

I raised my own pistol and heard the high, nervous laugh again.

"I counted," he said in thin triumph. "You shot six times. Your pistol's empty. You can't stop me."

The flashlight stooped suddenly and I saw his face again, a pale half-moon smeared with shadows, before he shifted the light and spoke in French, extending his right hand toward Blanchard's jacket for the key.

Blanchard muttered an answer through chattering teeth. I stepped closer. Magnus bent and Blanchard lunged upward toward his throat. A knife blade gleamed in the light, then buried itself in darkness, and Magnus screamed once in a cry that made the cave walls ring. His flashlight tumbled and went out and my own beam moved too slowly, finding them only as Blanchard's wrist wrenched the blade viciously upward, and I fired twice from no more than six feet away.

Even before Blanchard fell, I was kicking away his body and going down on my knees beside Magnus. The knife had entered just over the heart and the bright frothy blood was boiling out of his jacket, coating my fingers and painting the lens of the flashlight so that his shocked white face stared up to me in a lurid glow.

"Michael . . ." No more than a rattle. I made a cradle for his head with my left arm and pressed as hard as I could with my right hand against the wound. Blood spurted down my wrist and spilled through my fingers.

"I counted six shots," he said. There was no chance in all the world that I could reach the top of the cave with him before the blood stopped spilling. "But you had a Webbley."

"Hush, Magnus. I'll get you upstairs. We'll make it."

"You were letting me go. You still had two bullets." Blood bubbled from his mouth and stained the handsome face, the flight captain's moustache to make him look young. He swallowed and gagged. "I must have known it had eight shots," he said, swallowing after each word. "Because my father had a Webbley. In the war." And his head rolled out of the cradle.

# CHAPTER 19

"WHAT KIND OF FANCY DRINK CAN YOU MAKE WITH THIS tequila?" Dinah asked.

"Tequila mockingbird," I said from the desk where I was sorting through letters.

She laughed and put down the bottle. "There's more mail at my apartment," she said. "Fred brought it over one night when you were gone. He also gave me this recipe for something he calls Mexican chow mein."

I put aside a few bills and looked at a postcard of Cape Cod from my father. Merriman's advances would handle the bills. "Do you want me to make you a Margarita?"

She shook her head. "I put two bottles of wine in the refrigerator before I went to the airport for you. California Chardonnay. I didn't think you'd be in the mood for French champagne somehow."

"Not even French cuffs," I said. My father wrote that Provincetown was overrun all summer with hippies and politicians, and psychiatrists too in August. "I'm so glad to be back in America," I said, shoving the letters to one side and looking up at her. She stood near the big double windows, arms crossed, red head cocked curiously at me. "I'm so glad I'm going to buy a new Buick Terrorist like Fred's and get a luminous bumper sticker that says 'Honk If You're a Duck' and a six-pack of Henry Wienharts and drive up and down Van Ness till the tank runs dry."

"Open the wine," she said.

When I came back into the living room with the wine and glasses, she was curled on the couch, shoes kicked off, and staring out the window. Far below us, the lights of a ship were gliding across black waters toward the Golden Gate. At the bridge itself, the evening fog was pushing through, under the pale orange span and over it, sniffing the air. Fog never seems to billow through that stretch of water, but always advances slowly, massively, turning one way and then another like a giant blind animal. From the shape of the lights, the ship was probably an oil tanker.

"Was the funeral terrible?" Dinah asked.

"Worse." I sat down beside her on the couch and she put one hand on mine. "The general never spoke to me. Not a word. Not from the first. Just cut me dead, like a glacier. Susannah tried to be her normal mocking self, but halfway through the service, she started crying and one of the cousins had to lead her away. The other cousins stared at me and whispered."

"Poor Michael."

"Inspector Stock drove me down. The funeral was out in the country, near the general's house. Beautiful English landscape, old Norman church with stained glass from the sixteenth century. The minister read from the old Book of Common Prayer and the organist played something traditional and more or less military. Magnus would have liked it. Stock nearly went to sleep because of the painkillers for his ribs."

"I'm sorry."

"It rained the whole bloody day."

She squeezed my hand.

"It wasn't like losing my brother when I was eight," I said, sipping the Chardonnay and watching the ship's lights vanish one by one into the fog. "But Magnus was a kind of brother, an older version of myself. I understood what he was talking about, at the end. He felt l ost, and he envied his father's generation for having a war to give some shape to their lives, some point. He felt hopeless growing old. And he wanted to be admired by his father."

She drank wine. "One of my old teachers in medical school had a sign over his desk," she said after a moment. "He had painted and framed it himself. It was a quote from William the Silent, who was king of Holland during World War II."

"The war," I said.

"It said, 'It is not necessary to hope in order to undertake, or to succeed in order to persevere.'"

I smiled a little and tasted more Chardonnay. It had the golden, oak-touched flavor of a late fall afternoon in the Napa Valley, before the leaves have turned but after the heat has gone. We could drive out there tomorrow for a look around, a picnic. "You're telling me not to mope around feeling sorry for myself," I said, and she smiled back.

"That's not your major character flaw," she said.

"I smuggled in a box of Cuban cigars for your father," I said.

"I wrote him last week that you probably would, once you got free from all the police tangle in France. I wrote him all about your case."

"I begin to think of you as my Dr. Watson."

"You begin to think of me as your Lois Lane."

I grinned and got up from the couch. From the window, I could see the colored lights of the marina and the curling line of headlights coming into the city over the bridge. Not London, not the great gray Babylon, but home. Not 15 years ago either, but now. Dinah came and stood by me, one arm linked through mine.

"'I have no enemy but time,' Magnus used to say. One of his quotes. He was under the illusion that I lead a very glamorous life. I guess I encouraged him a bit."

"I have never understood what is so bad about being disillusioned," Dinah murmured. "Illusions are not true."

I bent down and kissed the top of her red head.

"Did I tell you the part about how the Frenchman said darkness releases primitive instincts?"

"Hands off, tiger. Finish your wine."

"Other primitive instincts."

"Ummm." She put down her glass on the sill abruptly. "Mike?" I looked at her serious round face. "Are you still thinking about the girl you went to find? Caroline? Did you see her again?"

I touched one finger gently to the corner of her mouth. "Caroline will be surrounded by a squadron of lawyers, consulting daily about how much of Angeletti's money she inherits outright and how much she has to sue for," I said. Goldilocks. I let myself remember for a moment my last glimpse of Caroline at Heathrow airport, walking away with two or three of Stock's plainclothes colleagues for a long discussion downtown. The lawyers would handle that too. Nobody could ever get her for Peter Angeletti's death, and the accessory-to-narcotics-dealing charges were unprovable for all practical purposes. She hadn't turned to say good-bye to me. All I had seen was the light blond hair and the slender figure walking away. She had never really looked that much like the picture.

"No," I said, "I didn't see her at all after Stock got us sprung from the gendarmes and back in London."

"I thought that when you left . . ." She hesitated. "You seemed to be growing a little tired of things."

When you're tired of Dinah, I thought, kissing her softly. She put both hands around my neck and lifted her face. I kissed her harder and her breasts and hips pressed against me. My hand found a button, then smooth, warm skin.

"Let me disillusion you," I said.

## ABOUT THE AUTHOR

Max Byrd is the award-winning author of 14 other books, including four bestselling historical novels and *California Thriller*, for which he received the Shamus Award. He was educated at Harvard and King's College Cambridge, England, and has taught at Yale, Stanford, and the University of California. Byrd is a Contributing Editor of *The Wilson Quarterly* and writes regularly for the *New York Times Book Review*. He lives in California.

Coming in October 2012

# THE PARIS DEADLINE

## A NOVEL

## MAX BYRD

# One

THE EIGHTH WINTER AFTER THE WAR, I was living in a one-room garret, a fourth-floor walk-up not much wider than a coat hanger, on the disreputable rue du Dragon.

And no, to get the question out of the way at once, I didn't know Hemingway, though it was Paris and the year was 1926 and every other expatriate American in the city seemed to trip over his feet or lend him money as a daily occurrence. (Years later I did stand behind him in the mail line at American Express and listen to him denounce Woodrow Wilson in very loud and Hemingwayesque French, which had the slow, clear, menacing cadence of a bull's hoof pawing the ground.)

The only literary person I actually did know, besides Gertrude Stein's landlord, was the journalist who sat on the other side of the desk we shared at the *Chicago Tribune* offices on the rue Lamartine.

He was a slender, amiable young man named Waverley Root. He was twenty-six that year, the same as the century, five years younger than I was, not quite old enough to have been in the army. Root was a remarkable person who wrote English like a puckish angel and spoke French as if he had a mouthful of cheese, and a decade or so later he was to find his true calling as a celebrated food critic for the *New York Herald*. The last time I saw him he wore nothing but yellow shirts and had gotten so fat he appeared to have inflated himself in one push of a button, like a rubber raft on a ship.

But in those days celebrity was far over the horizon, and Waverley Root was simply another vagabond reporter who had washed up on the cobblestoned shores of the Right Bank in search of a job. He had gone to Tufts. I had gone to Harvard. He had worked for the *New York World*. I had worked for the *Boston Globe*. He drank anisette and I drank Scotch, and this small divergence in personal character accounted for the fact that on the chilly, rainy Monday morning of December 7, he was leaning against my chair, nursing a French hangover (as he nicely put it), rigid, classical, and comprehensive.

"Toby," he said, "I will never drink alcohol again."

"I know it."

"An owl slept in my mouth last night. My teeth turned green. My poor eyes look like two bags of blood."

"They look like two bags of ink." I typed "30"— newspaperese for "The End"—on a sheet of yellow paper and swiveled to hand it through a hole in the wall—literally.

The Paris edition of the *Tribune* occupied the top three floors of a rambling nineteenth-century structure that had not been designed with modern journalism in mind. Apart from the Managing Editor's sanctum behind a frosted glass door, our editorial offices consisted of one long city room, which held a collection of sprung leather chairs, a long oval table covered with typewriters and ashtrays, and a string of smaller rewrite desks like ours, crammed off to the sides and in the corners. All practically deserted, of course, at this time of the morning. Bedlam arrived later, with the regular reporters, at the civilized hour of noon.

The composing rooms were downstairs (we lowered copy by force of gravity, through a chute in the middle of the floor) and the printing presses were in the basement. Our copyeditors had been banished to an interior room mysteriously inaccessible to us except by going down two flights of stairs and up again three, hence the hole in the wall. More than one visitor, seeing a disembodied hand waving vaguely through a slot in the plaster, had been put in mind of the House of Usher.

"And there is no health in me," Root said and sat down heavily on his side of the desk.

"It's nine thirty-one," I said. "She told us to be there at ten."

Our urchinish French copy boy plopped a thick stack of rubber composing mats on my blotter, murmured "Mon cher Papa," as he did every morning, and sidled away, smoking a torpedo-sized Gitane, to the dark little basement cubby he inhabited down among the rolls of newsprint. He called me "Old Dad," because even at thirty-one, my hair was mostly silver-gray, almost white, like a policeman's helmet. Many people, especially women, assumed sympathetically that something had turned it that way in the war, and if they were young and attractive, I had been known not to correct them. In fact, it had simply happened overnight when I was nineteen, and for some obscure reason, possibly modesty, probably vanity, I had never tried to dye it.

"Goddam 'The Gumps,'" Root said and picked up one of the composing mats.

I sighed and took it back. "The Gumps" had nothing to do with his hangover. They were the Paris edition's most popular comic strip (followed closely by "The Katzenjammer Kids" and "Gasoline Alley"). On Colonel McCormick's personal instructions, the comic strip mats were mailed to us from Chicago twice a month, filed in a cupboard behind the City Editor's desk, and delivered to me every Monday to be arranged in chronological order and chuted down to the printing room.

"She asked for both of us," I reminded him. "Tous les deux. Root and Keats, Keats and Root."

Root closed his eyes in anisette-induced meditation.

I sighed again like the Lady of Shalot and got to my feet. "Suite twenty-five, Hôtel Ritz, if you change your mind."

"Suites to the suite," Root said, with eyes still closed. And as I reached the door he added, sotto voce, "Lambs to the slaughter."

Outside on the rue Lamartine it was raining softly in the slow, sad Parisian winter way and the street was almost deserted: a few soggy shoppers, a gendarme in his cape, a pair of disheartened workmen on ladders stringing waterlogged loops of Christmas tinsel between the lampposts. Another crew was silently studying an enormous and inexplicable pit in the pavement, part of the endless cycle of street repair and excavations in post-war Paris.

I took thirty seconds to gulp a thimbleful of black coffee from the stall in front of our door, and another thirty seconds to frown at the cold gray sky and disapprove of our climate. Then I made my way around the pit and started out, an obedient lamb, for the Ritz.

The *Chicago Tribune* and its Paris subsidiary were owned at that time by Colonel Robert Rutherford McCormick, who had won the Medal of Honor at Cantigny (a battle I'd also attended, in a minor role), and who ran his newspaper along much the same military principles of fear and feudalism that he had evidently employed in the Army.

Fortunately for us, he managed the paper at a distance, coming to Paris only once or twice a year for what he jocularly called "little friendly look-sees," but which had the grim, white-gloved, pursed lips air of a regimental inspection. Like other monarchs he was invariably referred to by his title—in three years at the *Tribune* I had never heard him called anything except "the Colonel"—and like other monarchs as well, he was seriously burdened by family.

In his case, the burden was the Queen Mother, Mrs. Katherine Van Etta Medill McCormick, a grande dame about a hundred and fifty years old, daughter of the famous Civil War reporter Joseph Medill, eccentric even for a newspaper family, and much too fond (in the opinion of the *Tribune* staff) of visiting Paris. She called the Colonel "Bertie," which he hated, and had previously called him, against all evidence, "Katrina," until at the age of nine he rebelled.

Mrs. McCormick liked Root, as everybody did, and the Colonel liked me, because he thought I was a project in need of completing. When Mrs. McCormick had errands to be done in Paris, she summoned us both and reported the results, good or bad, directly back to Bertie.

I stopped at the corner of the rue de Provence and

watched a girl herding five or six goats down the street, still not an unusual sight in Paris in the twenties. An old man leaned out of a third-floor window and shouted to her, and while I crossed to the rue Rossini I could hear the goats' hoofs clattering as they went up the stairs to be milked.

I was a long way from Boston, I thought, or even Cantigny, and turned my gaze to the smallish blonde woman on the opposite sidewalk.

She was studying a tray of croissants in a bakery window, she had no herd of goats, and she was well worth looking at. She wore a nicely tailored green waterproof coat, which was beaded with rain and showed off her waist and her calves and her sensible brown brogues. Her hat was a blue trilby of a style I had never seen before and which, if I were not five thousand miles from home, I would have called foreign. And she had a brilliant red feather in the hatband, like a Christmas tree bulb.

In the buttery reflection of the shop window it was hard to see her face. She seemed to be counting coins in her palm. And despite the relative emptiness of the street, she also seemed completely unaware that she was being followed.

The follower in question was half a block down the sidewalk, a squat, broad-shouldered, gypsy-featured man about my age. He wore a dirty gray quilted jacket and a scowl, and carried a leather-covered billy in one hand, like a swagger stick, and moment by moment he was inching closer to her.

Up to no good. Obviously a pickpocket, I thought, and I took a step off the curb with the idea of making some sort of warning gesture to my fellow foreigner. The swarthy man transferred his scowl to me and then, to my utter astonishment, bared his teeth in a wolfish snarl.

At which precise moment the skies over Paris broke apart in a stupendous clap of thunder and a squall of freezing hard rain swept across the cobblestones with the rattling sound of coal going down a slide.

I don't mind rain. I grew up in New Mexico, where rain is so important that the Navajos have dozens of different names for it, the way Eskimos have for snow. But thunder and lightning are another story, another story for a soldier— ask Colonel McCormick about it. As the first boom rolled overhead I closed my eyes and clenched my fists as I always do, and counted silently till the last vibration had died away.

When I opened my eyes again both Red Feather and Dirty Jacket had vanished like a dream.

Printed in the USA
CPSIA information can be obtained
at www.ICGtesting.com
JSHW082154140824
68134JS00014B/239